"WHAT DO YOU SAY
WE GO TRY OUT YOUR BED FOR SIZE?"
RUSTY ASKED SOFTLY.

Blake's eyes widened in astonishment. "Uh, Rusty, I don't think so," she stammered as she scooted across the floor, putting vital space between them. "I never meant for things to go this far," she said quietly. "I'm not going to start an affair with you." She watched anxiously as his face reflected angry bewilderment.

"You mean that you're going to turn it off just like that?"

"My God, do you think it's easy for me to pull away from you?" Blake demanded angrily. "Don't you think I'm tempted? Do you know what I'd give to take you into my bed tonight and make love with you until morning?" She buried her head in her hands, her hair falling like a curtain around her face, hiding her anguish.

Rusty reached over and tipped her face up to his. "So, why don't you?" he asked softly.

A CANDLELIGHT ECSTASY SUPREME

JUST
HIS
TOUCH

Emily Elliott

A CANDLELIGHT ECSTASY SUPREME

To Lydia, who once upon a time assured a naive schoolteacher from Texas that yes, she could write.

My sincere thanks to Pilots Dennis Gilton and Frank Ellsworth for their most valuable input into this book.

To Our Readers:

Candlelight Ecstasy is delighted to announce the start of a brand-new series—Ecstasy Supremes! Now you can enjoy a romance series unlike all the others—longer and more exciting, filled with more passion, adventure, and intrigue—the stories you've been waiting for.

In months to come we look forward to presenting books by many of your favorite authors and the very finest work from new authors of romantic fiction as well. As always, we are striving to present the unique, absorbing love stories that you enjoy most—the very best love has to offer.

Breathtaking and unforgettable, Ecstasy Supremes will follow in the great romantic tradition you've come to expect *only* from Candlelight Ecstasy.

Your suggestions and comments are always welcome. Please let us hear from you.

Sincerely,

The Editors
Candlelight Romances
1 Dag Hammarskjold Plaza
New York, New York 10017

CHAPTER ONE

"Randolph!" Blake Warner muttered as she stared at the orders in her hand. "That's the last place I want to go!"

"What was that, Captain Warner?" Airman Stebbens asked politely as he carefully corrected an error on the order form that he was typing for the colonel.

"Nothing, Hal," Blake said, hoping that her outward calm successfully masked her inner turmoil. She read her orders again with disbelief in her eyes. She had not requested Randolph AFB in San Antonio. In fact, that was the last place that she would have wanted to be transferred. And as the maintenance officer of a bunch of training planes! Damn! She stared at the orders again, hoping that the word *Randolph* would magically disappear and that some other base's name would appear on the official paper. But no, the word *Randolph* stayed on the paper, as did the date that she was to report, the first of March.

Disgustedly Blake shoved the orders into her desk drawer and returned to her computer console, going over the specs for the New Generation Trainer one more time. Pushing thoughts of her transfer to the back of her mind, she directed all her attention to the figures on the console in front of her, trying to come up with the best possible combination of wing angles for the new aircraft. Absorbed in her work, she barely acknowledged the airman's quiet

"Good night" and did not even notice when her commanding officer, Colonel Henry Saunders, walked into her office and sat down in the only empty chair, the one recently vacated by the young airman. "Going to work all night, Blake?" he asked lightly.

"Sir!" Blake said as she surfaced from the glowing console. "I didn't hear you come in," she added softly.

"You wouldn't have heard it if World War Three started outside your office," he replied lightly, looking at Blake with tolerant amusement in his eyes. "Are the figures coming along?" he asked as he observed her admiringly.

"You bet," Blake replied, recording her newest manipulations and switching off the console. She stood and stretched toward the ceiling, shaking the kinks out of her back and arms. "All ready for Thanksgiving?" she asked lightly. Colonel Saunders nodded. Blake's face clouded as she faced the empty console. "I have to get those figures ready for you in the next four months," she said ruefully. "My orders came today. My three years here are almost up."

"I'm well aware of that, Blake," Colonel Saunders replied dryly, running a hand around the back of his graying head. Just over forty, he was tall and lithe and handsome, and he made most women's hearts beat a little faster, but to Blake he had just been her C.O. and her friend, although she had always felt he would have liked to have been more to her. "It's in your file, and you know that a three-year tour is routine."

"Yes, sir," Blake said rather shortly as she picked up her uniform jacket and slipped it on her shoulders. Pulling on her cap, she turned to Henry and grimaced. "And guess where I'm going next? Randolph!" She sighed audibly.

"You're not happy about Randolph?" Colonel Saunders asked in astonishment. "My God, that place is tops. The weather's nice, the base is beautiful, it's a training base—"

"And it's full of pilots," Blake broke in quietly. "It's a training base, and they train pilots."

"They train instructor pilots," Colonel Saunders corrected her. "They have some of the best pilots in the Air Force there, training future instructors."

"They're still pilots," Blake complained as she fished her purse out of her desk drawer. "I was hoping for something in design somewhere, away from planes."

"Something where you could bury yourself away for another three years?" Colonel Saunders asked dryly. "If you don't want to be around pilots, you're sure as hell in the wrong branch of the service. The business of the Air Force is flying, you know."

Stung by his criticism, Blake's face turned a slight shade of pink, and a shutter went down over her green eyes. "Sorry I mentioned it, sir," she said stiffly as she tucked her purse under her arm. "See you in the morning," she added as she headed for the door.

"Blake, wait," Colonel Saunders called as she opened the door. "Look, I didn't mean to come down on you like that. It's just that you have . . . the Air Force is . . . look," he said quietly. "Why don't I feed you over at the Officer's Club and we'll talk about this?"

Blake nodded, knowing this was the closest that Colonel Saunders would come to an apology, and they had shared many similar meals together at the Officer's Club here at Wright-Patterson. "All right. Let me freshen up in the washroom," she said as she reached into her purse for her lipstick. "Be with you in a minute."

Blake fled to the ladies' room and quickly washed her

face and hands, splashing cold water over her forehead to cool her stinging skin. The colonel's crack, although it had been honest and perfectly true, had hit home. Absently she rubbed blusher into her pale cheeks and over the high cheekbones, then painted her wide, rather firm lips with a pale peach lipstick that set off her natural blond coloring to perfection. She removed the pins from her bun and let the pale, honey-colored tresses fall around her shoulders and tumble halfway down her back. She ran her wide-toothed comb through the hair, smoothing the snarls, then reluctantly pinned it back up. Although she would have loved nothing better than to let her hair tumble down her back for the rest of the evening, it was against regulations to wear her hair down in uniform.

Shrugging, she replaced her cap and caught a glimpse of herself in the full-length mirror as she picked up her purse and turned to go. Tall, well-built, almost Junoesque in proportions, she managed to make her standard Air Force uniform look almost regal in spite of its unstylish cut. She wore the uniform proudly, unconsciously adding to its air of dignity. For Blake Warner, in spite of her feminine appearance, was every inch an Air Force officer. She glanced at the decorations on her left breast and un-consciously reached up and touched the wings that she wore above her pocket, a fleeting look of pain crossing her elegant face before it returned to its original calm look.

Colonel Saunders was waiting for her in the hall. "Shall we walk?" he asked as they left the building and walked toward the Officer's Club just a few blocks away.

Blake nodded. Together they walked in the leaden dusk toward the warm, brightly lighted club and home away from home of the Wright-Patterson officers. A light snow had fallen and melted, leaving the sidewalks wet and gushy and causing Blake's shoes to kick up little splashes as she walked.

They kept up a steady stream of light conversation as they entered the large club and were seated at a table. A waiter gave them each a menu and Blake ordered her usual Scotch and soda and they both ordered steaks.

Colonel Saunders glanced around the club as the waiter scurried away, then let his glance rest on Blake, assessing her thoughtfully. "So you aren't happy with the transfer to Randolph?" he asked slowly.

"You know I'm not, sir," Blake replied firmly. "You should have known that before I even said anything."

"Look, I mean it, Blake, the base is nice," Colonel Saunders protested. "I was stationed there right after 'Nam and it was a great tour."

"What were you doing there?" Blake asked as the waiter handed her a drink.

"Training instructors," he replied, sipping his water. Since his ulcer had been diagnosed six months ago, Colonel Saunders had sworn off all alcohol, and had not ordered his usual Scotch on the rocks. He spent a few minutes outlining the duties of an instructor trainer.

"You were flying, you mean," Blake corrected him quietly.

"Some flying, yes," Colonel Saunders replied. "And a lot of training."

"But you were flying," Blake protested quietly. "That's what I mean. Everybody at Randolph is flying. Or they're learning how to fly, or teaching others how to fly, or teaching others how to teach others how to fly. But damn it, sir, they're up in planes!"

"And that bothers you," Colonel Saunders said thoughtfully.

"Yes, it does," Blake said quietly as she pushed an

15

errant strand of hair back into her bun. The waiter arrived with their meal and Blake cut herself a piece of the succulent steak. She chewed her meat thoughtfully as she tried to formulate her thoughts. "I know I'm unreasonable, but it does bother me. It bothers me a lot."

"I guess it would bother any pilot who couldn't fly anymore," Colonel Saunders said thoughtfully as he speared a French fry with his fork, deliberately ignoring Blake's wince. "What will you be doing?" he asked casually.

"Maintenance officer," Blake replied, carefully keeping her face impassive. As a maintenance officer she would be supervising a hundred or so enlisted men and women, mechanics mostly, who would do the actual repairs and adjustments on the vast fleet of trainer planes that were in constant use. Realistically, she would not have that much contact with the pilots, but she would certainly see more of them than she had at Wright-Patterson.

"Not quite design, is it?" Colonel Saunders asked lightly as Blake chewed a too-large piece of steak until she had mangled it into more manageable proportions.

She shook her head ruefully as she swallowed the offending mass. "I had hoped to stay in design somewhere," she replied quietly.

"Oh, I don't know," Colonel Saunders replied. "Blake, you may be angry with me for saying so, but I think that this transfer and change of duties just might be the best thing that's ever happened to you."

"Colonel Saunders!" Blake protested, horrified. "How can you say a thing like that, knowing how I feel about flying?"

"That's exactly why I feel that it will be good for you," Colonel Saunders said. "Look, Blake, you used to love anything that had to do with pilots or flying. When I

16

trained your class at Williams, you were the pilot's pilot. You were the best pilot in that whole damned class, and you know it. I think what contact you do have with flying at Randolph will be good for you. You can't hide from your first love all the rest of your life."

"A lot of good that love does me now," Blake replied bitterly. "What good will being around flying do me these days, now that I can't fly anymore?"

"Maybe your expertise can help someone else who is flying," Colonel Saunders threw out lightly.

"Sure," Blake replied sardonically.

Colonel Saunders peered at her. "Blake, are you afraid to face it again?" he asked slowly. "Is that why you don't want to go to Randolph?"

Blake thought a minute as she absently pushed a French fry around on her plate. "No, sir," she said slowly. "I can honestly say that fear has nothing to do with the way I feel."

"Then how do you feel, Blake?" Colonel Saunders asked. "Why don't you want to be around pilots again?"

"Because they remind me of what I lost," Blake replied quietly, the eloquent ring in her voice more accurately mirroring her pain than tears would have.

They sat in silence a few moments, alone with their thoughts. Colonel Saunders finished his steak, and Blake picked at hers but finally pushed the plate away, the steak only half-eaten.

"Well, Blake, no matter how you feel about it, I guess you have to go," Colonel Saunders said softly as the waiter gave him the check. "This is the Air Force, and orders are orders. No, tonight's my treat," he protested as Blake started to open her wallet. He handed cash to the waiter. "Now, Blake, if you'll let me talk to you like a Dutch uncle, I suggest that you make the best of this stay at

17

Randolph and try to come to terms with the bitterness that's eating you alive. Yes, it is," he said, holding up his hand when she started to protest. "You're much too young to let a quirk of fate spoil the rest of your life. Give it a chance, Blake," he added as he took her arm to leave the restaurant. He walked her to her blue Datsun in the damp, gray night and waited until she had unlocked the door, then touched her hand gently and pushed her inside. "Think about it, Captain," he said softly.

"I will," Blake replied equally softly as she started the engine. She drove to her small off-base apartment and unlocked the door, shutting it behind her as the first swirling flakes of a new snowfall began to cloud the night. Once inside her bedroom, Blake shucked her uniform and wandered into the kitchen where Calico, her pet parakeet, chirped at her cheerfully. "Dumb bird," Blake said as she bent down and peered through the bars.

"Dumb bird," Calico chirped back merrily. "Want a bagel!"

"Bagel, my foot," Blake replied dryly. Still, she tore off a piece from her new loaf of bread and pushed it through the bars. Calico chirped and grabbed at the bread.

Blake wandered back into the tiny living room and sat down on the couch in her bra and bikinis, mulling over Colonel Saunders's words to her. Was she bitter? Yes, damn it, she was, and she couldn't help that, unreasonable as it was. Two little pieces of glass in the wrong place and a whole career down the drain. Damn! Angrily she picked up a pillow and threw it across the floor into the kitchen, narrowly missing Calico's cage. The little bird squawked in protest. "Sorry, Calico," she murmured.

Colonel Saunders had been right about her bitterness and he had been right about something else. She was in the Air Force, and she had received her orders. Whether she liked it or not, whether she wanted to or not, she would have to report to Randolph AFB in four months and work as a maintenance officer. There was no sense brooding about it. She would go, and that was that. Idly she flipped through the TV magazine that had come with her paper that Sunday and found a passable show. "Hey, Calico," she called as she stood up and switched on the television. "Think you're going to like Texas?"

Blake finished her work with Colonel Saunders with plenty of time to spare. She regretfully packed her things as February advanced, dreading the day that she would have to say good-bye to Dayton and the people she had met and learned to love there. On her last night in Ohio, her friends gave her the usual sendoff party that lasted until all hours, and then she flew to Chicago for a two-week stay with her mother before reporting to Randolph.

Chicago was even colder than Ohio had been, and very snowy, the weather matching Blake's dismal attitude. Mrs. Warner sensed Blake's dread of her new assignment and tried to ease her daughter's mind, telling her how nice San Antonio had been and how much she had enjoyed their tour of duty there right after World War II. Blake was grateful for her mother's reassurance and glad that at least she could expect to like the town, but she still had her doubts. Would she be able to work with pilots and planes again and not let it tear her up? She had to admit that a part of her wanted to be around planes again, even if she couldn't fly them anymore, but she wasn't sure how she would feel about that once she was actually there. So with more than a little apprehension she boarded the jet in Chicago that would take her to San Antonio.

Thank God that's finished, Blake thought as she placed

the last cup in the cabinet and shut it firmly. Although she had let the movers move all the heavy articles, she had not trusted them with anything breakable, and had insisted on unloading all her china, crystal, and her mother's heirloom silver herself.

She glanced at her clock and grimaced. It was after seven, and she had eaten nothing except a dry sandwich since early this morning. But it was her own fault, she thought as she headed for her shower, leaving a trail of clothes between the unpacked boxes in her new living room. This apartment was larger than her apartment had been in Dayton, and in a few days, after she had finished unpacking, Blake's habitual neatness would surface, but for now she would leave the mess and get ready to go over to the Officer's Club at Randolph for a bite to eat. She could have been finished arranging her kitchen a good two hours ago if she hadn't hopped into her car as soon as the movers left to get her first look at San Antonio.

I'm really going to like this city, she thought as she stepped under the stinging shower and tilted the spray onto her hair. The daytime temperatures were already in the high seventies even though it was barely March, and the bright Texas sun beat down on the unique blend of sleek modern office towers and old stucco buildings left over from San Antonio's years as a Mexican settlement. Armed with a street map, she had driven through the various neighborhoods and had even braved the confusing downtown labyrinth, promising herself that as soon as she had a free Saturday she would go back downtown and explore the Riverwalk and all the historic monuments, starting with the legendary Alamo.

Thank goodness San Antonio is more than just a military town, she thought as she soaped her body swiftly and shampooed her hair with her usual lemon shampoo. Although it boasted five military bases, six if you counted Medina just a few miles outside the city, San Antonio was also a commerce center and a tourist mecca. There would always be something to do on weekends! she thought with genuine pleasure.

So why was she going out to the Officer's Club for dinner? she asked herself as she pulled on a flattering coral sweater and a new pair of designer jeans. She could just as well go out to one of the interesting restaurants that was just a few blocks from her apartment. She toweled her hair and brushed it, but figured that it was warm enough to let it dry naturally. *You're going to the Officer's Club because you don't know a soul in this city,* she thought to herself. *And you know that there will be other lonely souls there too.*

She made her face up a little and grabbed her purse as she ran out the door, locking it quickly behind her. She did not realize what an attractive sight she was in her jeans and with her honey-colored hair floating free, but even if she had known, she wouldn't have cared much.

Blake hopped into her car and headed out the expressway for the base. Her apartment was just a few minutes away from Randolph by car, yet she felt that she needed the short distance from the base to keep from being totally submerged into military life. And she would need that distance now more than ever, she thought as she took the exit that was marked RANDOLPH AFB—NEXT RIGHT. She had visited the base briefly that morning to report for duty and had been quite taken with the picturesque white stucco buildings with the distinctive red shingle roofs that were uniform throughout Randolph. Even the hangars had white siding and red roofs. Driving through Universal City, the small bedroom community that had grown up to support the base, Blake gathered from the profusion of fast-food restaurants lining the main drag that Randolph saw a mass exodus every day about noon.

She drove through the gates into the base and was smartly saluted by the guard. *It's not me; it's just the officer's sticker,* she thought wickedly as she drove through the base and around the Taj Mahal. This morning the historic administration building, the trademark of Randolph that had been designed to closely resemble its namesake, had gleamed brightly in the sunlight, and tonight it was bathed in spotlights and dominated the small base. Blake was not sure, but she thought she remembered seeing the building in a couple of old World War II flying movies. Navigating slowly, she found her way to the Officer's Club and parked her Datsun in the large lot to one side of the building.

She wandered into the club and peered down a flight of stairs into what seemed to be an informal bar in the basement. It looked interesting, so Blake went down the stairs and stared into the large, smoky bar, full of young military types drinking, smoking, playing Ping-Pong, and picking each other up with great abandon. Not tonight, Blake thought with sudden amusement. She retraced her steps and asked if there was a quieter bar anywhere in the club where she could wait for a table in the restaurant. The young attendant took her name and pointed to another flight of stairs, this one going up, and Blake climbed the two flights of stairs to a smaller, more sedate bar that looked out over the base. She searched the crowded room for an empty table and chair, but gave up after a few minutes and sat down at the bar and ordered a drink.

"Mind if I join you?" a quiet voice asked at her elbow as a body slid onto the stool next to hers.

Blake turned around and suddenly found herself staring into the bluest eyes she had ever seen. Disconcerted, she stared right back, her own green eyes blinking a couple of times to see if the blue of those eyes was a trick of the light. It was not. Those eyes really were that blue, and they had faint lines around them, as though they had squinted a lot at the sun. And they were dancing. Yes, dancing. There was no other word for it.

Tearing her gaze away from the mesmerizing blue eyes, she examined the face that came with the eyes. Long nose, impudent mouth that was grinning at her outrageously, square chin, high cheekbones. Tan skin, with a smattering of freckles across the bridge of the nose. And auburn hair—no, not auburn, she thought. Red hair, the color of rust.

"Do you mind if I join you?" the man repeated, although from the look on his face he didn't much care whether she minded or not.

"Sure, be my guest," Blake blurted out, staring at the redheaded stranger.

Gracefully the stranger shifted on the stool, settling into a more comfortable position. Although he was not an overly big man, muscles rippled in his arms and in his shoulders under the knit shirt that he wore. He summoned the bartender with a raised finger and ordered Perrier while Blake tried in vain not to stare at him. Sex appeal with freckles, she thought in wonder as the bartender poured the man's drink. And the man did have sex appeal. *He has a ton of it*, she thought as a curiously pleasant sensation stole down her spine, *and I think he's about to turn it on me.*

Just as she imagined, the redhead turned to her with a lazy grin on his face. "I saw you coming back up the stairs from the cellar," he said, amusement in his eyes and voice. "Get enough of the single's scene down there?"

Blake smiled mysteriously and shook her head. "I never

went down there," she said simply. "I didn't need that tonight." She knew that she sounded deliberately provocative, but she didn't care. This man intrigued her, appealed to her, and seemed nice enough, so she could relax her usual hand's-off reserve at least a little, couldn't she? She sipped her drink and waited, letting him make the next move.

"New in town?" he asked as his gaze slid down her body, taking in the striking proportions of her figure, his blue eyes lingering on the swelling breasts, her trim waist, and her womanly hips.

Blake nodded wordlessly as the stranger continued his sensual survey. He was not speaking, he was not touching her, yet never had a man made her feel more desirable with just his eyes. She returned his gaze frankly, lingering on the wide expanse of chest that was covered yet not concealed by the tight knit shirt. His stomach was flat but well-developed muscles bulged in his thighs and calves.

Blake returned her gaze to the man's warm, friendly face, mesmerized once again by those dancing blue eyes. "How about you?" she asked. "Have you been here long?"

The stranger shrugged. "Just a couple of months," he said with a Southern drawl that was much thicker than most of the accents she had heard today from San Antonio natives. Deep South, she thought, comparing his own lazy speech patterns with her crisp Air-Force-brat accent. She wondered where he was from.

"I was delighted to get this base," the man said frankly. "How about you? To what do you attribute your good luck?"

"Would you believe the wicked old witch?" Blake answered wryly. She smiled grimly. "I would have preferred to be almost anywhere else."

"Why?" the man asked in astonishment.

"Would you believe that there are just too many pilots around here?" she asked lightly, hoping that her true feelings did not show. She glanced across the room and missed the strange look that passed across her companion's face. "So tell me what you've learned about our new home in the last two months," Blake suggested as she returned her gaze to his captivating blue eyes.

"It's a nice place," the man said thoughtfully. "Big, warm, friendly. Nice to the military. Nice to the tourists. Nice to the shoppers from across the border. Nice to everybody."

"They don't bite the hand that feeds them, huh?" Blake asked teasingly.

"Right," he said firmly. "Tell me what you like to do for entertainment, and I'll name you a few places that you'll enjoy."

"Dancing and the theater," Blake responded, and the man promptly named and described several places where she could indulge in either pleasure. Blake finished her drink and watched the mobile face in front of her as he animatedly recalled the melodramatic antics at one of the local theaters. The face was not strictly handsome, but it seemed to fit the lively, warm, appealing personality that went with it. Again Blake took in the strong, healthy body that went with the face and personality. Any one of the three alone would have made him rate a second glance, but the three of them together made for a fascinating combination. Normally rather reserved toward men, Blake found herself very drawn to this man and was a little bemused to find herself feeling this way. What is it about him? she wondered as he finished his hilarious description of his experience at the theater.

The man reached out and touched Blake's shoulder softly, yet a shock wave of response to his touch leapt from her, and she felt a fleeting urge to reach out and touch his flaming hair. But her interest in him was not just physical. Behind that compelling face there seemed to be a warm personality and, if those clear eyes were anything to go by, a fine mind and an intellect that would rival the best. Mistaking her stillness for a lack of response, the man touched her shoulder again. Behind her a young waiter from the restaurant downstairs stood patiently. "Captain, your table is ready," the boy said softly.

"Thank you," Blake said as she rose reluctantly. Damn! She hated to leave the man, but she couldn't very well stay here and drink all night. She picked up her purse and told the waiter to put the drink on her dinner bill.

"Young man, will there be a table for me soon?" the redheaded stranger asked quietly as he sipped the last of his Perrier.

"No, sir, I don't believe so," the waiter said regretfully. "The main dining room's full tonight, and it will be at least another fifteen minutes."

"You can share mine," Blake blurted out suddenly before she even knew what she was doing. She blushed a fierce shade of red when she realized what she had said and how forward she had sounded. "That is, if you want," she stammered, turning even redder. Never a forward woman, this was the first time she had ever flat-out asked a stranger to share a table with her, and her own boldness had embarrassed her.

"Why, thank you, ma'am," he drawled as he stood beside her. He was taking in her embarrassment and his eyes were laughing at her, although his lips did not crack a smile. *Oh, well. So what if he knows I'm not really the forward type,* she thought matter-of-factly. *I don't suppose he minds, since he's coming with me.*

As they walked behind the waiter, Blake noted with

26

surprise that the redhead was not more than a couple of inches taller than her own five foot eight, but saw with appreciation that he walked gracefully and that his tight-muscled physique was even more striking when he was standing. *He really keeps in shape,* Blake thought as the muscles in his legs rippled powerfully.

The man turned to her in the door of the dining room. "By the way, do you have a handle I could call you?" Blake looked at him in bafflement. "You know, a handle. A name."

"Oh," Blake laughed. "Sure. I'm Bebe." *Now why did I tell him that?* she wondered as she took in the amusement in his eyes at the provocative sound of that name. Actually, the name was just the initials of Barbara Blake and used only by her immediate family, but she had to admit that it sounded sexy.

"I'm Bill," the man said simply as he extended his hand. She put her hand in his and they shook hands solemnly.

By the time the waiter had seated them at their table, Blake had made a supposition that she had to verify. "I bet you're a runner," she said as the waiter handed them their menus.

"Five miles a day, unless it snows," Bill replied enthusiastically. "And I don't think that will be a problem here. You, too, I guess."

Blake nodded. "Three miles every afternoon," she confirmed, surveying her menu. Skipping over the dishes with foreign names, she decided on broiled fish, and shut her menu. "It was the muscles in your legs," she said by way of explanation.

The waiter came to take their orders. Bill ordered a plate of Mexican food and Blake ordered her fish. "Where did you start running?" he asked curiously.

"High school track team," Blake replied, her eyes smiling at the memory. "Cross-country. Of course, I was a little smaller then."

"Not too much, I hope," Bill replied as he caressed her feminine curves with his eyes. "You would have been rather bony."

"Oh, I was," Blake laughed, never one to be self-conscious about her figure, past or present. "I was this tall at fourteen and as skinny as a rail. I danced with many a chin on my shoulder." She laughed and patted her right shoulder lovingly.

"And I would have been one of those chins," the redhead said ruefully. "I didn't manage to get this tall until I was almost out of high school."

"I wouldn't have minded," Blake assured him warmly. "Some of the nicest chins you ever met danced there." She laughed out loud at the memory and Bill joined in.

Their meal came and they had a hilarious time exchanging funny stories about things that had gone on in their high schools when they were students. Blake had attended a very affluent school in Chicago, where the students were wearing designer clothes before it became the thing to do, and she and Bill laughed together at her description of the boy who didn't like his new BMW and left it in the parking lot with the keys in it, hoping it would get stolen. Of course, it was still waiting for him when he got out of class that day. No one else had wanted it either!

She laughed in turn at Bill's description of the tiny high school he had attended in a small town in Alabama, the kind of school where the agricultural students would put a cow in the gym for a laugh, and she laughed even harder when he admitted that he had been the one who had put the cow there. Blake laughed until tears ran down her face at his funny tale of climbing up the fire escape to the window that he had unlocked that afternoon, and how he had to drag the unwilling cow through the gym doors while two of his buddies pushed her from behind.

Not willing to be outdone, Blake admitted that she managed to walk off with a pad of official office passes with the principal's signature on them during her sojourn as a student aide, and that she and her friends would write themselves passes to class when they had been gossiping in the bathroom past the bell. Bill told her of winning a state championship in track during his senior year, and Blake admitted that she had done almost as well, coming in second in her division at the state level. They talked and talked, oblivious to where they were or what they were eating, only conscious of a striking rapport that neither had expected to find in the Officer's Club with a total stranger.

Blake finally looked down in astonishment to find she'd finished eating, the scraps of her delicious dinner cold. They had been talking for almost two hours. "Good grief, it's almost eleven!" she yelped as she looked at her watch. "My first day on the job is tomorrow."

"Coffee before you go?" Bill asked wistfully, staring at her.

"Sure," Blake replied softly, unable to refuse this delightful man anything. He signaled and the waiter brought them each a steaming cup. "Mmm, this is good," she murmured as she sipped the rich brew.

"Sure beats the coffee we make in the office," the man teased as he stirred cream and sugar into his cup. "That stuff is enough to make a grown man cry." He sipped his coffee and looked at her curiously. "What do you do for good old Uncle Sam?" he asked genially. "I can't believe we spent the whole evening and haven't talked about our jobs yet."

Blake froze for just a second, her mind working furiously. She did not want to admit that she was a maintenance officer, because she was not particularly proud of that job. Yet, she didn't want to say she was a pilot, since that was not really true anymore. And if she told Bill the whole story, they would be here all night. Smiling a little, she compromised. "Oh, I'm on a new assignment and I'm not sure what all it involves," she said, which was the truth and enough to discourage further questioning. "How about you? What do you do?"

Bill hesitated for a second, then grinned. "Quality control," he said as he set the cup down and added more sugar and Blake tried not to shudder at the ruination of a perfectly beautiful brew. "I want to thank you for this evening," he said as he sampled his doctored coffee.

"Thank me? I ought to thank you," Blake replied warmly as she enjoyed her coffee and her last few minutes with this interesting man. "This was my first night in a new city, and I was a little lonely. I enjoyed your company immensely."

"The enjoyment was mutual," he replied. A faintly troubled expression crossed his face, and his eyes temporarily lost their sparkle. "I'm not looking forward to tomorrow," he said quietly, "and you helped me take my mind off of it."

"Oh?" Blake asked with quiet concern. "What happens tomorrow?"

The man grimaced a little. "No big deal. Just a new man in the unit. You know what I mean."

Blake nodded. "One of those whose reputation precedes him," she said understandingly. "A troublemaker?" she asked.

"No, just the opposite. A real hard-assed career type. Everything by the book. Looks for regulations to follow."

Blake nodded understandingly, although she personally

had never had any run-ins with that type of person. She was much more likely to clash with the lax unprofessional types who treated their jobs as a joke. "At least you've been warned," she said gently.

"Yeah, my buddy called me all the way down here to give me the good news," Bill replied.

Blake set her coffee cup down and picked up her check before Bill could do so. "I really do have to go," she said quietly, loathe to leave him because of the magic spell they had woven. Would they feel the same way about each other the next time they met? Blake looked at her companion and smiled to herself. Yes, they would meet again; Randolph was a small base. And the magic would be there, and maybe they would go with it.

Bill rose quickly. "Let me walk you to your car, Bebe," he said as he picked up his own check.

They walked to the almost empty parking lot and Blake fished out her keys. She unlocked the door and was about to open it when he laid a gentle hand on her arm and turned her around gently. "A kiss, Bebe," he said as he reached around her waist and drew her to him, capturing her lips with his own. The touch of his lips was electric, sending chills of delight down Blake's spine. Unconsciously she swayed closer to him, savoring the rough touch of his tongue as it traveled around her lips, yet did not presume further intimacy.

Blake gave in to the desire she had been suppressing all evening and wound her hands into the luxurious red hair, short and thick at his nape, feeling it surprisingly soft under her fingers. They clung together, lost in a world of their own, unconscious of the stares they were receiving from the young officers leaving the club. Bill ran his hand down Blake's arms and slid them around her waist, holding her close to his tough, muscular body. Blake pressed herself closer to him, every inch of his body impressed upon her tender skin. All reason was forgotten as Blake kissed him with a passion that she had never even known she had.

After long moments, sanity prevailed and they separated slowly. Bill was breathing hard, and Blake's face wore a distinctly bemused expression. Fighting an urge to throw herself back into his arms, she forced herself to climb into the car.

"Good night, sweet Bebe," he said as he shut the door after her.

"Good night, Bill," she whispered, touching her lips tentatively with her fingers.

Now why didn't I get her number? he asked himself as he drove home in the sparse late-night traffic. Stupid, stupid. He hadn't even thought about that until he had driven out of the parking lot, he was so shaken by that kiss. And no wonder. The evening had been magic, he had to admit, even for a thirty-one-year-old man who knew the score. And score was not in the cards with Bebe, he thought as he pulled into the driveway of his new subdivision house. Even though she had that sexy name and a beautiful body, she was not the kind who indulged in passing around her favors. Her quick exit from the cellar had proven that! It was a good thing that she had not guessed that he had deliberately followed her out of the cellar. He wandered inside the house and headed for the refrigerator, reached for a beer, then stopped himself. It was too late for a beer if he had to fly tomorrow morning.

Bill stood in front of the refrigerator and stared in, then broke off a chunk of cheese and nibbled on it. What did Bebe have against pilots? he wondered as he nibbled his cheese. She had tried to hide it, but something had been eating her when she had mentioned pilots. Probably a temporary thing, he reassured himself. By the time she found out that he was a pilot, she would be over it.

Yawning, he headed for the bathroom and stripped and showered quickly, staring at his nude, muscled body for a moment before he turned out the light and padded into the bedroom. Too bad he wasn't a little taller, he thought for the millionth time, but if he were, he'd be miserable in a small cockpit. He threw back the covers and climbed into the bed, lying on his back and staring at the ceiling. *I wonder if I'll ever see Bebe again,* he thought. Sure he would. Word of a gorgeous woman like her would get around the small base quickly. God, what a body! Yes, word would get around quickly. Of that he was sure. Just as word had gotten to him of the new maintenance officer they were getting in the morning. A by-the-book type. Real military hard-ass. Hooray, he thought disgustedly. His brow wrinkled and he frowned into the darkness. Well, tomorrow he would meet the man and be able to decide if Ralph had been right. And if Ralph were right, he was going to do his damnedest to stay out of the path of the infamous Blake Warner.

CHAPTER TWO

Blake jumped and swore as the alarm jangled into the still, early morning quiet of her gloomy bedroom. Groggily she groped for the button on the side of the clock and mashed it in with her thumb, then she lay back on the pillow, hoping to catch a few more minutes of silent rest. She had not gone to sleep until very late last night, her thoughts returning to a pair of dancing blue eyes every time she closed her eyes. She raised her hand and touched her lips gently. *I can hardly wait to see him again,* she thought as a dreamy smile curved her mouth and she snuggled down deeper into the covers for a ten-minute snooze. Unfortunately at that moment Calico decided to make the acquaintance of the sparrow outside the window and began a series of spirited chirps that would have raised the dead. Any possibility of snoozing eliminated, Blake shrugged her shoulders and climbed out of bed, moving swiftly before she stumbled into the bathroom for a shower.

Her shower over quickly, Blake wandered into her bedroom and pulled on her lacy underwear, then stood before the closet trying to decide what to wear on her first day at Randolph. Her choice of attire was very simple. She could wear either her regular uniform or she could wear green fatigues and combat boots. At Wright-Patterson she had worn her regular uniform all the time in the office, but here she would be around greasy airplanes much of the time, and on most days the fatigues would be the best choice. But today, her first day on the job, feminine vanity won out and she removed a regular uniform from a hanger and pulled it on. As she rummaged in the cardboard boxes for her shoes, she opened the wrong box by mistake and found her custom helmet, the one she had worn as a pilot, and had to blink back bitter tears that took her by surprise. Angrily slamming the lid of the box, she tried another one and located the shoes. A quick trip to the bathroom to put up her hair and fix her face a little and an even quicker trip to the kitchen for a glass of milk, and Blake was ready to report for duty.

It was still early when Blake drove into the base and was saluted by the guard, but the hangars were already buzzing with activity. She parked her car in a designated slot and wandered into the hangar where she had been told that her office would be. Wandering inside the huge, barnlike building, she felt an involuntary quickening of her heartbeat at the sight of the sleek T-38 that was parked in the middle of the hangar. Involuntarily she walked up to the plane and touched the side of the aircraft gingerly with her fingers. It was the first time she had been this close to an airplane since her accident, and she had to literally make herself turn around and walk away from it to keep from climbing into the cockpit and taxiing down the runway. Abruptly she strode into the small office that was marked MAINTENANCE. It was typically sparse, with three desks and a table with a grubby coffeemaker and plastic foam cups and plastic spoons scattered all over the table. A half-full can of coffee was sitting open, and two jars of nondairy creamer stood in their spilled-over powder at the end of the table.

Blake glanced around, hoping to find a clerk who could be told to straighten the table. Spotting no enlisted types who could be asked to take on the job, Blake sailed in and had the table spotless in minutes, then she carefully measured the coffee and put it into the coffeemaker. As she poured in the last of the water, the door opened behind her and in walked a short, stocky officer in greens. He shut the door behind him, muffling but not blocking out the sound of activity in the increasingly noisy hangar. Blake looked at his decorations and quickly determined that this was probably her commanding officer. She saluted smartly and waited for the man to acknowledge her presence.

The man acknowledged her salute, then stopped and stared at the name on her uniform. "Captain Blake Warner?" he asked as his astonishment turned into a smile of welcome.

"Captain Warner reporting for duty," she replied.

"I'm Colonel Alda, your new C.O." He reached out and gripped Blake's hand in his own, causing her to stifle a quick wince at the strength of his grip.

"I'm glad to meet you, sir," Blake said sincerely. Although she had never heard of Colonel Alda before and knew nothing about him, she sensed from the cheerful but businesslike attitude he radiated that he would be good to work for. She sensed that he was much like Henry Saunders, and that in him she would find a friend as well as a commanding officer.

He released her hand and walked to the coffee table, his eyes widening in astonishment at the neatness and the brewing coffee. "You mean that damn-fool airman finally did something about that mess?" he asked in astonishment.

"No, sir," Blake admitted. "I did, and if you like, I can give your airman careful instructions as to the care and feeding of the watering hole."

"That would be fine, Captain Warner," Colonel Alda said with satisfaction. "I take it you're not one of those sensitive women officers who gets offended by doing a chore that could possibly be regarded as female?"

Blake fought to keep her lips from twitching. "No, sir, the only thing that offends me is terrible coffee," she said, deadpan. "Besides, I've already proven myself a capable officer."

Colonel Alda nodded and poured himself a cup of the steaming coffee. "Mmm, this is good," he said as he sampled the brew. He looked at Blake's decorations and

36

frowned in puzzlement. "Are you on a rated supplement?" he asked finally.

Blake's cheeks burned with embarrassment. A rated supplement was an assignment given to a flying pilot to broaden his or her horizons, and most pilots hated them because it took them out of the cockpit. "No, sir," she said simply, a bitter smile playing around her mouth. "I was injured and can't fly anymore."

Colonel Alda frowned, commiserating. "That's tough, Captain," he said, and Blake could sense real compassion behind those words. "Although, frankly, it will probably make you just that much better at this job." He motioned to the desk in the middle of the room. "Have a seat, and we'll go over some of the aspects of your new job."

Colonel Alda spent nearly two hours going over her new duties in great detail, until Blake's head was spinning at the vast amount of information she was expected to remember. Basically, her duties were to oversee the small army of maintenance personnel who kept the aircraft on Randolph operational. They would repair and maintain the airplanes, then one of four test pilots would take the planes out and test them on over a hundred factors that determined operational safety. If so much as one factor was not repaired to the pilot's satisfaction, the plane would not be released for use by the instructors. As he was winding down, Colonel Alda mentioned his test pilots again. "You'll find them a pleasure to work with. They're a great bunch of pilots," the colonel said warmly.

Blake nodded. "I'm sure they are," she replied in what she hoped was an enthusiastic enough voice. Stupidly, the possibility of having to work that closely with a group of pilots had not occurred to her, although someone certainly had to test the planes after they were repaired. "They have to be," she added.

"Yes, they do," the colonel replied, suddenly serious. "Although the maintenance personnel do their best, the reason that pilot is up there is that there was, or is, something wrong with the plane. If something does go wrong up there, those guys are on their own. Frankly, it's a hell of a lot more dangerous than instructor flying."

And a lot more exciting, Blake thought to herself.

"I'm not having a Commander's Call this week, so the guys will probably wander in on their own today to meet you," Colonel Alda added, and Blake could have sworn his eyes glinted with humor over a private joke. "Jim Rogers is the youngest pilot on the squad, but he's good and I have no complaints about him. Patrick Gordon and Tommy Ochoa are both newlyweds, Pat to a local girl and Tommy to his high-school sweetheart." Colonel Alda paused in his recital and Blake wondered for a moment if her new C.O. had maybe just a little taste for gossip.

Colonel Alda poured himself another cup of coffee and sat back down. "But you aren't going to believe the fourth pilot." Blake smiled to herself. Yes, Colonel Alda did like to gossip! "He's been here only a couple of months, but that guy has to be the best damn pilot you ever laid eyes on! I swear, he could fly a mosquito if we could ever get an engine screwed on! He's an ace if there ever was one."

Blake nodded, unreasonable jealousy boiling up in her. The man must be good, for his C.O. to carry on about him like that. Damn, she could have been that good! Adjusting her expression carefully so that her resentment did not show, she nodded and said again that she was looking forward to meeting all the pilots.

"Oh, you'll especially enjoy meeting William O'Gorman," Colonel Alda replied with that hint of humor in his eyes again. "Absolute tops as a pilot, but loves nothing better than a good joke, and has every lady on the base panting after him." Colonel Alda rose. "Think you can manage to take over now?" he asked briskly.

I better be able to, Blake thought. Out loud she replied, "Yes, sir," as they rose from their chairs.

As Colonel Alda left the office, she thought again about the four pilots whom she would be working with on a regular basis, and resentment reared its ugly head once again. She had known so little about this job that it had not dawned on her that she would have four pilots in the office next to hers. *It's ridiculous to resent them,* she thought, *but I do.*

She sat down in her chair and sipped her coffee, wondering especially about the ace pilot, William O'Gorman. Why had the colonel looked so amused when he had mentioned him by name? Was the man likely to come on to her? Not that she would have any problem repelling that type. She never did. She wondered fleetingly about Bill. Was he thinking about her today? Had he enjoyed their kiss?

Blake waded through paperwork for the rest of the morning, then walked over to the Officer's Club for a light lunch. She was just returning to her office when a plump young airman, barely out of her teens, collided with her in an attempt to open the office door. When the young girl realized that she had almost sent an officer sprawling, she blushed a fiery shade of red and stood at attention, ready for the inevitable tongue-lashing that would follow such an accident.

Blake looked at the clumsy girl and immediately took pity on her. "At ease, airman." The girl visibly relaxed. "Just be more careful next time, all right?"

The girl nodded vigorously. "Yes, sir—uh, ma'am," she stammered. Without really knowing why, Blake took an immediate liking to the awkward young girl.

Blake walked into the office and motioned for the girl to follow her. "I'm Captain Warner," she said to the airman.

"I'm Airman Sally Du Bois," the girl piped up proudly. "I'm your clerk." The girl's eyes darted toward the coffee table and her eyes widened in astonishment. "What happened to the table?" she asked, forgetting that she was talking to an officer.

"I cleaned it up, Sally," Blake replied. "Please take a look at it. From now on I expect to find it in this shape." Blake's words were polite, but they were an order.

"Yes, ma'am," the girl assured Blake.

Since the coffee that Blake had made this morning was almost gone, she asked Sally to make another pot, then she turned to her desk to begin her afternoon's work. She happened to glance up at Sally and watched, horrified, as Sally dumped in twice as much coffee as the unit called for. "No, Sally!" she cried, making Sally jump and spill coffee all over the table.

"I'm sorry, ma'am," the girl mumbled.

Blake took a deep breath and got up, schooling herself not to laugh out loud at the poor girl. "Airman, I'm going to give you lessons in how to make a good cup of coffee," Blake said in her best military voice, unaware that a twitching smile had given her away and put Sally at ease. "Listen closely, because in the morning I want you to do it, and I want you to do it this way." She took the scoop out of the girl's hands and measured out the proper amount of coffee, shaking it very carefully into the basket. "Did you see how much coffee I put in there?" she asked the girl.

"Yes, ma'am," Sally replied crisply.

Blake then took the pot and filled it with water and

poured it into the machine. "Did you see how much water I poured in?" she asked.

"Yes, ma'am," Sally replied again.

"Good. See that you do it this way in the morning." Blake switched on the machine and turned to find the door open and three men standing there in sweat-ringed flying suits, helmets in hand, staring in open-mouthed astonishment at Blake and Sally. Momentarily disconcerted at being caught giving cooking lessons, Blake recovered quickly and turned a cool and remote eye on the three pilots in the doorway. "Are you the test pilots?" she asked unnecessarily.

The men nodded as they walked into her small office, crowding in and gathering around the coffeepot. "And you must be the new maintenance officer?" one of them asked.

"Yes, I'm Blake Warner, the maintenance officer," she said stiffly, her formal behavior contrasting sharply with the casual attitude of the pilots.

A dapper young pilot with a Clark Gable moustache came forward and shook her hand. "I'm Captain Patrick Gordon," he said as he looked at her with admiration and a surprised amusement in his eyes. It was the same amusement that Colonel Alda had regarded her with, and frankly it puzzled her. "Pleased to meet you."

The other two pilots, also captains, introduced themselves to her. Jim Rogers was a lanky, quiet man, and judging by his accent from the Midwest, and Tommy Ochoa was a friendly California native. All three were personable and friendly and would probably be very easy to work with, yet Blake found herself being very proper and formal with them, even more so than she usually was with fellow officers. If the other pilots found anything amiss in her attitude, however, it didn't show, and all three waited until the coffeepot was full and poured themselves a cup.

"Boy, is this coffee going to come as a shock to old Rusty!" Tommy laughed.

Who's Rusty? Blake wondered.

"He's been bitching about this coffee ever since he got transferred here."

"I'm willing to bet it won't be any better in the morning," Jim said laconically. "Sally'll be making it again."

"It should be considerably better in the morning," Blake replied crisply. "I showed her how to make it properly."

All three men burst into loud guffaws. "Yes, and you're about the sixth person to show her how!" Patrick laughed. "Mark my words. It won't be any better, we promise you!"

The pilots finished their coffee, picked up their helmets, bade her good afternoon, and wandered across the hangar to the planes they were to test.

As she watched them go, Blake felt waves of resentment against the three men well up in her chest, and she fought them down as best she could. She could not afford to resent four competent colleagues just because they were pilots. Briefly she wondered about the fourth pilot, O'Gorman, the one who was supposed to be so good, then she pulled the door of her office to and sat down at her desk, ignoring the sound of engines roaring and the T-38's taking off.

She had been working for most of the afternoon when the sound of footsteps coming up the hangar disturbed her concentration. Stretching, she laid down her pen and wiggled her toes inside her shoes, then checked her watch and sighed with relief. It was almost five and in a few minutes she could go home.

"You should have seen the new maintenance officer

showing Sally how to make a pot of coffee!" Patrick Gordon's voice said as the footsteps passed her door. A strangely familiar voice murmured something in reply. "Naw, Rusty, it's not too late. Go on in and meet him before you go on home."

Him? Blake thought. Patrick Gordon, are you blind?

The man murmured something else quietly. "Oh, go ahead," Patrick's voice chided. "I think you'll be surprised."

Blake straightened in her chair as firm footsteps approached her door. She deliberately looked down at her papers, then glanced up as the footsteps entered the room, freezing in positive shock as she looked up to meet a pair of blue eyes, no longer grinning at her outrageously, but smiling at her with the proper formal politeness. The eyes widened in astonishment but quickly returned to their previous state of polite interest, although Blake knew that it had taken him a great deal of effort to hide his feelings so quickly.

She rose from her chair slowly and took in the sight of the man she knew as Bill. His flaming hair was flattened down to his head from his tight-fitting helmet and his flight suit was sweat-ringed from the test flights he had made in the sweltering cockpits, but his sensuous virility could not be disguised even by his disreputable appearance. She looked at the patch the left side of his shirt. Above the wings the name read O'GORMAN and the rank was captain. Her Bill was the ace pilot, William O'Gorman! Bitter disappointment surged through Blake at the discovery, although she should have known last night when he ordered only Perrier. Blake's cheeks burned as she realized that she was the hard-assed officer he had not wanted to meet today. No wonder the other men had been

43

looking at her with such amusement. Thank God none of them knew the whole story!

A mixture of emotions, none of them pleasant, flared in her, but she was too much a military officer to let her feelings show on the outside. "I'm Blake Warner," she said in her chilliest military voice. She extended her hand and shook his purposefully, ignoring the sensation of awareness that shot through her fingers and up her arm. Involuntarily she remembered the way those same fingers had felt caressing her just last night. "And you're Bill O'Gorman?"

"Rusty O'Gorman," the man corrected her quietly as he let go of her hand and walked over to the coffeepot. "I seldom use Bill anymore." So why did you use it last night? Blake asked herself, admitting inwardly that Rusty really fit his personality better than Bill ever would.

He poured himself a cup of her coffee and tasted it tentatively. "Good coffee," he said finally. "I hear you've been teaching Airman Du Bois," he added, grinning a little as he had last night.

His smile left Blake unmoved. "I've shown Sally how to make coffee," she acknowledged frostily. "I think we'll see an improvement in the next day or two."

"Don't count on it," Rusty said under his breath as he sipped his coffee.

"Is there anything I can do for you?" Blake asked pointedly as Rusty settled himself into the chair opposite her desk. She was in no mood for a social visit, especially with this man.

In response he placed several papers on her desk and, commandeering her pen, signed three and handed the fourth to her. "I've released these three planes, since they passed inspection with flying colors," he said as he tossed those three papers in the middle of her desk. "Now, this one just isn't fixed yet. The engines aren't burning right." He proceeded to explain to Blake with surprising precision exactly what each engine was doing wrong, and made a couple of good suggestions as to what might correct the problem. In spite of her animosity, Blake had to admit that he obviously knew his way around a T-38.

Their business quickly taken care of, Blake rose and took her purse out of her desk drawer. Rusty made no move to rise, even after Blake had put on her jacket. Instead, he slowly finished the rest of his coffee and tossed his cup into the trash, eyeing her with wary speculation. She returned his gaze with one of cool hauteur, looking at the door pointedly. "Captain O'Gorman, it was a pleasure meeting you," she said formally, taking her keys out of her purse. "I'm sure we'll have a long and very pleasant working relationship." Such was her control that she only lightly stressed the word *working*.

"Make it Rusty," he replied genially as he stood slowly and walked toward her and the door. He halted when he was just a few inches from her and looked into her green eyes, today opaque and cold, then noticed with concealed surprise the wings on her jacket. Although she didn't move a muscle, he could feel her mentally retreat all the way across the room from him.

Blake looked at him impassively, determined not to let his nearness affect her, even though he was so close that she could smell the manly sweat from the flight suit. Bitter disappointment flooded her and drove away all of the warm, sensual feelings she had had for Rusty O'Gorman when she had met him as Bill last night. Last night he had been a lovely stranger. Today he was a pilot, and he had dreaded meeting her because she was a hard-assed military type.

Rusty leaned forward and opened the door, brushing

45

against Blake and sending little shivers down her side. Disconcerted by the contact, she stepped back involuntarily, and Rusty's mouth tightened. He started through the door and then turned back around to her. "Would you like to have dinner in town this evening, Bebe?" he asked quietly. "I know a nice place that has dancing that you might enjoy."

"I don't think so, Rusty," she said curtly. "And please make it Blake."

His fingers tightened on the doorknob and his mouth thinned with displeasure. "I don't suppose an apology would matter much, would it?" he asked tightly.

Blake shrugged. "It doesn't matter. Besides, you ought to know by now that you can't believe all the gossip you hear anyway," she replied dismissively.

To her surprise, Rusty turned a bright shade of red. "I guess you're right," he mumbled. "But the offer's still good."

Blake shook her head, not even remotely tempted. "I didn't think so," Rusty replied as he turned on his heel. "Good night, Bebe-Blake," he said softly as he walked out the door.

He thinks I'm mad about the hard-assed part, Blake thought as she watched his stiff-shouldered figure stride out of the building. Actually Blake could forgive him that. She had crossed swords often enough with some of her fellow officers at Wright-Patterson to have honestly earned the title, and it was easy to imagine the glee with which one of them would have recounted her attitude to Rusty, deliberately setting him up by not telling him that she was an attractive woman. But a pilot! Damn, why did he have to be a pilot? She thought about the sweat-soaked flight suit that he wore and the helmet that he carried, and she had to bite her lip to keep tears from forming in her eyes. The fates have a cruel sense of humor, she thought as she slammed the door of her office behind her. The most attractive man that she had met in years, and she was so jealous of him that she couldn't stand to be in the same room with him!

Well, O'Gorman, you really blew it, Rusty thought as he slammed his small pickup into gear and roared out of the parking lot. How the hell could he have known that Bebe was really Blake Warner, and that Blake Warner was a woman, and a knockout at that! Quickly he controlled his temper and eased his foot from the accelerator, at least until he was off the base, for he had no desire to tangle with the strict M.P.s.

Once off the base and out of Universal City, he stomped on the accelerator again and took out a little of his aggression in speed, although he would really have preferred to cross-country to Ohio and punch Ralph in the damn mouth. Although Ralph had certainly had no way of knowing that Rusty was going to spill the beans to her at the Officer's Club like he had.

Damn your big mouth, man, he thought as he darted around a semi and received a rude gesture from the aggravated driver. Returning the gesture, Rusty took the exit to his house and pulled up in front of it. Of course, she knew that she was the hard-assed officer he had dreaded, and she had frozen up like a Popsicle, he thought as he climbed out of the truck and unlocked his door. Stripping off the flight suit and boots, he dumped them on the entryway floor, flopped down on the couch, and stared at the ceiling, his frown of disgust turning into one of puzzlement. She was a maintenance officer, yet she was wearing wings. So why wasn't she flying? At three quarters of a million per pilot to train, the Air Force didn't take a pilot out of the cockpit unless there was a damn good reason. Well, maybe she wasn't out of the cockpit. Maybe she was on a rated supplement. Was that why she had made that crack last night about too many pilots being around?

Rusty reached over and picked up the remote control, flipped through the channels, and turned the television back off again in disgust. He wondered again why Blake Warner wasn't flying anymore. *Maybe I'll just ask her,* he thought, then decided against it for the time being, remembering the frost in the green eyes that had smiled at him so warmly the night before. There was no sense stirring up any more antagonism in her than he already had. Restless beyond belief, Rusty ignored his weariness and changed quickly into shorts and jogging shoes. The only way he could work off this agitation was to run, and in spite of the five miles he had already run this morning, he banged out the front door and loped down the street.

Blake sat on the couch in her new apartment, a half-eaten hamburger sitting in front of her on the coffee table. She had picked up the hamburger on the way home, thinking that once she got back to the privacy of her new home, she would feel like eating. But once there, her imaginary appetite deserted her and it had been all she could do to gag down half of the burger. Sighing, Blake ran her fingers through her long, silky hair and held a strand up in front of her face, tugging on it a little. Even her hair was a painful reminder of how much her life had changed, how different it was from what she had always wanted it to be. During her pilot training she had been required to keep her hair short in order to wear the tight-fitting flight helmet, but in the three years since the accident that had so changed her life, she had let her hair grow out to its present luxurious length.

Sighing, Blake cradled a pillow in her arms and stared at the boxes of unpacked paraphernalia that littered her living room. She knew that she should get up and unpack just a few, but her mind kept returning to the painful reality that her new job only emphasized. She was a pilot, yet not a pilot. She could fly a T-38 better than almost anybody she knew, yet she couldn't fly one an inch. What a cruel irony, she thought. If this was to be her fate, why, oh, why couldn't she have flunked out of training or something? Why had she gotten so close only to have her dream snatched away?

Blake settled back on the couch and let her mind drift back to her childhood and the years that followed, letting herself remember everything for the first time in a long time. Her father, Charles Warner, had been an Air Force pilot, and some of Blake's earliest memories were of standing on the edge of a runway with him as he pointed out each plane blasting into the air, roaring up into the sky. He would lean over and whisper to her that she could fly away like Daddy someday, and she believed him, and promised herself that she would do just that. Blake never lost that vision, even when her father was shot down in Vietnam when she was in junior high. Instead of killing her dream, losing her father seemed only to intensify her desire to fly, even though she knew there were no women pilots in the Air Force.

She sampled her first real flying in high school in a local flying club, and she had loved every moment, adoring the reality of flying as much as the dream. At the time, Blake's mother had tried gently to discourage her daughter's interest in flying, but when Blake was a freshman in college, the Air Force opened pilot training to women, barring them only from actual combat experience. Blake was elated. Now her dream was a real possibility. She not only could fly, but she could fly with the Air Force. She quickly enrolled in Air Force ROTC, since it was too late to get into the Air Force Academy, and changed her major from business to engineering. The proudest day of her life was the day that she both graduated from college and received her commission into the Air Force.

Although Blake had flown some in college, she could hardly wait to graduate from the small Cessna and into a "real" plane. The next few months tried Blake's patience as she worked in a small office in Chicago and waited to go on active duty. Finally her orders came. She was to report to Williams AFB to begin her fifty-week training as an Air Force pilot. Blake's features clouded as she recalled the painful confrontation with Andy, her college sweetheart, and the subsequent breaking of her engagement when her orders finally came. When faced with the reality of a pilot for a wife, Andy, who had no interest in the military, had balked and demanded that Blake resign her commission. Blake had loved Andy dearly, but she had loved flying more, so tearfully she returned his ring and reported to Williams to begin the most exhausting, satisfying year of her life.

An involuntary smile touched Blake's mouth as she remembered that year. She had naively reported to Williams, expecting to be turned loose in a T-38 the next day. Instead, it was six weeks before they let her near an airplane. She and the other trainees spent hours on academics, learning every nut, bolt, and vector involved in flying an Air Force plane. They also spent days learning lifesaving skills and how to use a parachute. Blake laughed out loud as she remembered being towed with her chute open behind a truck, and jumping off innumerable water towers, and recalled the rigorous survival training in the desert, but she and the other pilots learned. She would still cringe as she remembered the miserable experience of having her custom helmet poured, literally, right on her head. But she did well, sitting up at night with her roommate Suzanne Henderson to study, and finally the day came when she got inside a T-37 for the first time. In spite of her lack of experience, and the fact that it was the smaller of the two training planes, she felt like she had come home.

Blake reached out and picked up her hamburger, munching on it absently. She had learned quickly in the T-37, spending the next three months mastering the operation of the little plane. She had spent the first ten hours with an instructor with her, then she had taken it out for over eighty hours of solo time. Of course, her instructors had plenty to criticize, but she learned and she learned fast, and when she and her class had mastered the slower plane, they graduated to the small but powerful T-38s, which Blake and the rest of the pilots loved. They went well over the speed of sound, and the glamorous little jets were a joy to fly.

As she had in the 37s, Blake mastered both contact flying, where she would do rolls, figure eights, stalls, spins, and other maneuvers designed to improve her skill as a pilot, and formation flying, where she and the other pilots learned to hold a formation. She also mastered instrument flying and got to fly several interesting cross-countries.

Although the days were long and the training grueling, with twelve-hour days and long study sessions lasting deep into the night, Blake had thrived during this period, becoming obsessed with flying, as did most of the young pilots, and could hardly wait for the day when she would receive her beloved wings.

A bitter smile touched Blake's mouth as she thought of the day she had gotten her wings. If she let herself remember, she could still taste the giddy excitement of that after-

51

noon on her tongue. She had made it! Not that there was any doubt in her mind that she would, but she was beside herself with excitement nevertheless. Her roommate Suzanne was even more excited, since she had seriously doubted that she would even make it through the program.

The girls were properly solemn at the ceremony, but then their exuberant spirits took over and they danced around the parking lot like a couple of foolish teenagers. The pilots were being honored at a party at the Officer's Club there on base, but Suzanne had wanted to pick up her boyfriend who lived in Phoenix, so Blake suggested that they ride together in Suzanne's little car. As they drove closer to Phoenix, their high spirits got the best of them, and Suzanne was laughing so hard at one of Blake's jokes that she did not see the carload of teenagers that was trying to pass them on the right. She swerved into the car and then bounced into a car coming in the opposite direction, finally coming to rest in a ditch on the opposite side of the road. The windows shattered into a million pieces and sprayed both girls with a hailstorm of flying glass.

At first Blake's concern had been purely cosmetic. When the doctors assured her that she would be unmarked, she relaxed and rejoiced that she had not been killed, and that she was going to be all right. But then the bandages had come off her right eye, and subsequent testing revealed that she had sustained a permanent blind spot in the peripheral vision in her right eye. Blake had sat in stunned silence as the young doctor explained as gently as he could that she could no longer pass the vision test for an Air Force pilot. She would be able to wear her wings with pride, but she would never fly an airplane again.

At first she was so stunned that for days she couldn't even cry, then, once home from the hospital, she cried every day for weeks until bitterness replaced her grief. She was so bitter that she refused even to see Suzanne, who was actually hurt worse than Blake, but who would be back in the cockpit in just a few months, even though the girl begged Blake to see her.

As she recuperated from her injuries Blake considered getting out of the Air Force, but thought again when she learned that her injuries would bar her from flying for most of the civilian airlines also. Although she didn't really want to fly civilian, since she felt deep down that it wasn't as important as military flying, she was still bitter. She had stayed in the Air Force and had asked for an assignment that would take her as far from pilots and flying as she could get. In the Air Force that was hard to do. But miraculously an opening in design on the Next Generation Trainer had come up, and so Blake had gratefully followed her orders and had worked at Wright-Patterson for the last three years while her classmates at Williams had taken to the skies. Thankfully, her earlier bitterness was fading some, but she still found it hard sometimes to believe that such a rotten piece of luck had actually come her way.

Blake reached up and was surprised to find tears on her cheeks. Brushing them away, she stared at the cold hamburger, then wrapped it up in disgust and tossed it into the trash. She had not thought about her accident much at Wright-Patterson, willing herself to put it behind her, but it seemed that here at Randolph she was going to be confronted with her feelings of resentment and loss every day. Her feelings of disappointment had faded but not disappeared, and in the last three years she had begun to resent other pilots with an emotion that more than bordered on jealousy. She not only was jealous of their flying status, but she did not want to be around them because they reminded her sorely of her loss.

Unbidden, the memory of two dancing blue eyes cavorted across her mind, to be replaced by the vision of her handsome Bill standing there in a sweaty flight suit. Damn you, Bill, why did you have to be Rusty O'Gorman, ace pilot? Why couldn't you have been a flight surgeon, or a lawyer, or an engineer? Throwing a pillow at the wall, Blake groaned in frustration. The magic with Bill was gone, as though it had never been. It had disappeared the minute she realized who he was. Unreasonable as her attitude was, apparently she was stuck with it. *I'm sorry, Rusty, Bill, whoever you are,* Blake thought as she stood up and started to unload a box of records into the stereo cabinet.

CHAPTER THREE

Blake poked around in the pile of frozen steaks and winced. Even at the base exchange the price of meat was ridiculous! Oh, well, it was still significantly cheaper here than at the civilian grocery stores, she thought as she selected two small rib steaks and tossed them into her basket. She wandered down the meat counter and picked up a few cheaper cuts of meat and a chicken breast, then headed out to the aisles to stock up on staples. Although she had been in town for nearly a week, this was the first chance she had to come shopping and stock her kitchen. She had either eaten out or bought fast food every night since she had arrived, and she was ready to eat a little of her own cooking again.

Wandering up and down the aisles, she found all the usual staples, plus a few things that were necessary to her even if they weren't for everyone else, such as canned mushrooms and exotically flavored tea. Absently, she pushed her cart around a corner and banged it smack into the cart of a tall, dark-headed woman who was picking up a box of cereal.

"Sorry," Blake said as the woman turned around to see what had happened to her basket.

Both women gasped in shock. Blake stared, speechless, into the face of Suzanne Henderson. Blake blinked a couple of times to be sure that it really was Suzanne, and not just a woman who looked like her. But, no, it was Suzanne, a little older, a little more shapely although still thin. The liquid brown eyes and the shining dark cap of hair were the same, although now Suzanne's dark hair was cut into a sleek wedge rather than permed into tight curls. Blake swallowed as the shock assaulted her. This was Suzanne, the woman who had cost her a flying career. Yet, this was also the Suzanne who had been her closest friend for the better part of a year, and that was the only part that mattered now.

Blake saw the shock on Suzanne's face turning into distinct apprehension. *She's scared of me,* Blake thought in shock. *And I'm so glad to see her!* All the bitterness toward Suzanne had dissolved long ago and she opened her arms. Suzanne stepped into them, hugging Blake tightly.

"I've missed you, Blake," she said simply, tears in her eyes.

"I've missed you too," Blake replied honestly, not realizing until that very moment just how much she had missed Suzanne.

"So what are you doing at Randolph? Are you stationed here?" Suzanne asked excitedly.

Blake nodded.

"Are you flying again?" Suzanne added hopefully.

"No," Blake said shortly. "I'm a maintenance officer." Seeing Suzanne's face start to fall, she rushed on. "I've just spent three years with Colonel Saunders on the Next Generation Trainer at Wright-Patterson. Got to use a little of that fancy engineering degree."

"And they put you in as a maintenance officer?" Suzanne asked curiously.

"Yes, and don't ask me why," Blake replied honestly. She swallowed and asked the next inevitable question. "How about you? Still flying?" she asked a little too casually.

"I'm a training instructor in the T-37s," Suzanne said. "We've been here almost six months now."

"We?" Blake asked. "Did you marry Sammy?" Sammy was the boy they were supposed to pick up in Phoenix the night of the accident.

Suzanne's face looked momentarily bitter. "No, he dropped me like a hot potato after the accident," she said quietly. "I didn't have too many friends crowding around me after it happened."

Ouch, thought Blake to herself. "So whom did you marry?" she asked as she looked down at the graceful diamond set on Suzanne's hand. It was expensive, obviously out of the price range of the average military officer.

Suzanne followed Blake's gaze down to her ornately ringed hand. "John is an instructor like me," she said laughingly. "These rings are a family heirloom. He comes

56

from a banking family in Upstate New York. Lots of old money." At Blake's puzzled frown, Suzanne laughed understandingly. "So what's he doing in the service? He just loves to fly, can't stay out of planes, you know?"

"Yes," Blake said quietly. "I know." She spoke levelly, keeping as much of the resentment as she could out of her voice.

In spite of Blake's self-control, Suzanne's face flamed a bright shade of crimson and her eyes blinked quickly several times, as though forcing back tears. "I'm sorry, Blake," she said with a voice that was suspiciously wobbly. "I've been sorry every damn day for the last three years. That's what I wanted to tell you at Williams. I realize what I did to you and I hate it."

Blake swallowed the lump in her throat. "And I'm sorry that I wouldn't come and see you after the accident," she replied honestly. "That was inexcusable of me." Taking a deep breath to control her tears, she looked Suzanne in the eye and spoke from the heart. "The accident's in the past," Blake said quietly. "Let's leave it there and go on. Our friendship was deeper than that, wasn't it?"

Suzanne nodded wordlessly, tears in her eyes.

Blake looked down at her pile of groceries and grimaced. "I better get this stuff home before it melts," she continued. "Please call me—I'll have my phone in a couple of days and you can get the number from Information," Blake begged. "You're looking wonderful, Suzanne," she added. "Marriage must agree with you."

"Blake, wait," Suzanne said quickly. "Would you like to come over to dinner on Friday night? I'd love you to meet John and get to know him. He's a very special person."

"I'm sure he is," Blake replied. She smiled at Suzanne,

her heart suddenly light with joy. She and Suzanne were going to be friends again! It would be wonderful to be able to talk to her like they used to. Knowing that she had completely forgiven Suzanne, and glad that she no longer resented her friend, she nodded eagerly. "Sure, I'd love to come," she said brightly. "What time do you want me to be there?"

"About eight?" Suzanne asked, obviously delighted that Blake had accepted her invitation. "That will give me a little time to fix something really nice for supper."

"I hope you've improved a little since Williams," Blake said dryly, winking. Suzanne's cooking had been a constant source of amusement between them.

"Oh, I've improved." Suzanne laughed, her eyes sparkling with pleasure in the shared joke. She reached into her purse, pulled out her checkbook, and took out a deposit slip, handing it to Blake. "This has our address and telephone number on it," she said. "If something comes up, call me, but otherwise we'll see you on Friday." She reached out and placed her hand on Blake's arm. "It's good to see you again, Blake," she said softly, a suspicion of tears in her eyes. "I missed you."

"Don't I know it," Blake replied, reaching out and hugging Suzanne again. "I'm looking forward to meeting John."

"Thanks," Suzanne said as she turned her cart around. "'Bye!"

Blake watched as the tall, pretty woman made her way to the meat counter, presumably to buy meat for Friday night. She looked down at the deposit slip in her hand and noted that Suzanne's name was now Parks, then shoved the paper down into her purse, looking forward to Friday night. Yes, she was sincerely glad to see Suzanne. They had been so close, and Blake had missed her so much. And she was glad that she had seen her again. The accident had not really been Suzanne's fault anyway, Blake thought to herself as she turned her basket around and headed for the paper goods. It was hardly Suzanne's doing that the car had passed them on the right, and she had been distracting Suzanne terribly. No, she had stopped blaming Suzanne a long time ago. In fact, she blamed herself a whole lot more than she had ever blamed Suzanne. Perhaps if she had not been acting silly and distracting Suzanne, the accident would never have happened. Sighing, Blake threw a package of toilet paper into the basket and headed for the checkout.

Blake leaned back in her chair and sighed audibly. The little office was hot, and her fatigues and boots were almost as sweaty as the pilots' flight suits. She had spent the better part of the day in the sweltering shop supervising the repair of a difficult engine, and she still wasn't sure that the repair had been done correctly. Oh, well, the only thing to do with the damned thing was to put it back in the T-38 and send one of the test pilots up in it. If it came back thumbs-up, then she could be sure that it was all right.

Sighing, she pushed a strand of hair back into the loosely braided knot that she wore for work these days, having given up her elegant chignon after her first day in the shops, when she had had to put it back up three times before noon. Blake had been surprised to find that she actually enjoyed the job that she had turned up her nose at just a few months before. It was a real challenge to keep those airplanes in top shape, and she found that she enjoyed the occasional piece of detective work necessary to find out what was wrong with a particular plane.

Blake reached up and pulled on her collar a little, trying

to let a little cool air touch her hot skin. This town was hot! But except for the heat, San Antonio was not a bad place to be. In fact, Blake, to her surprise, had found herself not only liking San Antonio itself, but she was finding a lot to like about this entire tour. As she had predicted on her first day at work, Colonel Alda was a peach to work for, and she had spent a delightful evening in his home with his wife and three lively teenagers. And little Airman Du Bois, with her funny chatter and even funnier mistakes, kept Blake chuckling for most of the day. Blake had taken the girl under her wing, patiently showing her such mundane details as how to place the carbon between the forms with the carbon side down, and had been rewarded by Sally's unwavering devotion and gallons of still-terrible coffee. And in spite of herself, she found herself warming to the three other test pilots, their infectious good humor impossible to resist, even though she was still very reserved toward Rusty.

Blake reached into her purse and pulled out the slip of paper with Suzanne's address on it and smiled a little. Tonight was the night she was supposed to go to dinner at Suzanne's, and she had looked forward all week to meeting Suzanne's husband. She shoved the paper back into her purse and wandered over to the coffeepot, pouring herself a cup of coffee and making a face at the taste of the foul brew. Was a decent cup of coffee totally beyond Airman Du Bois? she wondered ruefully. "Sally!" she called, for once a little exasperated with her young friend. There was no answer, nor did the plump little airman come running as she usually did.

"I think Colonel Alda sent her over to the Taj Mahal on an errand," a familiar voice said as Rusty stepped into Blake's office with a stack of release papers in his hand.

Blake jumped and spilled hot coffee on her hand.

"Damn it, Rusty, did you have to startle me like that?" she demanded, wiping her hand off with a paper napkin, grateful that the coffee hadn't been as hot as it sometimes was. She rubbed her hand absently and picked up the coffeepot. "And that was the last cup," she said disgustedly. "Oh, well, it probably wasn't worth drinking anyway." She measured out some more coffee and placed it in the coffeemaker, conscious of Rusty's eyes watching her every move. In spite of his disturbing presence, she moved quickly and gracefully, switching on the machine and wiping up the last of her spilled coffee. "I still haven't been able to teach that girl to make a decent cup of coffee," she said ruefully.

"Oh, well, at least the table's clean," Rusty observed as he lowered himself into a chair and watched her with his intensely blue eyes.

His eyes are dancing again, she thought as he handed her some signed release papers. She riffled through the papers and gratefully added four more planes to her roster for next Monday. One of her duties was to schedule planes for the instructors to use each day, and if too many planes were tied up in maintenance, it was hard to schedule as many flights as were necessary. Placing the papers on her desk, she flopped down in her chair and surveyed Rusty through lowered lids. *I wonder if I'm still the hard-assed officer he dreaded so,* she thought as she met his mocking glance with a cool look of her own.

"What are you doing this weekend?" he asked teasingly, making the mundane question somehow not mundane at all. His teasing manner made the question into something of a challenge, but one that Blake did not choose to meet.

"Nothing much," she said shortly, not mentioning her dinner at Suzanne's this evening.

Rusty looked at her with amusement. "Not going to the

Officer's Club?" he asked with laughter dancing in his eyes.

"No," Blake said firmly, blushing a little. Even after two weeks the memory of their passionate embrace could make her heart beat a little faster, and her cheeks burned with the memory of her uninhibited response to his touch.

For the first week after their meeting in the Officer's Club and the subsequent mutual disillusionment the next day, they had been coolly polite to each other, and Rusty appeared to be almost indifferent to her. But in the last week Rusty's attitude had thawed even if hers hadn't, and he had returned to being the teasing, arrogant, appealing man she had met in the Officer's Club. And in spite of her resentment, her magnetic attraction to him was returning, much to her dismay. She had thought last week that knowing that he was a pilot would be enough to permanently squash anything she felt for him. But it had not, and she felt herself drawn to him as strongly as she had been that night in the Officer's Club. Knowing that such a feeling could only lead to further misery for her, she had firmly ignored the way she felt when he was near, and had kept her outward response to Rusty on a purely professional level.

"Too bad," Rusty said, his eyes dancing. "The fellows over there could use the treat!" His eyes traveled down her body, most of its allure camouflaged by fatigues and boots. "I swear, the things you can do to those green things!" His eyes went up in an attitude of a prayer of thanksgiving.

"Funny, Rusty, real funny," Blake replied as she got up and poured herself a cup of the freshly made coffee. Automatically she poured Rusty a cup and handed it to him, accidentally brushing his hands, his touch invoking the memory of him touching her body intimately, tenderly, passionately. She moved away quickly, before she betrayed herself, but Rusty grinned knowingly as he reached over and picked up the sugar dispenser and liberally dosed his coffee with sugar. "How can you do that to a perfectly innocent cup of coffee?" she asked incredulously.

"I need the energy," Rusty replied wickedly, sipping the hot coffee enthusiastically. "Blake, you make a marvelous cup of coffee."

"How would you know, with all that sugar in it?" she asked sardonically.

"Now, don't be nasty," Rusty replied. "There's a lucky lady who can't wait for me to show up tonight, just bursting with energy for her."

"Oh, you're going out?" Blake replied stiffly, jealousy of the unknown woman shooting through her.

"Sure am. I've got a hot one tonight!" Rusty crowed, never taking his eyes off Blake's face. "We don't all do the old-maid routine, you know," he added wickedly.

If you let him know you're jealous, you'll never live it down, she told herself firmly. "You don't?" she asked indifferently. "Have a good time then." She refused to rise to the bait about being an old maid. "And thanks for the planes."

Rusty's eyes narrowed at her apparent indifference to his remarks. "See you Monday, beautiful," he said as he swallowed the rest of his coffee and sauntered out the door, twirling his helmet on his finger.

Damn, Blake thought as she locked her office five minutes later and marched to her car. This was ridiculous! She had never even dated Rusty, had only kissed him once, and she was almost insanely jealous of this "hot date" of his. Disgusted with herself for her ridiculous emotional response to him, she drove home, stripped off her fatigues and boots as soon as she was in the door, shivering a little in delight as the cool air touched her heated flesh, then walked to the refrigerator and poured herself a cup of cold mint tea.

Curling up on the couch, she forced herself to think rationally. She didn't want Rusty. A relationship with a pilot would only bring her pain. And besides, even if she had been interested in Rusty, she would never have been the "hot date" that he was so excited about. Although Blake was certainly no prude, she simply did not sleep with every man she went out with. She had to know a man very well and care for him a lot before she would become intimate with him, and it had been a long time since she had felt that way about any man. Blake sighed and sipped the cold tea. Yes, if circumstances had been different, she probably could have felt that way about Rusty. But now she would never know.

Glancing down at her watch, she jumped up from the couch, drank the rest of her tea quickly, and hurried to the bathroom. It was almost seven, and she was supposed to be at Suzanne's by eight. Shedding her underwear quickly, she turned on the shower and stepped under its stinging spray.

Blake squinted at the street map and peered again at the number on the mailbox, then checked the deposit slip that Suzanne had given her. Yes, this was the street and this was the address, so this huge, sprawling mansion must belong to Suzanne and her husband. John must have brought some of his family's "old money" with him! There was no way that two Air Force pilots could afford to live like this. Well, good for Suzanne, Blake thought as she climbed out of the car and tucked her cream-colored blouse back into the waist of her black velvet slacks.

She shook out her hair and strode to the front door, bouncing a little with anticipation of the pleasant evening ahead. She pressed the doorbell and was amused to hear the expensive, melodious chime sound throughout Suzanne's house. Firm footsteps came toward the door, then the door was thrown open and Blake found herself staring up into a face that, although it was cordial enough, was definitely a little wary of her. Blake swallowed as she smiled up into the man's face, hoping that his wariness was only a figment of her imagination. Then, determined to get to know Suzanne's husband and make him like her, she extended her hand and smiled at him warmly. "I'm Blake Warner," she said simply. "And you must be John."

The man smiled politely, but the lurking wariness did not go away. "Yes, I'm John Parks," he said as he shook her hand and moved aside so that she could enter. "Suzanne's in the kitchen." He gestured for Blake to follow him through the large entry and past the huge, sunken living room into a large, comfortably decorated family room with a spacious kitchen off to one side. Suzanne's dark head was bent over a dish that was on the drainboard, and Blake threw her purse on the couch and walked into the kitchen, wondering if John was always so reserved.

Suzanne looked up and smiled at Blake brightly but a little nervously, even the slight unease very odd for the usually outgoing Suzanne. "I'm so glad you could make it this evening," she said as she came over and gave Blake a quick hug. Blake hugged Suzanne back, noticing over her shoulder that John Parks was watching her intently. "Please, sit down," Suzanne said as she gestured to a chair in the family room. "John will get you a drink."

"Is there anything I can help you with in the kitchen?" Blake asked, hoping that she would have a chance to visit a little with Suzanne.

"Oh, that's all right, I have everything under control,"

Suzanne assured her blithely. "John, Blake always liked daiquiris. Is that all right, Blake?"

"A daiquiri will be fine," Blake said as she wandered toward the kitchen. "Are you sure I can't help?"

"Well, if you insist, you can put the silverware on the table," Suzanne said as she nodded toward the silver box. "The dining room's through that door."

"I'll have your drink made by the time you're through," John added, his expression warming into genuine friendliness for the first time. "Can I help you with anything, sweetheart?" he asked as he turned to Suzanne. Almost as if by magic, his face softened and he looked at Suzanne with such love in his eyes that Blake was almost embarrassed to see it. Lucky Suzanne, Blake thought, to have a man love her like that. *I bet he isn't reserved with her!* Blake thought wickedly.

Blake picked up the silver box and pushed open the swinging doors to the dining room, which was as opulently decorated as the rest of the house. Blake opened the box of silverware and suddenly realized there were four places set at the table. Uh-oh, had Suzanne been expecting her to bring a date? Surely not, since she hadn't been in town long enough to know anyone to bring. Well, maybe they had invited another friend over, someone who could even up the numbers. As Blake set the last spoon on the table, her theory was confirmed when the doorbell chimed.

She returned the silver box to the kitchen as the front door opened and the sound of men's voices filtered from the entry into the family room. Blake followed Suzanne's retreating back into the room where the men were standing, and her eyes widened in surprise when Rusty O'Gorman stepped forward and grinned at her impudently.

"Rusty, this is Blake Warner," Suzanne said as Rusty reached out and grasped Blake's hand, bowed, and kissed her knuckles regally. Although Rusty was kissing her hand for a laugh, the touch of his warm lips on the tender skin of her fingers sent a frisson of excitement through her.

"So glad to make your acquaintance, my beautiful lady," he said as Suzanne and John laughed.

Blake blushed, as much from her own response as to what Rusty was doing to embarrass her. "You didn't kiss my hand this afternoon when it was all greasy," she complained mockingly.

"Ah, well, it's a wonder what Jergens can do," Rusty said as he sniffed at her hand a little, sending Suzanne and John into gales of laughter.

"Have you two already met?" Suzanne sputtered between laughs.

Blake shot Rusty a warning look, which he promptly ignored. "We certainly have," he said meaningfully, causing Blake to blush to the roots of her hair.

"I'm his maintenance officer," Blake added quickly lest Rusty tell Suzanne and John about their meeting in the Officer's Club.

"Of course they would have already met," John said as he ushered the party into the family room. He handed Blake her drink and turned to Rusty. "Will it be your usual killer, my friend?" he asked with a warm smile on his face.

"The usual," Rusty replied as he sat down on the couch and subtly pulled Blake down beside him with a firm arm around her waist. "Looks like my hot date for the evening has gone distinctly lukewarm," he whispered into her ear.

Blake blushed, but without making a scene she could not very well get up and move. "Sorry about your date," she muttered, reddening further when Rusty laughed softly. She and Rusty were sitting where her thigh was brushing against his, and the warmth of his strong leg burned

67

her through her slacks. Surreptitiously she eased her leg away from his, only to have Rusty inch his leg over so they were in contact once more. Damn him, Blake thought as she sipped her drink. He was disturbing her equilibrium and he knew it!

John handed Rusty his drink, a rather strong one made with Scotch, and Rusty sipped it slowly. Suzanne retired to the kitchen to put the finishing touches on dinner, and Blake watched John and Rusty. *Well, John seems friendly enough with Rusty,* she thought noncommitally as she sipped her drink. *Maybe it's all in my imagination,* she thought. *Or maybe it just takes him a while to warm up to people,* she thought as John and Rusty rattled on. It seemed that the two men had trained together at the base in Del Rio, then they had renewed their friendship when they were stationed together at Randolph. Thankfully for John, Suzanne and Rusty had set up an immediate mutual admiration society, and the three of them had become close friends.

Suzanne called them in and dutifully they followed her through the kitchen into the dining room. *I'm glad Suzanne hasn't gotten all stuffy about her money,* Blake thought as her friend unselfconsciously ushered them through her spacious but messy kitchen. *A lot of women would have made us go around the kitchen.* Blake wondered why, with such a wealthy family background, John stayed in the service, then she remembered Suzanne saying how much John wanted to fly. Of course, Blake thought, if he were in the family business, he couldn't fly all that much. That familiar pang of jealousy gripped her once again as she thought about John. She, too, would have turned her back on a family business to fly.

Gallantly Rusty jumped to Blake's chair and pulled it out for her. She smiled at him with what she hoped was the proper amount of gratitude, and was rewarded with an impudent grin that told her that he knew how she really felt. John seated Suzanne and they passed around the dishes of roast beef and vegetables and mouth-watering rolls family-style in spite of the formal atmosphere.

When their plates were full, Blake sampled Suzanne's vegetable casserole and rolled her eyes appreciatively. "When did you learn to cook like this?" she asked in astonishment. "When we lived together, you couldn't boil water!"

Suzanne smiled at Blake impishly, winking at her husband. "I've been practicing on poor John for the last two years," she admitted. "And then, he likes to cook and he taught me a lot."

"You've been married for two years?" Blake asked in surprise.

"We met at Vandenburg," John volunteered, smiling warmly at Blake.

"Were you flying transports there?" Rusty asked eagerly.

"Those, and T-38s too," John replied enthusiastically. "Those transports are like taking a tank up."

"They're better than a B-38," Suzanne interjected with spirit. "Those little suckers are scary."

"She doesn't like my Porsche either," John said confidingly to Rusty. "Says it's scary too!"

I should have known it would come to this, Blake thought as she consumed Suzanne's delicious meal in silence. *You get more than one pilot together, and all they can do is talk about airplanes.* Suzanne, Rusty, and John droned on, comparing the virtues and the drawbacks to the various airplanes they had flown in their careers. They laughed and they argued spiritedly, not noticing when Blake quietly dropped out of the conversation. Since she had only flown two planes in her aborted career, she simply could add nothing to what was being said.

Stoically she ate her dinner, letting the conversation float around her as she fought back tears, the happy evening she had anticipated down the drain. Damn it, couldn't they talk about the weather, or the awful movie on television last night? Why did they have to sit there and rub it in? Did they have to remind her of all that she had lost?

John and Rusty were still rattling about airplanes when Suzanne and Blake started gathering up the dishes and taking them to the kitchen. Suzanne started scraping the plates and Blake returned to the dining room for three more loads, then she helped Suzanne rinse the dishes and load the dishwasher. "Your dinner was excellent, Suzanne," Blake volunteered as she fitted a plate into the rack in the machine.

"Thanks, Blake," Suzanne said as she cleaned out a large pot. "But you sure didn't say much this evening."

"What would I say?" Blake snapped without thinking. "I didn't have anything to contribute to that conversation!"

Suzanne's already fair skin turned pale at Blake's caustic remark. "Oh, Suzanne, I'm sorry," Blake said quickly, but not before Suzanne could stem the tears that were welling up in her eyes. "I didn't mean that."

"I'm sorry, Blake," Suzanne whispered. "I didn't mean to hurt you before, and I didn't mean to hurt you tonight. I guess that hurting you is my specialty."

"Look, forget I said anything, all right?" Blake pleaded desperately, knowing that she had spoiled her friend's evening with her frustrated outburst but not knowing what to do about it. "Where are your cake plates?" she added in an effort to take Suzanne's mind off her remarks.

"In that cabinet," Suzanne said as she glanced toward the dining room and quickly wiped the tears from her eyes.

Blake took the plates out and Suzanne cut four generous slices of cake. By the time they had returned to the dining room, Suzanne was again composed, and she smiled tremulously when John looked suspiciously at her too-bright eyes. John's lips thinned as he stared into his wife's distraught face, and he shot Blake a look that said he would have killed her if he could have. Blake stood rooted to the spot, horrified by the unadulterated rage on John's face, and Rusty stared from John to Blake in astonishment. As John opened his mouth to speak, Suzanne rushed in hurriedly. "Pour the coffee for me, will you, John?" she said too quickly.

They ate their dessert and Suzanne subtly steered the conversation to more general topics, but the tension was thick. John stared at Blake with cold rage in his eyes, making her miserably uncomfortable, and Suzanne tried desperately hard to cover for John. As they retired to the living room for brandy, Blake turned somewhat in desperation to Rusty to salvage what was left of the evening. Ignoring her common sense, she sat down beside him, hoping he didn't notice the way her pulse beat in her throat, and asked him a leading question about the local theater.

Rusty winked at her wickedly and launched into a hilarious tale about the last production he had seen, quickly reducing John and Suzanne to helpless laughter. *He knows I'm using him to save this miserable dinner party,* she thought resentfully as he tormented her with his devilish grin. *And he knows how attracted I am to him, and he's determined to get to me one way or the other!* Yet, at the

71

same time, she genuinely appreciated him for smoothing over the tension.

The conversation drifted, Rusty and John carrying most of it, then Suzanne admitted that she had a cross-country that she had to start early in the morning, so Blake said her good-byes and took her leave. Rusty lingered in the entry, talking to John, and Blake was grateful to slip away without having to say good-bye to either of them.

Blake climbed into her car and turned the ignition. The car tried to turn over, but instead of a catch and a pleasant purr, it yelped a little and was silent. Blake tried again, and again the car failed to start. She pumped the gas pedal and tried for a third time. Still nothing. Swearing, she got out of the car and lifted the hood, staring futilely into the shadowed interior of her small car. Seeing nothing whatsoever, she found a small flashlight in the glove compartment and peered under the hood again. Although she was unusually knowledgeable about things mechanical due to her training, she could see nothing wrong with her engine. Groaning in frustration, she slowly ran the flashlight up and down, but when a second search proved fruitless, she put the flashlight back into the car and started back up the walk. She could see the front door shut and Rusty's figure walking toward her in the dim light of the half moon overhead.

"Having a problem?" Rusty asked as they met on the sidewalk.

"Car won't start," Blake said shortly. "I've got to go call a cab."

"Did you check under the hood?" he asked.

"Of course," Blake said derisively. "And I couldn't see anything wrong there."

"Sorry," Rusty said easily. "But you won't have to call

a cab. I bet John will run you on home, and you can come back and tend to your car in the morning."

Hooray, Blake thought. A thirty-minute ride across town with a man who had turned unexplainably hostile. Her face mirroring her thoughts, she started to walk around Rusty, but he reached out and grabbed her arm lightly. "I tell you what. Don't bother John and Suzanne this late," he said. "I'll run you on home."

What a choice! Pruneface or the hangar flirt! Blake stopped and turned around. "Thank you," she said softly. "I'll take you up on that." Whatever her feelings about Rusty, it would be foolish to drag John out at this late hour, and she would honestly rather go with Rusty anyway.

Reluctantly she followed him to a small red pickup and waited while he opened the door for her, then climbed in and joined her in the small cab. Although they were not as close as they had been on the couch, Blake could smell Rusty's tangy aftershave in the close confines of the little truck, and the intimacy was somehow intensified by the confining cab. Blake watched Rusty start the truck, then asked him why he drove a pickup and not a small, snazzy sports car as did most of the single pilots.

"I use it to tow my boat," Rusty said as he pulled onto the expressway. "I can only afford one vehicle if I want to own the boat too."

"Must be a nice boat," Blake ventured. Rusty nodded. "No old money in your family?" she teased.

"Not a penny," Rusty admitted nonchalantly. He cut his eyes toward Blake, then back to the road. "Does it bother you that Suzanne married someone with money?"

"Heavens, no," Blake replied honestly. "Her family doesn't have much, and Suzanne has had to work her butt off for everything she ever had. I'm delighted to see someone giving something to her for a change."

Rusty said nothing more, and they drove the rest of the way to her apartment in silence, with only Blake's softly spoken directions disturbing the quiet. She watched the traffic on the expressway, but every fiber of her being was aware of the virile man who sat beside her. She was more strongly drawn to him than ever, and it was all she could do to stay on her own side of the seat. Damn, she could not afford to get involved with Rusty. A relationship of any sort between them would be a disaster for them both.

Rusty parked in the driveway in front of Blake's apartment. Before he could kill the engine, she said "Goodbye," and snapped open the door of the truck.

She was halfway out the door when strong fingers gripped her arm and tugged on her gently. "Just a minute," Rusty said softly but with a thread of command in his voice. "I'll see you to your door."

"That isn't necessary," Blake said breathlessly, but she waited even after Rusty had let go of her arm until he had come around to her side. He offered her his hand and she got out of the truck, and once out, he continued to hold hers as they climbed the stairs to her second-story apartment. She unlocked the door with her free hand, then turned to Rusty. "Thanks for the lift," she said in a voice that was strangely husky.

"My pleasure," Rusty said gallantly. Instead of freeing her hand, he twirled Blake around until she was just inches from him, then reached for her with his other arm and wrapped it around her waist. "A kiss from Bebe, no?" he asked as his lips bent to capture her own.

Her "No, Rusty" was muffled by the soft, sensuous pressure of his mouth closing over hers. She melted, her resistance forgotten, as Rusty explored her lips and teeth with his tongue. Blake's hands, acting as though they had a will of their own, reached around Rusty's waist and explored the hard, rippling muscles of his lower back, then they moved upward until they found the sharp, pointed wings of his shoulder blades. Trailing her hands to the center of his back, she pressed her palms into his spine, forcing his sensual body even closer to her own.

Startled by her unbridled response, Rusty's hold on Blake lessened, but his questing fingers sought out first her tender neck, then strayed lower to one of her breasts, where his fingers closed over the nipple. Blake gasped as his fingers stroked her nipple through her blouse and bra, taunting it into a hard button of desire. Then his other hand reached up and gently palmed her other breast into a turgid state of arousal. Blake moaned and unconsciously thrust her body outward, trying to prolong the delightful, sensual pleasure that he was bringing to her. She had been kissed before, she had been made love to before, but nothing in her past experience could quite match the feelings that this man could arouse in her.

Her heart hammering, the blood pumping in her ears, she moaned as Rusty's lips left hers and tenderly explored one soft eyelid, then the other. He rained gentle kisses over her face as Blake drew him to her once again, then recaptured her mouth as she swayed against him helplessly. As she moaned his name against his lips she realized that her control was nearly gone, and that his couldn't be in much better shape. If she didn't put a stop to this lovely insanity now, she would never be able to pull away from this magnetic man. Reluctantly she broke her hold on Rusty's waist and pushed him away gently.

Surprisingly Rusty did not try to draw her back into his arms. It was as though his control was as fragile as her own, and he had no desire to jump off the deep end with her tonight. As they untangled themselves from their embrace, he smiled ruefully and ran his hands down her arms. "Thanks, Bebe," he whispered as he pushed her in the door and shut it behind him.

Blake stared at the door stupidly for a moment, then stumbled to the couch and sat down, her head buried in her hands. What in the world had come over her? She must have been out of her mind! But she knew that she could no more fight the attraction between them than she could restore the flawed vision in her eye. "Damn it, Blake, you *can't* get involved with him!" she said out loud. She stood at the front window and stared out into the night, her mind spinning. Did she dare get involved with Rusty? Could she overcome her resentment and jealousy of him? Or would a relationship with him spell only pain and heartbreak?

Rusty put his truck in gear and eased it out of the parking lot, a guilty grin on his face. He sure hoped John remembered to correct the wires to Blake's electronic ignition that he had reversed on his way into the house tonight! *You shouldn't have, Rusty,* he chided himself, *but it worked so well!* Blake had accepted his ride home from dinner and had kissed him so delightfully. If he had left her car alone, his conscience would be clear, but then his lips wouldn't be throbbing from the wonderful way she had responded to him. *I almost had Bebe back,* he thought as he pulled onto the thoroughfare in front of Blake's apartment.

Why doesn't John like her? Rusty mused as a small frown flitted across his face. Rusty had known John a long time, and had known the minute he had walked in the door that his friend simply couldn't stand Blake. Come to think of it, Rusty mused, something had been wrong the entire evening. John had been wary at first, then downright unfriendly to Blake, Suzanne had been nervous and too eager to please, and Blake had clearly wanted out of there the first chance she got. And then it would have taken a fool to miss the tension between Blake and Suzanne when they came back with the cake, or John's reaction to that. But Blake hadn't appeared to be jealous of Suzanne's house or her wealthy husband. In fact, she had seemed genuinely delighted for her friend.

As Rusty pulled off into his subdivision's entrance, he thought about the way Blake's breasts thrust against the material of her fatigue shirt and desire stirred inside him. She could even make combat boots sexy when she wore them. As he again remembered the wings resting above her left breast, he wondered for the hundredth time why she wasn't flying, and what had made her turn from the warm, tender woman he met in the Officer's Club into his cold, indifferent maintenance officer. It was more than the gossip about her that he had unwittingly repeated. He had even heard her laughing about it with Colonel Alda later. No, it wasn't the gossip. It had to be more than that.

Rusty unlocked his house and pulled a beer out of the refrigerator. Flopping down on the couch, he unbuttoned his shirt and drank a long gulp of the beer. *So how do I get back to the warm woman I met before?* he asked himself. *How do I find Bebe again? She was there a few minutes tonight, when she kissed me. Now, how do I get Bebe back for good?* He laid back on the couch, his mind spinning, and planned his slow, subtle campaign to get back to Bebe, the real Blake Warner.

CHAPTER FOUR

I swear I don't know what to make of that man, Blake thought as she hunted around in her kitchen cabinet for a vase. *This is the third time in the last month he has sent me flowers!* Shaking her head, she located a graceful green vase that was her grandmother's and ran a little water into it, then carefully arranged the dozen roses and the greenery in the vase, stopping often to drink in the delightful fragrance of the beautiful red flowers. *Now, how does he know I have a passion for roses?* she asked herself as she pulled on her fatigues and her boots over her lacy pink underwear. Anyway, she did love the flowers and she would have to be sure to tell him so today when he came by for his daily chat and flirting session.

Shaking a little food into Calico's feeder, Blake pushed open the sliding door to the balcony and breathed in the warm sweet April air, the tang of wildflowers growing in the vacant lot across from the apartment complex delicately perfuming the breeze. She wondered if it was the warmth of spring that was causing her to thaw toward Rusty, or if she would have fallen victim to his charm under any circumstances. For thawing she was, although that was the last thing Blake wanted to happen to her.

Shutting the sliding door, she left her apartment and crawled into her car to make the short drive out to Randolph, her thoughts returning to the redheaded pilot who had dominated them all too often recently.

It isn't that I haven't tried to resist him, Blake thought as she took the exit to the base. She had greeted his daily stop by her office with cool indifference, responding to his casual flirting with careless disregard, even though a part of her waited eagerly for him to come by every day. She had thanked him dutifully for the other two bouquets of flowers he had sent, but had not confessed that they had taken the place of honor on her dining room table. Any other man would have given up long ago in the face of her continued lack of response, but Rusty simply didn't seem to notice or care, and this confused Blake. *I've never seen that kind of persistence before in a man,* she thought as she drove through the gates into the base. Yet, at the same time, Rusty had made no attempt to ask her out again or to put their relationship on a more intimate level and this she found bewildering.

Anybody else would have made his move, asked me out before now, she thought as she parked her car and wandered into the hangar. *Why hasn't he?* Blake opened the door to her office and poured herself a cup of coffee, noting with surprise that it wasn't nearly as bitter as it usually was. She would have refused to go out with him, of course, and he knew it. Or would she? Blake sat down at her desk and sipped her coffee thoughtfully. Four weeks ago she would have turned him down flat. Even a week ago she would have found an excuse. But now she was not so sure. In spite of herself Blake was tantalized by the persistent pilot who courted her ever so patiently. *Maybe I would say no and maybe I wouldn't,* Blake thought as she twirled her swivel chair around a little faster than she should have, sloshing coffee on the floor. "Slob!" she said out loud.

"Or maybe just a kid on a merry-go-round," Rusty

laughed as Blake jumped out of the chair and began wiping up the coffee with a napkin. "Never fear, I won't tell Sally that the officer she idolizes is really a kid at heart," he teased as Blake's cheeks reddened.

"I think she already knows," Blake murmured as she threw the napkin into the wastebasket. "She caught me flying a kite on the vacant lot behind the apartment."

"And what did she say?" Rusty teased.

"Nothing," Blake admitted as she poured herself another cup of coffee. "But a day or two later she laid a deluxe roll of kite twine on my desk and said that it doesn't tangle as badly as the regular old stuff. And she's right—it's great." Blake sipped her coffee. "She's even learning to make decent coffee."

"Not really," Rusty said. "It was so bad this morning that I dumped it and started over."

Blake laughed out loud. "Well, thank you," she said. "And thanks for the roses. How did you know they're my favorite?"

"Because you look like a roses lady," Rusty said, his voice softening a little. "I'm sure looking forward to Fiesta," he added in a normal conversational tone.

"What's Fiesta?" Blake asked in puzzlement.

"Oh, these characters down here have a week-long celebration every April—something about winning some war with Mexico," Rusty said. "I don't know my history, but Pat Gordon said that it's a week's worth of fun and parades. Going to any of it?"

"I—I don't know," Blake stammered. "I didn't know anything about it until just now."

"Well, you really should get down to an event or two," Rusty said as he handed her some signed release forms. "I'm not releasing 3447 yet," he said as he showed her a

80

paper on one of the more troublesome planes. "I don't think the throttle is as tight as it should be."

Blake blinked. "Sorry, we thought we fixed it," she said. "I'll run it through the shop once more." She thought a moment. "Damn, that's going to make me short a plane today," she said to herself. "Don't worry about it," she added to Rusty. "It will be fixed next time."

"Okay, Blake. Be seeing you," Rusty said as he sailed out the door.

Now why does he keep telling me all about Fiesta if he doesn't intend to ask me out? Blake wondered for the next three days. According to the papers, San Antonio was indeed gearing up for a giant party, and every day Rusty managed to say something about the various events coming up. Apparently he intended to go, but he made no mention of including Blake in his plans, and she was beginning to get worried. She would really like to go to some of the events, maybe a parade or two, but if Rusty didn't intend to ask her out, she would have to find someone else to go with or make plans to go by herself. Suzanne and John? She had seen Suzanne several times since the disastrous dinner party, but she had not seen John since then, and she did not particularly want to. Suzanne would probably be going with him, and she did not want to be the third wheel. The secretary next door? No, she would want to go with her boyfriend.

Blake searched around in her mind for someone to go with, but everyone she had made friends with already had someone to go with or had made other plans. *Oh, well, it won't be the first time I've gone somewhere alone,* she thought as she completed the last of her paperwork on Friday afternoon. Actually, the thought didn't bother her, except that she would rather go with Rusty and she knew it. He would be a lot of fun at something like that, she thought as she made up the flying schedule for Monday, grimacing when she discovered that she was two planes short.

"Hi there. Looks like you could use another plane," Rusty said as he breezed into her office waving release papers in her face.

"Oh, thank you!" Blake cried as she snatched the papers out of Rusty's hand eagerly and plopped them on the desk. "I wasn't sure whether I could make the schedule or not."

"Glad to oblige," Rusty said as he plopped his tired body into one of the chairs and unzipped his flight suit a little. "Well, they officially kick off Fiesta tomorrow."

"That's nice," Blake said absently. "What event?"

"The Rey Feo parade. I think Tommy said that meant ugly king."

"Are you going?" Blake asked innocently. *And if you are, why don't you ask me?* she added to herself.

"No, I have a cross-country," he replied. "Won't get in until late Sunday."

"Too bad," Blake said, really meaning it.

"Oh, well, I can always go to the River Parade Monday night," Rusty said. "In fact, I think I'll do just that."

Blake fit the last plane into her schedule. *Ask me, ask me,* she screamed inwardly, hoping her face remained impassive. "Well, have a good time," she said slowly.

Rusty got up and walked toward the door. "Oh, by the way, care to go with me?" he asked casually as he leaned against the door frame.

"Yes!" Blake burst out. "Uh, I guess so," she added in her best neutral voice.

"Pick you up about five thirty on Monday," Rusty said as he walked out the door, twirling his helmet on the tip of his finger. "See ya, Blake," he threw over his shoulder. He walked nonchalantly to his truck and got in, not allowing himself to whoop with triumph until he was all the way off the base.

I think I've been manipulated by a master, Blake thought as she drove home in the thick Friday-evening traffic, a wide grin on her face. But she didn't care! Rusty had finally asked her out, and she was going to have the time of her life. *Now, what do you wear to Fiesta,* she asked herself as she took the exit to her apartment. Once home, she searched through her closet but could find nothing appropriately festive. Blake slammed the closet door in despair. She had to look her best for this date!

In a panic she called Suzanne, who gave her directions to a small flea market that was held in an old shopping center every Sunday. Blake found the flea market and was astonished to find dealer after dealer with cotton dresses from Mexico in every color of the rainbow, richly embroidered with flowers across the yoke and down the front. She picked one out and gritted her teeth as she asked the price for the handmade item, but when she found out how astonishingly inexpensive the dresses were she picked out two more and left the flea market feeling that she had truly found a treasure.

Blake put the finishing touches on her makeup and carefully pulled her dress over her head so as to wrinkle it as little as possible. She had debated long and hard over which of her new dresses to wear tonight and had finally settled on the white one with red, pink, and green flowers embroidered on the bodice. She pulled her hair out of her collar and brushed it until it shone, then wiped off her lip gloss and put on a brighter one that matched the red in the embroidered flowers. Pulling her hair back on one side with a red cloisonné comb, she put her purse items into a small straw bag and declared herself ready for Fiesta.

Rusty rang the doorbell just as she was strapping on her high-heeled sandals. She deliberately made herself not hurry and answered the door leisurely, her smile of welcome fading a little when she realized that her tall strappy heels made her tower over Rusty. He walked in and grinned at her outrageously, then stood up on his tiptoes to kiss her cheek and slid his chin onto her shoulder. "Perfect fit," he quipped.

"I'll change the shoes," Blake murmured.

Rusty looked down at her expensively clad feet. "Under any other circumstances I would tell you not to be ridiculous, but we're going to be walking for a good half mile in a crowd, and those things are going to be uncomfortable. Why don't you put on your boots while I wait?"

Blake laughed out loud and kicked off the offending shoes, relieved that they were on eye level once more. "I think I can find something a little better than those glamorous boots!" she said as she disappeared into her bedroom. Soon, suitably shod, she was sitting in Rusty's pickup truck on the way into downtown San Antonio. They kept up a running stream of conversation as Rusty dodged his way through the narrow, winding streets of downtown and parked in an almost full parking garage. "So what's going to happen tonight?" she asked. "Dinner and then the parade?"

"That's it," Rusty replied as he took her hand and walked with her toward the exit. "We have reservations at one of the restaurants along the river, and then we watch the parade from there."

"Now, how are we going to watch a parade from a restaurant along the river?" Blake asked as they headed into the mass of people on the sidewalk. The combining crowd of offices letting out and those coming to see the

84

parade filled the sidewalks, but the people were universally in good spirits and the sidewalks rang with happy chatter.

"Somebody didn't do her homework," Rusty chided her as he headed down a flight of stairs that would take them to the river level. The river, meandering through downtown San Antonio below street level, was normally a haven of peace, but tonight it was even more crowded than the upper sidewalks.

Rusty and Blake weaved their way through the gathering crowd and past a couple of restaurants, then Rusty stopped at a small Italian restaurant and gave the harried headwaiter his name. Soon they were seated at a table on the balcony that looked out over the river. "Now, to answer your question, this is a river parade, and the parade will come floating right by you on barges."

"No marching bands tonight?" Blake asked with mock ruefulness.

"'Fraid not," Rusty replied as he opened his menu. "But they tell me it's really a nice parade."

They ordered lasagna and a robust red wine to go with it. "So are you liking this tour of duty?" Rusty asked as he poured her a glass of wine.

Blake nodded, sipping the wine. "I didn't think I was going to, but, yes, I like it very much," she said sincerely. "Everyone was right," she added, explaining her statement as Rusty looked at her curiously. "I wasn't at all happy about being assigned here or being a maintenance officer," she said frankly.

"Well, most people don't like rated supplements," Rusty said, wondering at the strange expression that passed across her face. "Or is there another reason why you aren't flying right now?"

"You're right, most people hate rated supplements," Blake said honestly, not answering Rusty's question about her own flying status, since she had no desire to talk about her own aborted flying career tonight of all nights. "Have you ever gone on one?"

Rusty looked at her shrewdly, not missing the fact that she had expertly changed the subject from her career to his. "No, never have," he said casually as the waiter brought them overflowing bowls of salad laced with a tangy dressing.

"What made you go into test-piloting?" Blake asked as she sampled the delicious salad.

"The flying," Rusty said eagerly, his blue eyes burning with enthusiasm. "Getting up there, just me and my machine, all alone, looking out over the countryside. You know?"

"Yes, I know," Blake said softly, her thoughts stirred by memories of just such moments in her past. "Great, isn't it?"

"Sure is," Rusty replied, watching her face closely and surprised to see an expression of wistful longing cross it before she resumed her friendly smile.

"You must like it," Blake said teasingly, her dreamy expression gone. "To get up there and test the planes! You don't even know whether they're fixed or not," she laughed.

"Oh, I've flown planes a lot less secure than an Air Force jet that needed testing," Rusty replied.

"Such as?" Blake prompted as she sipped her wine and gazed down at the thickening crowd on the sidewalk.

"Oh, when we were in college we used to rent old crop dusters and buzz the cows in the field. Now, that was some flying!"

"I'm sure it was fun, but surely that can't compare to what you're doing now, can it?" Blake asked as the waiter set a steaming plate of lasagna down in front of each of them.

"Yes, it certainly can," Rusty protested as he gingerly forked up a bite of the steaming dish, blowing on it a little before he popped it into his mouth. "That was some of the greatest flying I ever did."

"You're kidding!" Blake protested as she cut out a small square of lasagna and put it into her mouth, chewing it and swallowing it gamely before grabbing her water glass. "Damn, that was hot," she muttered.

"If you blow on it a little, it won't burn you," Rusty offered helpfully, forking up another bite of the cheesy concoction as his eyes danced in amusement.

"Thank you," Blake said with great dignity, blowing delicately on her next bite.

"I would think the flying you're doing now would be the best kind of flying there is, unless you were to go into fighter piloting," Blake probed, interested in spite of herself in Rusty's rather unorthodox attitude toward flying. Most of the pilots she knew, herself included, felt that the more powerful and faster the plane, the better.

"Well, I like it because I get to fly all the time," Rusty admitted. "It's worth putting up with the Air Force to get to fly their planes."

"You don't like the Air Force?" Blake asked in astonishment, thinking of her own attitude of respect and admiration toward the military.

"Not particularly," Rusty admitted calmly. "Although I hesitate to admit that to a hard-assed military type." Blake burst out laughing as Rusty grinned at her. "But no, I stay in for the benefits and mostly to get to fly. You've got to admit that not too many people are going to pay me that well to do something that I love."

"And if you couldn't fly for the Air Force anymore?" Blake asked quietly.

Rusty shot her a piercing look, but she was cutting another bite of lasagna and did not see the expression on his face. "I'd stay in for the benefits and fly on weekends, of course," he replied. "Unless someone offered me a job flying on the outside. Oh, I've thought about getting out and flying a crop duster back home, but I like the pay here."

Blake choked on a bite of her dinner. "Don't put me on," she scoffed. "There's no way you'd willingly leave Air Force flying and go fly a crop duster."

"Why not?" Rusty challenged. "It's flying, isn't it?"

"But it's not flying jets for the Air Force," Blake countered.

"So what? Flying is flying," Rusty laughed. "I don't give a damn if it's the best T-38 the Air Force has to offer or a used Cessna. A plane is a plane is a plane, as long as I'm up it it."

"Do you ever fly those used Cessnas anymore?" Blake asked. "Maybe you've forgotten what they're really like."

"Oh, on weekends I fly nearly every kind of small plane there is," Rusty admitted as he poured himself another glass of wine. "I'm the Air Force liaison for the Civil Air Patrol, and I fly missions for them all the time." He looked down at the river and pointed over at the bridge. "Look, the parade's starting." He motioned to Blake.

Blake's eyes followed his pointing finger. "They do it on barges," she said in astonishment. "Will you look at that?" she said excitedly as the first brightly decorated and lighted barge floated past the restaurant, a group of small girls valiantly doing an intricate Mexican dance on the swaying boat. Soon that barge was followed by another, and another, and before long the music from the various barges made further conversation impossible.

Blake glanced over at Rusty every so often as he watched the unique parade with interest. His attitude toward flying frankly astonished her, and she didn't know quite what to make of it. She loved to fly, but she honestly felt that there was no flying like what you could do in the Air Force. Anything else would be a step down to her, and since the accident she had not flown a plane. But Rusty sincerely didn't seem to care what he was flying as long as he was up in the air.

I wonder if he really means all that, or if he just says it because it sounds good. But since Blake could not imagine Rusty saying something that he really didn't mean, she thought that he was probably sincere in his attitude toward flying and she simply could not understand it.

As the last barge floated by, Rusty signaled the waiter and handed him a credit card. The waiter promptly returned with the receipt and Rusty signed it, then he took Blake's hand and together they left the restaurant and walked along the crowded sidewalks to the stairs, making very slow progress but not really caring, as long as they were in each other's company. As they walked under one of the arching bridges, Rusty reached over and kissed Blake's cheek lightly. "Thanks for coming with me," he said softly.

"My pleasure," Blake replied as she returned his gentle kiss. The skin of his cheek felt soft against her lips, and she would have liked to have had the freedom to explore his entire face with her tender mouth. They climbed up the stairs and entered the crowded parking garage, waiting patiently as the cars gingerly nosed out onto the busy streets. "You know, that was fun," she said as Rusty edged his little truck out of the garage.

"Well, if you enjoyed that, would you like to go to NIOSA with me tomorrow night?" Rusty asked.

"What in the world is NIOSA?" Blake asked.

"Night In Old San Antonio," Rusty explained. "It's a citywide block party, I hear. Lots of food and beer and music. Street dancing."

"Sounds like a lot of fun to me," Blake said with sincere enthusiasm. "I'd love to come." And she meant it. Tonight had been a lot of fun, and she had enjoyed getting to know Rusty a little better.

They chatted about the parade on the way to Blake's apartment, comparing notes as to which were the better floats. Blake had liked the one with the huge rainbow arch, but Rusty's vote went for the float with the real Playboy bunny riding in the front! He parked in front of her apartment and opened the truck door for her, sliding an arm around her waist as together they mounted the stairs. When they reached the top of the landing, Rusty took her key from her and proceeded to open her door. He edged her inside and, following her in, shut the door behind him.

Blake opened her mouth to protest, but Rusty laid a gentle finger on her lips. "I have no intention of staying. I know you're not the type for a casual sleepover, and neither am I, if the terrible truth be known. But I would like to kiss you without all of your neighbors watching us." As Blake nodded in agreement, Rusty's mouth lowered to hers and he captured her lips with his own.

The kiss began as a gentle thing, but before either Blake or Rusty could realize what was happening, the passion between them ignited suddenly, engulfing them both in its torrid fury. He curled his tongue temptingly around hers, fencing with her until she surrendered to his passionate possession. At first only their mouths were in contact, but Rusty reached out and drew Blake to him, putting one arm around her waist and drawing her close to the hard warmth of his body, every inch of his powerful frame plastered to hers in intimate contact.

Whimpering softly in her throat, Blake returned Rusty's kiss eagerly, sliding her arms around his shoulders and pressing the upper part of her body closer to his. As his fingers wove a spell up her back, she daringly unbuttoned his shirt and slipped her hand inside, feeling his hard warm chest and the soft red hair that covered it, her fingers eagerly exploring its strength. Without breaking off their kiss, Rusty swung her up into his arms and carried her to the sofa, sitting down with her in his lap.

"You're crazy," she murmured as Rusty finally broke the kiss and started to nuzzle her neck lovingly. "I probably weigh almost as much as you do."

"Naw, I have a few pounds on you," Rusty protested as his lips traveled down her neck and onto her shoulders. "You were as light as a feather."

Blake giggled, knowing that she was no such thing, but was warmed by Rusty's teasing. His hands crept up and found her breast through the cotton fabric, and he caressed it gently through her clothing. He felt around the edge of the dress, but found no way to slide the dress down Blake's body to gain access to her turgid nipples. "Damn," he muttered. "How'd you get into this thing anyway?"

"Over my head," Blake admitted, her own frustration with the uncooperative neckline mirrored in her expression. Suddenly coming to a decision, she reached down and pulled the dress up and over her body, exposing her bra and slip to Rusty's hungry gaze.

Gently Rusty reached out and unhooked the front closure on Blake's bra, gasping as her swelling breasts spilled out of the cups. "I can't believe how beautiful you are," he whispered as he reached down and captured one salmon-colored nipple in his lips, kissing it first lightly and then tormenting it with his tongue as Blake squirmed with delight at his tender touch. He brought one peak to rigidity, then proceeded to torment the other one into a similarly aroused state.

Blake tugged open the rest of the buttons of Rusty's shirt and pulled him close to her, reveling in the feel of the soft hair on his chest as it tickled her breasts. "Oh, Rusty, you feel so wonderful," she whispered. For long moments he nibbled and caressed her breasts, turning them into hard peaks of excitement as Blake cooed with pleasure.

Finally Rusty pulled back and lovingly examined Blake, naked to the waist, then he reached down and kissed each breast softly. "You're a tempting sight and I'd love nothing more than to stay tonight, but we're not ready for that yet," he whispered.

Blake nodded wordlessly as she reached for her bra. "No, don't," Rusty said as he stilled her hand. "I want to remember seeing you like this, your lips swollen from my kisses and your breasts bared to my eyes." He reached out and planted a tender kiss on her mouth, then buttoned his own shirt slowly. He ran his fingers down between her breasts, then tilted her chin up to meet his gaze. "Tomorrow night then?" he asked, his eyes glazed with passion.

Blake nodded. "Good night," she said softly as Rusty let himself out the door.

Blake sighed and twirled around in her swivel chair, sipping a cup of bitter coffee and humming absently. She was supposed to be scheduling airplanes for tomorrow's flights, but her thoughts kept returning to the devastating kisses and caresses she and Rusty had shared the night before, and her cheeks grew warm as she remembered the way she had wantonly removed her dress to give Rusty better access to her breasts. It was a wonder he hadn't insisted on staying all night, with the encouragement she had shown him. *And I wouldn't have objected either,* she thought as she got out her plane schedule for the next day. *I would have been delighted!*

Color staining her cheeks, Blake realized that a part of her had actually hoped that Rusty would stay. She had been left restless and unsatisfied by their caresses, and had laid awake half the night wishing with both her mind and her body that they had taken their embraces to their natural conclusion. Blake was glad that Rusty had been able to call a halt while he still had the good sense to do so. It was too soon to get involved in an affair with him, and Blake knew it, but she still longed for the touch of his body on hers.

Dragging her thoughts away from Rusty, she juggled her plane schedule for the better part of an hour, breathing a sigh of relief when Rusty walked through the door with a stack of papers. "Oh, am I glad to see you!" she exclaimed, her cheeks warming as his eyes traveled down the length of her fatigues, clearly recalling how she looked under them. "I need a couple of planes."

"Sorry, I can only release you this one," Rusty replied as he poured himself a cup of coffee.

"One! That will never do," Blake muttered as she grabbed the release paper he handed her. "How about 3447—the one that we redid the steering on?"

"The yoke still isn't right," Rusty replied. "It's still too loose."

"It can't be," Blake said positively. "I personally made sure that they got it as tight as it can legitimately go."

"Sorry," Rusty said firmly. "Look, Blake, I'm sure you did your best, but it simply isn't ready for release." He held up his hand when she opened her mouth to protest.

"I'm the pilot and I'm the one to make that decision, all right?" His face softened at the angry light that came into her eyes at those words. "I'm sorry—I know you'll have to juggle the planes tomorrow, but I just can't release that plane yet. Have Maintenance look at it again." He turned around and wandered out the door. "See you tonight," he added as he left.

Over my dead body, Blake thought as she slammed down the release paper and juggled with her schedule. Yes, she could schedule around the plane, but did he have to throw his status as a pilot right in her face?

I'm the pilot, I'm the pilot, drummed through her head as she drove home and ran up the stairs to her apartment, slamming the door behind her. *Damn you, Rusty, you're the pilot and I'm not,* she thought as she poured herself a glass of orange juice and drank it down in three gulps. *And I'm crazy for having anything to do with you.* Resentment welling up in her and brimming over, she picked up the receiver and dialed Information. When the nasal-voiced operator had given her Rusty's number, she dialed it, her finger trembling in fury.

"Rusty? This is Blake."

"And what can I do for you?" Rusty asked genially.

"I'm not coming tonight," Blake said curtly. "I've got a screaming headache and wouldn't be any fun."

"Blake—" Rusty began as she hung up the telephone.

She wandered into the bathroom and shed her fatigues, stepping into the shower. After showering and washing her hair, she pulled on underwear and a pair of shorts. She was toweling her hair dry when a knock sounded on the front door.

Swearing softly at the interruption, Blake threw open the door and stood back astonished as Rusty barged into

94

her apartment. "What's all this nonsense about a damned headache?" he demanded.

"I have a headache and don't really want to go out tonight," Blake said with dignity.

"Headache, hell," Rusty snapped. "You're just mad because you can't meet tomorrow's schedule."

"I met tomorrow's schedule just fine, thank you," Blake replied.

"Then what's the problem? And don't tell me you have a headache, because that's a lie and we both know it."

Blake searched her mind for a plausible excuse as to why she didn't want to go, and found nothing. Unwilling to admit that she resented him because of his status as a pilot, she shrugged expressively. "Isn't it a lady's prerogative to change her mind?" she asked.

"Not when the gentleman in question has shelled out for advance tickets," Rusty replied firmly. "So unless you can give me a very good reason why you don't want to go, I think you better get your purse and come on."

Damn, Blake thought as she looked at the implacable face that was staring into hers. She was too proud to tell him the truth. Kicking off her clogs, she shrugged expressively. "All right, all right, I'll go."

"So where are you going?" Rusty demanded imperiously.

"To change clothes," Blake replied patiently. "You wouldn't want to be seen with me in a very very short pair of shorts, now, would you?"

Rusty grinned, his annoyance with her forgotten. "Well, it would be one way to find out if you're really hard-assed or not," he jibed as Blake stormed into the bedroom and slammed the door behind her, throwing a pillow at the offending door that did nothing to muffle Rusty's delighted laughter.

CHAPTER FIVE

Blake and Rusty walked through the gates into NIOSA and Rusty handed the volunteer his tickets. Blake peered around at the crowded street that was lined with booths selling every imaginable food and drink and handicraft. "When you said it was a big block party, you weren't kidding," she said as Rusty took her hand.

"I wasn't expecting this though," Rusty admitted as they made their way through the milling crowd down historic old Villita Street. Blake guessed that this area of old buildings that had been converted into quality shops was normally a rather peaceful area in which to stroll, but the presence of NIOSA turned it into happily crowded bedlam. Nevertheless, Blake found herself eagerly anticipating this evening, even though she was still annoyed with Rusty over the afternoon's disagreement.

Determinedly thrusting her annoyance with him to the back of her mind, she pointed over to a booth that was selling something with a Mexican name. "Want to try one of those?" she asked as they started to make their way to the booth.

"Sure," Rusty replied, relieved that she didn't intend to sulk all evening. He fished the proper change out of his pocket and soon they were munching on buñuelos, a fried pastry dusted with powdered sugar that absolutely melted in their mouths. "These were a good idea," he said between bites.

"They're delicious," Blake acknowledged. "I wonder what else there is to eat here."

"Why don't we wander around and find out?" Rusty asked as he reached out and brushed a speck of powdered sugar from Blake's upper lip, his casual touch reminding Blake of the passion they shared the night before. Forcing that memory to the back of her mind, she followed Rusty's lead through the crowd and through a corridor between a couple of buildings, finding a whole new block of food and drink booths selling everything under the sun to the thirsty, hungry crowd.

"We're never going to be able to try everything here tonight," Blake muttered as she looked around at all the different booths.

"Well, we can give it a try," Rusty replied as he headed toward the booth that proudly proclaimed to be selling fried rattlesnake. "And I'm starting here."

"I'm sure they're not serious," Blake said as Rusty leaned over and ordered a plate of the fried meat. "Excuse me, sir, what is that meat really?" she asked the volunteer dishing up the meat.

"Rattlesnake," he replied, laughing at the horrified look on Blake's face. "Yes, ma'am, it really is."

"Rusty, that's real rattlesnake!" Blake cried. "You can't eat that!"

"Why not?" Rusty asked as he bit off a strip of the peculiar meat. He chewed it quite deliberately and swallowed it, nodding his head thoughtfully. "Tastes a little like frog's legs."

"Well, you can have it," Blake said positively as Rusty cheerfully finished the rest of the small pile of meat. "I think I'll tackle a ranch steak, thank you."

Rusty obligingly bought her a ranch steak that was folded into a tortilla, then after he had sampled hers bought himself one too. They wandered around, trying the sausages, shish kabobs, tamales, nachos, pizza, fried chicken, and went back for two more of the delicious buñuelos, then washed it all down with brimming cups of cold beer.

Since the shops were all open, Blake and Rusty wandered through them, admiring the artwork and handmade crafts and clothing and jewelry, some made locally and others imported from Mexico, but all in the finest of taste. Blake found a candle factory that actually made candles while the customers watched. On impulse Rusty bought Blake a wide brass bracelet from one of the local artisans and slipped it onto her wrist before she could protest. Blake held her wrist out and turned it this way and that, sincerely admiring the carefully crafted band. She complimented the artisan and thanked Rusty, leaning over and kissing him gently on the cheek before she could stop herself.

"You like it?" he asked.

"I like it," she confirmed.

They walked around the huge party for a while longer, sipping beer and watching the street-dancing inspired by a country and western band, and finally taking a spin around the street themselves, mutually surprised at how well they danced together. Blake had to admit to herself that she was having a good time in spite of her initial reluctance to come. Rusty really was fun! If only he hadn't been a pilot. But then, he wouldn't be Rusty if he weren't a pilot, Blake acknowledged to herself as they wandered out of NIOSA and made the long trek to Rusty's truck, parked some blocks away.

"Have a good time?" Rusty asked as he opened the door of his truck for Blake.

"You know I did," Blake replied warmly, hoping against hope that he didn't ask her why she didn't want to come in the first place. "And I love the bracelet," she said as she lovingly touched the metal cuff. "There are certainly some fine artisans here, aren't there?"

Rusty took the hint and they talked about some of the various local crafts they had seen and admired as he drove her home. Blake held up her end of the conversation, but in spite of her efforts to put it out of her mind the incident this afternoon kept popping into her thoughts, and Rusty's unknowingly painful words kept coming back to haunt her. He was a great person, but he was also a pilot and he had not hesitated to remind her of that fact. By the time they had arrived at her apartment, Blake's resentment toward Rusty had returned in full force and she quickly opened the door on her side of the truck. "If you don't mind, I'll go on up. Thanks for a good evening!"

She was halfway up the stairs by the time Rusty caught up with her, his arm slipping around her waist, his expression one of irritation. "I'll see you to your door," he said impatiently as he took her keys from her hand and unlocked her front door. He followed her inside and shut the door behind him. "Just a good night kiss," he said softly as he took her into his arms and his lips lowered softly onto hers.

Blake willed herself to melt into his arms, hoping that the sensual longing for Rusty that she had experienced last night would return and wipe the resentment from her mind. But as she returned Rusty's caresses, this afternoon's argument returned to haunt her and it was all she could do to keep from pulling away and scrubbing her hand across her mouth. She forced her hands up around his neck and let her fingers play with the hair on his nape, hoping that his soft skin under her fingers would awaken the passion that was so sorely missing in her tonight. Rusty explored her mouth hungrily, and she let him, passively accepting his torrid embrace.

Blake made no attempt to move away when he unbuttoned her blouse and slipped his hand inside, one finger sliding back and forth across her nipple, and let her hands slide around his waist and pull him closer, hoping that the further intimacy would set fire to her emotions. Rusty deepened the kiss, probing her mouth sensuously, desperation driving him to plunder its depths. Finally, just as Blake thought she could stand no more of his touch, Rusty pushed her away abruptly and impatiently tucked his shirt into his jeans.

"You were faking it," he accused her quietly.

"Yes, I was," Blake said honestly as Rusty's face flamed with anger.

"What went wrong tonight?" Rusty demanded.

"I don't know," Blake lied desperately. "Damn it, Rusty, I tried to respond to you!" she snapped.

"I don't need that," he ground out quietly. "If you knew you felt this way tonight, why didn't you just say no?"

"Would you have accepted that?" Blake asked quietly. "I didn't think so," she added as Rusty shook his head honestly. "Besides, I didn't want to hurt your feelings."

"You think you didn't hurt them just now with that fake display of passion?" he replied bitterly. "Look, next time you plan to go frigid on me, just tell me to get lost and I will."

"I didn't plan to go frigid on you; it just happened. And I tried to tell you to get lost earlier this afternoon, but you wouldn't take no for an answer," Blake pointed out tremulously.

"Well, I'll sure as hell listen to you the next time," Rusty snapped as he headed for the door. "But you sure had me fooled, Blake. I thought you were warm and caring. I didn't think you could turn passion on and off like a faucet!"

Blake watched Rusty's retreating back as he opened the front door and slammed it behind him, tears welling in her eyes as she watched him go. She sat down on the couch and cradled a pillow on her lap, tears spilling out of her eyes as she remembered Rusty's taunt. She was warm and caring, especially toward Rusty the person. But Rusty was also a pilot, and she resented that side of him and she resented him for reminding her of it. Wiping the tears from her eyes, she stared, unseeing, into her small living room, wondering if she would ever be able to ignore the fact that Rusty was a pilot, or if it would forever come between her and Rusty the person.

Blake rubbed her sleepy eyes and stared at the flight schedule once again. Damn it, she needed two more planes if she was going to have everybody flying tomorrow, and unless Rusty released 3447 she was going to have to disappoint someone. Sighing, she scratched a mosquito bite on her neck and sipped a cup of cold coffee, remembering with dismay her lack of response to Rusty the night before. *Maybe I am cold,* she told herself ruefully as she moved 8214 to an earlier flight. But a woman who was cold would not have responded so passionately that night after the river parade. No, she wasn't cold. Confused and resentful maybe, but not cold.

Rusty peeked around the door and looked at Blake warily, her tired head bent over her chart. *Doesn't look like she got any more sleep than I did,* he thought as he rubbed his palm across his forehead. *And this isn't going to endear me to her, not at all.* "Blake," he said softly.

Blake looked up, a cool professional mask slipping across her face. "Hello. Do you have some planes to release yet?"

"Yes, 5235's ready to go," Rusty replied.

"And 3447?" Blake asked quietly. "I really need that plane."

"I know you do, but it's just not ready," Rusty said.

"Damn it, Rusty, that plane's fixed!" Blake snapped irritably, her lack of sleep the night before robbing her of patience. "I saw to it myself. I went up in that cockpit and I turned that yoke myself, and it was fine."

"Fine on the runway and fine in the air are two different things," Rusty pointed out reasonably, valiantly holding on to his own temper. "Now, I was the one flying that plane today and I know that it isn't ready to go yet."

He had done it again. He had pointed out to Blake that he was the pilot. Her face flaming, she whirled on him. "Damn it, Rusty, I'm a pilot, too, and I checked that plane out! It is fixed!"

"It is not!" Rusty bellowed back, his own restraint snapping. "Damn it, Blake, I'm the pilot that took that plane up and I'm the one to make the decision. If somebody were to crash in it, it would be my career and my conscience."

"Yeah, you're the only one qualified to make any decisions around here," Blake taunted unreasonably. "You're the one to arbitrarily decide that another professional pilot doesn't know what she's talking about and do it rather rudely and arrogantly, just like every other pilot the Air Force has ever produced. You think you're a cut above the rest of us mere slaves, don't you?"

"Well, what about you?" Rusty jibed. "You wear

wings, too, lady. You're one of those rude, arrogant pilots, too, aren't you? But it's obvious you haven't flown in a while, isn't it, Blake?"

Blake sucked in her breath and her face turned white. Rusty had just handed her the ultimate insult that one pilot could give to another. Hands shaking in fury, she clutched the back of her swivel chair and stared him in the eye, cold calm rage overcoming her first impulse, which was to dissolve into tears and run away. "You know, Rusty, it's real easy to hit somebody with an insult like that when you don't know the whole story," she began quietly. "No, I can't fly anymore. But I want you to think about this the next time you're up in that cockpit, Rusty O'Gorman, ace pilot, thinking you're the best. Once upon a time, before something bad happened to her, there was one who was better than you. I was the best. I could fly the pants off you, O'Gorman. Easily. And that's why I know the damned plane's fixed. Now, will you please get the hell out of my office so that I can schedule these planes without your precious 3447?"

She watched calmly as Rusty walked out the door, his face white, then sat down at her desk and wiped a single tear from each eye. Oh, why had he goaded her into losing her temper and telling him off like that? But every word she had said to him was true. She had seen Rusty fly, and although he was good, he honestly wasn't any better than she had been, or could have been if she had been able to keep flying. He had no right to disregard her professional opinion.

Blake glanced down at her watch and noted that it was nearly five. *Well, I guess I get to go home and brood all evening,* she thought morosely. But there was no sense in that. Picking up the telephone, she called Suzanne's work extension. "Suzanne? This is Blake. Want to go out to supper tonight?—No, I don't want to face that apartment alone. Officer's Club about six? Thanks, Suzy." Relieved that she would have Suzanne to talk to, she bent her head and struggled with the airplane schedule for Thursday.

Rusty shook his head as he sipped his daiquiri at the bar in the Officer's Club. It had been over an hour since his confrontation with Blake. His temper had cooled and his conscience was giving him a very hard time. How could he have said something that cruel to her? He may as well have slapped her in the face! And from the way she had paled at the taunt, he had hurt her deeply by his crack.

Staring out the wide windows overlooking the base, Rusty pondered Blake's response to his cruel words. So she obviously wasn't on a rated supplement. She had said distinctly that she couldn't fly anymore, that something bad had happened to her. Had she gotten in trouble with the brass? Sometimes pilots were removed from flying status because of too many hijinks, but Blake would have been the last pilot to be disciplined for something like that. Did she wash out? No, she wore her wings, so she definitely had made it through training. Searching for clues, Rusty remembered the dinner party at Suzanne Parks's house last month. Blake had said very little during dinner when the three other pilots at the table had been discussing the various airplanes they had flown in their careers. Had Blake been busy eating, or had she had nothing to contribute to the conversation?

Rusty finished his drink and ambled down the stairs, freezing halfway down when he saw that familiar head of honey-blond hair gliding into the dining room, Suzanne's dark head beside her. Not wanting to spoil Blake's dinner, he waited until the women had entered the dining room, then came down the stairs and left the club quickly, his mind spinning. *I'm going to talk to her, and I'm going to do it tonight. I'm going to get some answers from her this time if it's the last thing I do,* Rusty promised himself as he put his truck in gear and drove away.

Blake smiled at Suzanne across the table. "You know, I'm selfish, I guess, but I'm sure glad John's on a cross-country and you were free tonight."

"Me too," Suzanne admitted. "It's been hard getting to see you as often as I'd like to."

Blake nodded. The two of them had gotten away for a few lunches together, but between Suzanne's desire to spend her evenings with her husband and Blake's evenings spent settling into her apartment and exploring the city, the women had not been able to get together but once in the evening since Suzanne's dinner party, and that was also at a time when John had been away.

Blake stared at the menu for a while and finally ordered steak. Suzanne ordered a plate of Mexican food and handed her menu to the waiter. "Okay, out with it, Blake," she demanded.

"Out with what?" Blake asked.

"Whatever's eating you," Suzanne demanded.

"Nothing's eating me," Blake murmured, not wanting to unburden herself to Suzanne.

"Your nose is going to start growing like Pinocchio's if you keep telling fibs as big as that one," Suzanne chided her. "We lived together for the better part of a year, Blake. I know when something's bothering you, and you know how much it used to help you when you would talk to me about it."

"Oh, it's just a stupid fight I had with one of my test pilots," Blake said ruefully.

"Rusty?" Suzanne asked shrewdly.

"How did you know?" Blake asked as her eyes widened.

"You wouldn't care enough to fight with any of the others," Suzanne teased her. "So what did you fight about?"

"A damned plane that he wouldn't release," Blake admitted. "It's stupid, really. I needed that plane and I made sure that it was fixed properly, only Rusty swears that it isn't yet, and he won't release it."

Suzanne shrugged. "Test pilots and their maintenance officers squabble about releasing planes all the time. So what was so bad about this one?"

"It got out of hand," Blake admitted. "He threw it up to me that he was the pilot and that it was his decision, and I told him that he was rude and arrogant just like every other pilot I'd ever met, and he said that he could tell that I hadn't flown in a long time!"

Suzanne wrinkled her nose. "You both got a little personal, didn't you?" she asked.

Blake nodded miserably.

"But Blake, did he really throw it up to you that he was the pilot, or did he just point that out to you? It isn't like Rusty to throw anything up to anyone. He's usually the soul of humility."

"I don't know," Blake replied miserably. "I just know that it kills me to hear him say it, even if he is being reasonable. Damn it, it kills me every time he or one of the others takes off in one of those pretty little planes and leaves me behind!"

"It's eating you alive," Suzanne muttered hoarsely, her face paling and her fingers shaking slightly. "You're desperately unhappy because you can't fly, and I took it away from you. It's all my fault."

"No, Suzanne, you didn't and it isn't and you have to stop thinking that way," Blake cried sharply, sorry she

106

had even let Suzanne worm the story out of her. Damn it, why couldn't she had kept her mouth shut? "Suzanne, look at me," Blake commanded her firmly. Suzanne raised tear-filled eyes to meet Blake's. "That damned accident was as much my fault as it was yours, if not more."

"How can you say that?" Suzanne demanded tearfully. "I was driving, wasn't I? I'm the one who didn't see the car coming."

"And who was doing her best Joan Rivers monologue?" Blake asked dryly. "I was distracting you and we both know it. Now, wasn't I?" she demanded.

"But—"

"But nothing. And furthermore, that carload of kids certainly had something to do with it! Yes, I blamed you in the beginning, because I was looking for someone to blame and you were convenient. But Suzanne, that wreck wasn't your fault! Will you please get that through your head?"

Suzanne looked at Blake miserably. "But you're so unhappy," she said softly.

"Yes, I'm unhappy sometimes," Blake admitted quietly. "And frustrated. But because of an *accident*, Suzy, not because of anything you 'did' to me. Now, Suzanne, you have to promise me one thing," she added firmly. "You have to stop blaming yourself for what was an unfortunate accident, and get on with being my friend. Do you hear me?"

"Yes, Mother." Suzanne giggled at Blake's firmly issued order, glad that she could lighten the mood by making Blake laugh, because if Blake had pressed her, she would have had to admit that she was no closer to forgiving herself than she had ever been. How could she forgive herself as long as Blake was miserable?

Blake looked over at Suzanne as the waiter brought

their meals. *I'm glad that's settled,* Blake thought as she cut a bite of steak and popped it into her mouth. Suzanne had no reason to torture herself with guilt, and Blake was glad that she would no longer be doing so.

The conversation drifted to other matters, and Suzanne regaled Blake with stories of John's antics during their courtship. From the stories that Suzanne told, Blake gathered that John was or at least had been on a par with Rusty, and she remembered the way he had glowered at her during the dinner party. As they laughed together at a particularly funny stunt that John pulled, Blake looked at her friend thoughtfully. "I'm glad that John can be fun," she said frankly. "I got the feeling that night over at your house that he didn't care for me a great deal, and I wondered if he was always that reserved with people."

Suzanne shook her head vigorously. "Oh, he liked you j-just fine," she stammered nervously as the waiter cleared their table. "He just had a bad headache that night, and he's never much good when he feels badly."

Sure, Blake thought as the waiter handed them the check. *Headache, my foot. John just plain didn't like me.* But if Suzanne wanted to cover up for him, that was her privilege as his wife. Blake and Suzanne chatted for a few more minutes, then agreed to meet one day next week for lunch.

As Blake drove home in the purple dusk, her thoughts returned to her bitter quarrel with Rusty, and she wondered if indeed she had overreacted. Had he actually thrown his status as a pilot up to her, or was she just overly sensitive? Had she provoked his cruel taunt about her lack of recent flying time? Dreading their meeting tomorrow, she parked her car and climbed the stairs to her apartment slowly, stifling a scream when out of the shadows a man stood up on the top step. "Don't be frightened, Blake, it's me," Rusty's softly accented voice called out of the gloom.

"What do you want?" Blake asked rather shortly.

"I want to talk to you," he replied firmly.

"I think you've said quite enough already," Blake said dismissively.

"I have, but you haven't," Rusty countered smoothly. "Blake, let's not create a scene out here on your front porch. Let me come in. Please."

And he would make a scene, Blake thought as she noted the firmness of his jaw, and that was the last thing she needed tonight. "All right, come in," she replied ungraciously. "But no more insults like the one this afternoon, all right?"

"All right," Rusty agreed softly as she unlocked her door and ushered him in.

CHAPTER SIX

Blake shut the front door behind her and motioned to the couch. "Have a seat," she said quietly, sitting down in the large wing chair that had been her father's. Rusty sat down on the couch and leaned forward, his elbows on his knees, his expression uncomfortably self-conscious. Blake stared him in the eye, her own shadowed eyes revealing a little of the hurt she had felt earlier in the afternoon.

"Blake, I'm sorry," Rusty said suddenly. "That was a

cruel thing to say to you and I had no excuse for saying it."

"That's right, you didn't," Blake replied steadily. "Although unfortunately in my case the statement is all too true." She stopped and stared at Rusty's blue eyes, which managed to be apologetic yet firm at the same time.

Rusty jumped off the couch and paced the carpet, the soft fabric muffling the sound of his footsteps. "I suppose you want an excuse and I really don't have one, except that I had reached my breaking point with you. I was mad when you tried to break our date yesterday and I was hurt last night when you wouldn't or couldn't respond when I kissed you, and then today when you accused me of being arrogant—well, Blake, I've always done my damnedest not to be rude or arrogant like so many of our fellow pilots are, and then when you said that I was just like them, well . . ." Rusty trailed off and shrugged his shoulders.

"I guess you weren't being rude and arrogant," Blake said slowly. "And I shouldn't have accused you of being that way. I'm sorry." She got up out of her chair and extended her hand to Rusty. "Friends?" she asked softly.

"Not quite, Blake," Rusty said as he took her hand in his and stroked it lovingly. "Of course I'm accepting your apology and I hope to goodness you'll accept mine. But it goes deeper than that with you, doesn't it, Blake?"

Blake withdrew her hand and sat back down in the chair. "Not really," she said softly, unwilling to say anything more about her feelings to him.

"Oh, yes, it does," Rusty said softly as he sat down on the floor beside her chair and leaned his back against it. "You've had a chip on your shoulder ever since you've been at Randolph," he said softly. "Yes, you have," he added as Blake opened her mouth to protest. "That first night in the Officer's Club you came out and said that you

110

didn't want to come to Randolph because there were too many pilots around. Then you froze up on me the minute you saw me in a flight suit. We were getting closer and then yesterday I did something, I don't know what, that made you so mad that you could hardly stand me to touch you, and then today we got into it so badly that I said something you may never forgive me for."

"Oh, I've forgiven you," Blake said softly.

"But you haven't told me what's eating you in the first place," Rusty said. "You're bitter toward me, Blake. And it isn't just me. It's every pilot you come around. Yes, Pat and I have talked about it a few times," he added as Blake's head shot up in surprise.

"I thought I had hidden it," she admitted ruefully.

"You've tried, but it hasn't worked," Rusty replied. "Once before I asked you and you deftly changed the subject," he said. "Now I want to know what on earth happened to you to sour you against everybody with a set of wings on his chest?"

"Rusty, I just don't want to talk about it," Blake said softly, drumming her fingers on the arm of the chair.

"Why not?" Rusty demanded.

"Because there are some things that are just too painful even to talk about," Blake replied quietly. "I'd really rather not bring it all back up again to torture myself with." *Please, Rusty,* she thought, *please don't make me go back into all of that with you. I don't want your pity, I really don't.*

"Well, then, how are you going to justify the claim that you're a better pilot than I am?" Rusty asked arrogantly.

"I never said that!" Blake protested.

"Oh, yes, you did," Rusty replied. "You stood there in your office and informed me that you're a better pilot than

I am. I think your exact words were to the effect that you could fly the pants off me."

"Bothered you, did it?" Blake asked caustically. "The thought that someone else might just be better than you?"

"Not at all," Rusty replied. "If you really are better than I am, then more power to you. But so far I haven't any proof of that, or any reason to think you might be any good at all, except for those wings on your uniform. So tell me about it, Blake. I dare you."

Blake sucked in her breath and got up out of the chair, pacing the floor as Rusty had done earlier. "Okay. First off, I'm not better than you, at least I wouldn't be if I had to get into one of those jets and fly it tomorrow. I haven't flown in three years. But I sure would have been, Rusty, if I had been able to keep flying. I was the best pilot in my class at Williams." She stopped pacing and looked Rusty straight in the eye. "Yes, you're good, but I would have been better."

"So what happened?" Rusty asked quietly.

"Well, the day I got my wings my best friend and I were going to pick up her date in Phoenix. A carload of kids tried to pass us on the right and we bounced into them and then hit the car in the other lane. We were showered with glass and a nasty little piece got into my right eye. I have damaged peripheral vision, and the Air Force doesn't let people with damaged peripheral vision fly their planes."

"How badly damaged?" Rusty asked.

"Oh, not very. For ninety-nine percent of the jobs in this world, I could have many times over that vision loss with no problem. But not in the Air Force. So my career was over before it ever started. And yes, I resent the rest of you sometimes, because if my career hadn't gone down the tube I would have been the leader of your pack."

"I wouldn't say that your career's down the tube,"

Rusty said slowly, measuring his words carefully. "You made your rank on schedule, didn't you?"

"Of course," Blake replied. "But I would hardly call being a maintenance officer a career."

"But you're a good one!" Rusty replied firmly.

"Yes, and I was a good engineer at Wright-Patterson, and I'll be a good whatever at the next base they station me at," Blake replied honestly. "But that isn't what I wanted to do with my life," she continued. "I wanted to fly. I still want to fly."

"So what's stopping you?" Rusty asked calmly.

"What do you mean, what's stopping me?" Blake replied indignantly. "I told you, I can't pass an Air Force physical to fly anymore."

"So is the Air Force the only game in town?" Rusty asked thoughtfully. "Can you fly civilian?"

"Not for an airline," Blake replied. "I wrote them and explained the problem, and they wrote me back and explained that with so many applicants with no physical problems whatsoever, there was no way that they could even consider sending me an application."

"All right, the airlines are out," Rusty said.

"And most other commercial jobs too," Blake replied morosely.

"So fly on weekends," Rusty said.

"What do you suggest I do, borrow the Air Force's T-38s for an occasional joy ride?" Blake asked derisively. "I don't think Colonel Alda would think very highly of that."

"Of course not," Rusty said impatiently. "There are other planes in the world besides Air Force jets. There are a lot of civilian flying clubs you could join. I know there's one out at Kelly Air Force Base that's very popular, and the Civil Air Patrol is always looking for a good pilot."

113

Blake whirled around in her tracks in astonishment. "Rusty, you have to be kidding," she exclaimed in wonder. "I flew Air Force jets. You know, the big ones. The fast ones. The ones that broke the sound barrier. Are you seriously suggesting that I should go out to Kelly and rent a dinky little plane for an hour or two at a time and take it up for a joy ride?"

Rusty's lips thinned impatiently and he got up off the floor and faced Blake squarely. "Yes, I am, if it's all that's left to you."

"I should have known better than to expect any understanding from you," Blake muttered as she twisted away from Rusty. "I'm talking about a career, a whole way of life down the drain, and you start talking some nonsense about flying little prop planes on the weekend as though that will make up for what I lost."

"Oh, I do believe I detect a note or two of self-pity in there somewhere," Rusty drawled as Blake whirled around to face him, too angry even to speak. "Yes, Blake, you just plain feel sorry for yourself. Your career's not down the drain. On a different path, perhaps, but at least you're still an Air Force officer and a damned valuable one." He took a deep breath and walked up to where he was right in front of her. "And you could still fly if you wanted to. You're not the first pilot to lose his or her flying status with the Air Force, and you won't be the last. Yes, I'm sorry you can't fly Air Force jets anymore, contrary to what you may be thinking about me right now. But if you wanted to fly badly enough, you would be out there doing it."

"I told you, that isn't what I want!" Blake snapped. "Rusty, I'm an Air Force pilot! What Air Force pilot would fly a little prop plane?"

"This Air Force pilot does," Rusty snapped back. "I fly

them nearly every damned weekend. And you know what, Blake? I enjoy it. I enjoy it a lot. And if you would come down off of your high-and-mighty I'm-an-Air-Force-pilot pedestal, you might enjoy it too. And furthermore, a lot of the civilian flying isn't just joy riding. We do a lot of search-and-rescue work that has saved lives."

"The Air Force didn't train me for that kind of stuff," Blake said stiffly.

"No, they just taught you to be a snob," Rusty said coldly. "All right. Be a snob. Be miserable. See if I care. Good night, Maintenance Officer Warner."

"Good night, Ace Pilot O'Gorman," Blake muttered as Rusty marched out of her front door and slammed it behind him. *Snob be damned,* Blake thought as she threw herself down on the couch and glowered into her living room. *That man has to be the most insensitive idiot that has ever climbed into a cockpit. To think that I would even want to fly a silly little prop plane after those jets I used to fly!*

Knowing she had to work off her anger if she ever expected to get any sleep tonight, Blake put on her jogging clothes and let herself out into the warm April night, the soft breeze caressing her body as she pounded out her fury on the soft dirt path that she liked to run. Snob! She was no snob. She just didn't particularly want to fly the little planes, not after flying jets.

But she hadn't been so picky during her year at Williams, she remembered suddenly as she stumbled on a rock. She and Suzanne had regularly rented a Cessna on Saturdays and flown over the desert, dipping and whirling high above the shimmering sand. She hadn't objected to piloting a small plane then. It was only after the accident, only after the Air Force no longer wanted her as a pilot, that she had begun to feel that the little planes were beneath her dignity.

Blake turned around and jogged back to her apartment, her fury cooled somewhat but still unconvinced that Rusty was right. Would she enjoy the little planes after her sojourn with the jets? Or would it make her even more dissatisfied with her life? Shrugging, Blake let herself into her apartment and shed her clothes in the bathroom. Deciding that she needed a treat after a long day, she ran a tubful of warm water and sprinkled her favorite bubble bath into it, sinking up to her neck in the delicate bubbles and letting the soothing bath wash her cares away.

Rusty stared unseeingly at the Johnny Carson show, completely unmoved by the earnest young comic who was trying so hard to be funny and failing so miserably. The scene with Blake had shaken him, and if he were not due behind the throttle of a jet in just seven hours, he would have had a good stiff drink. So now he knew why she was so bitter toward him and the rest of the pilots that she came in contact with. She hadn't flown in three years! He could hardly stand to be out of a cockpit for three days, much less three years.

And it's a shame, Rusty thought, *that she's so turned off by the thought of civilian flying.* Sure, the Air Force jets were great, but some of his best flying had been done on weekends, either flying a mission with the C.A.P. or just flying for the pure joy of it. But how could he convince Blake of that when those bastard instructors at Williams had brainwashed her so thoroughly about the superiority of Air Force flying?

Rusty got up and switched off the TV, then wandered back toward his bedroom and slipped out of his robe, sliding naked between the sheets. He remembered the feel of Blake's body against his, the sight of her generous breasts exposed to his hungry gaze, and his body tightened with desire for her, both her body and her mind. *Damn,* he thought, *I'll never be able to get to that woman as long as she is miserable about not flying anymore, because every time she looks at me she's going to remember what I have that she doesn't.* The only way he would ever be able to reach her was to help her ease the miserable frustration that was eating her alive.

Rusty, you wouldn't, he chided himself as a beautiful plan started to formulate in his mind. *Oh, she's going to hate you if you do it,* he thought later as his plan grew and took shape. *You sneaky pilot you! You're asking for it this time.* Rusty rolled over and went to sleep, a grin of pure devilment on his lips as he dreamed of Blake's body curled up next to his.

Blake wandered into her kitchen and peered into the refrigerator, poking around in search of something for supper. It had been a week since she had been shopping at the commissary and she was woefully low on anything substantial to eat. Finding nothing in the refrigerator, she checked the freezer and again came up with zero. *I'll go shopping tomorrow when I get off work,* she promised herself as she changed into a pair of jeans in the bedroom and checked her wallet. Yes, she had plenty of money, and she didn't think that McDonald's would dent her budget too badly anyway. Grabbing her sunglasses and her keys, Blake bounced out of her apartment and shut the door behind her.

She was about halfway down the stairs when she spotted the familiar red pickup truck pulling into the parking lot of her complex. *I wonder what he wants,* Blake thought as she slowed her step on the stairs. She had barely spoken to Rusty in the last five days since their argument in her apartment and they had both gone out of their way to avoid each other. But the accusation that she was a snob still rankled Blake, although a part of her acknowledged that it just might be true. However, she still wanted no part of civilian flying, of that she was sure.

She watched as Rusty bounced out of the pickup cab and banged the door behind him, leaping over the retaining wall and bounding up the steps two at a time. "Blake, wait up," he called.

Blake stopped halfway down the steps. "You wanted to see me?" she asked very coolly.

"Are you leaving?" Rusty asked as he noted the wallet and the keys.

Blake nodded as Rusty's face fell. "I'm going for a hamburger," she explained quietly. "My refrigerator's empty."

"Ah," Rusty replied, his face splitting into a wide smile, "then I got here just in time. Would you like to go out for a decent meal with me? I can feed you better than an assembly-line hamburger."

"Well, I don't know," Blake replied reluctantly. She was still angry with him over calling her a snob, but she was hungry and certainly wouldn't mind a decent meal. Slowly she nodded her head. "All right," she replied. "Where do you want to go?"

"I've heard of this little place on the other side of town that's supposed to be very good. You know, one of those holes in the wall where the food is delicious. How about that?"

"Isn't that awfully far to drive?" Blake asked doubtfully.

"Pat Gordon swears the food's worth it," Rusty replied as he took Blake's arm and led her to his pickup.

She climbed in and before long she and Rusty were whizzing along the expressway, past downtown into the older, south part of town. Rusty chattered nonchalantly to Blake, their argument apparently forgotten, as he got off the expressway and drove down a narrow winding road lined with an occasional small home. Blake peered out the window of the car and saw a sign that read MISSION ESPADA and promised herself that she would either bring Rusty back to see the old mission or she would come by herself. Peering ahead, looking for something that looked like a hole-in-the-wall restaurant, she turned her head sharply when Rusty turned into a gate marked STINSON FIELD.

This was no restaurant. This was a small airport! Blake whipped her head around and glared at Rusty. "What in hell do you think you're pulling?" she demanded. "Where are we?"

"Stinson Field," Rusty replied calmly.

Blake looked resentfully around at the various small aircraft parked at the little airport. "And what are we doing here?" she demanded.

"Tonight's the monthly Civil Air Patrol meeting," Rusty replied calmly. "I thought you might like to attend."

"That's a pile of horse manure and you know it," Blake replied scornfully. "You know how I feel about this civilian junk. You sneaky little redhead, you tricked me into coming all the way out here, didn't you?" Rusty nodded smugly. "Well, it isn't going to work. You can just take me right back home—or better yet, out for that meal you promised me."

"You want your meal, you come in to the meeting," Rusty replied calmly. "Otherwise, you sit out here while I go and then I take you home hungry."

Blake looked Rusty straight in the eye. "All right, I'm calling your bluff. Go on in to the meeting, and then you can take me home and I'll go on to McDonald's from there." She settled back into the seat and rolled the window down, crossing her arms in front of her.

"Damn it, if you're not the most hardheaded woman I've ever met in my entire thirty-one years!" Rusty snapped disgustedly. "Look, the only reason I bothered to drag you out here was because there just might be something in it for you. You just might get to fly again, and you might even enjoy it a little. All right, so it isn't Air Force flying. These people fly small planes, and they do it on a volunteer basis. But there are some really good pilots in there, Blake. Some of them are on par with the best the Air Force has to offer. And their flying isn't just joy riding either. They fly search-and-rescue missions and they save lives. But I guess that isn't noble enough for you, is it?" Thoroughly disgusted, Rusty got out of the truck and slammed the door behind him.

"All right, all right, I'll go to your meeting," Blake said as she got out of the pickup and slammed her door. "I'll go and see these paragons of the civilian flying world." She caught up with Rusty in the middle of the field and glared at him angrily. "Just this once. And then I don't want to hear another word about it. Ever!"

"Fine," Rusty replied with satisfaction as he took her by the elbow and escorted her to the door.

They were met by a chorus of "Hello, Rusty" from a group of about twenty men and women and five or six teenagers. Rusty nodded a greeting to everyone and Blake sat down beside him on a folding chair.

A tall, dark-haired man came and sat down on the other side of Rusty. "How you doin', Bob?" Rusty asked genially.

"Well, I did three open-hearts this afternoon and Mar-

120

gie wants to redecorate the living room in Oriental, but other than that I'm fine."

Rusty and Blake both laughed out loud at the man's outrageous comment. The man stuck out his hand and Blake shook it. "I'm Bob Merrill," he volunteered warmly.

"I'm Blake Warner," she replied. "And I want you to know that I heard from the best of sources the other day that Oriental is very in this year!"

Bob laughed. "Are you Rusty's date tonight?" he asked.

"Not exactly," Blake stammered.

"Blake's a pilot," Rusty volunteered. "She's interested in doing some flying sometime." Blake shot Rusty a murderous look, which he patiently ignored.

At that moment the meeting was called to order and the chatter stopped. The commander, a retired Air Force colonel, reviewed the organizational events that had taken place since their last meeting and mentioned that there were several events coming up in the next few weeks. Then the meeting got down to the business at hand. The performance of several of the new pilots on the last search-and-rescue mission was reviewed and critiqued. Two of the pilots had done just fine, but one had been a little too concerned with the safety of his own craft and had been flying too high to really be effective as a search plane. The members offered the man several suggestions as to how to improve his technique.

Blake listened closely as a new observers class was scheduled, a practice search-and-rescue was set up for the next Sunday morning, and a new ground team was organized. A possible arrangement with one of the local hospitals to transport organs around the Southwest was discussed and voted on. As the meeting continued, Blake had to admit to herself that these pilots, whether they were active military, retired military, or civilian, were surprisingly knowledgeable, and that if their skill in the air matched their expertise on the ground, she was sitting in a roomful of very good pilots. Bob Merrill particularly impressed her. Although he was a heart surgeon and flew only on the weekends, his comments were extremely well-informed and she felt sure that his flying would be tops. But does this kind of flying really matter? Blake asked herself over and over. Sure, it sounds good, but do they ever do anything besides sit around and prepare for a bunch of what-ifs?

The meeting was finally adjourned after two hours. Blake stood up and was attacked by a sudden case of pins and needles in her bottom from sitting still for so long.

As the group milled around the room, laughing and chatting, the commander wandered toward her and Rusty. "I'm Colonel Prescott," he said as he extended his hand to her.

"Blake Warner," Blake said as she shook his hand.

"Captain Blake Warner," Rusty corrected her gently. "Blake's an Air Force officer."

"Pilot?" Commander Prescott asked.

"Not exactly," Blake said.

"Blake is no longer able to pass the Air Force physical to fly, but, yes, she's a fine pilot," Rusty volunteered as Blake glowered at him resentfully.

"Well, Captain Warner, we could sure use you here if you're at all interested in flying with us," Commander Prescott said eagerly, ignoring the shuttered look that came down across Blake's face. "I doubt that you would have any trouble passing our physical, and you would, of course, keep your same rank with us that you have in the Air Force. We'd love to have you."

"Thank you," Blake murmured as her stomach growled

loud enough for the two men to hear. "Sorry about that."
She blushed.

"I promised this lady dinner and I need to feed her
before she starts gnawing on my arm," Rusty teased.
"Come on, woman, before you faint on me and I have to
carry you all the way to the truck."

"Funny, Rusty," Blake murmured. "It was nice meeting you, Commander."

"Hope to see you back here next week," Commander
Prescott said as Rusty steered her toward the door.

CHAPTER SEVEN

Rusty escorted Blake to the car and unlocked her door.
"Well, am I forgiven for kidnapping you?" he asked impudently.

Blake laughed. "You know you are. I could forgive you
just about anything, and you know it." She reached out
and ruffled the hair on his forehead.

"Where to?" Rusty asked as he walked around the
truck and unlocked his door. "I guess you earned your
supper."

Blake reached over and grabbed Rusty's wrist. "I guess
this is as good a place to start as any," she teased as she
lovingly nibbled the sensitive skin on the underside of his
forearm.

"Cut that out, Blake, or I'm going to ravish you right

here," Rusty said with a thread of sexual tension in his voice.

In response, Blake ran her tongue up the side of his arm. "That's what I keep hoping," she murmured as Rusty firmly withdrew his arm from her sensual caress. Blake's stomach rumbled again. "Oh, well, first things first," she said as Rusty started the engine. "That little hole in the wall? Or is there no hole in the wall?"

"Nope, none that I know of," Rusty admitted cheerfully. "So how about I take you downtown for the best plate of Mexican food you ever ate?"

"Is it good?" Blake asked.

"Tops. I promise," Rusty assured her as they drove out of the parking lot and got back on the little street. They chattered about this and that as Rusty got on the expressway that would take them into downtown, but neither of them said anything about the meeting that they had just attended as Rusty made his way into the heart of the city. Blake's attention was captured by the picturesque group of buildings that Rusty was parking in front of. "Where are we?" she asked eagerly.

"I think it's called the Mercado," Rusty said as they climbed out of the truck.

"Whatever it is, it's nice," Blake replied.

They wandered hand in hand into Market Square, one of the oldest continual markets in America. Although most of the shops were closed by this time of night, they could still see the colorful merchandise, all shipped in from Mexico, that the individual little shops were selling. Besides the usual souvenir-type merchandise, some of the shops had perfume and leather goods, and several of them carried dresses similar to the ones that Blake had already bought, but at a considerably higher price than she had paid. Blake grimaced as they peered into the windows of a small "pharmacy" and saw rows and rows of herbal treatments for various ailments. "By looking in there you would never know it's 1984," she said in wonder.

Rusty shrugged. "I'm sure there are still a lot of people who believe in that kind of thing," he replied.

In spite of their hunger, they took their time wandering around the square, finally ending up in front of Mi Tierra, a combined restaurant-bakery that Rusty said was a San Antonio landmark. A friendly young waiter seated them and handed them each a menu.

"You're going to have to help me," Blake said as she surveyed the menu. "I've never eaten Mexican Food before."

Rusty leaned over and pointed to one of the combination plates. "That one has nearly everything that a novice would like." He ordered the same dish for himself and asked for two Mexican beers.

"Where did an Alabama boy like you learn all about Mexican food?" Blake asked as she sipped her water.

"I trained down in Del Rio for a year," Rusty reminded her. "We used to go across the border all the time for a meal. And how about you? You trained in Phoenix, didn't you?"

Blake nodded. "But somehow we just didn't get into the ethnic cuisine very much," she admitted. "I know Mom and Dad liked Mexican food, because Dad was stationed here before I was born, but after I came along he was always stationed somewhere farther north or out of the country."

"Where are your folks now?" Rusty asked.

"Dad was shot down in 'Nam," Blake said softly. "I still miss him sometimes. Mom and I moved to Chicago and Mom got a good job with an insurance company. She dates a lot, but she's never remarried."

"Was your dad a pilot?" Rusty asked.

"Yes, he was," Blake said, her eyes shining. "They tell me he was a fine pilot."

The waiter brought them two bottles of beer and a basket of complimentary chips. Blake poured her beer into a glass and sipped it curiously. "This stuff is delicious," she said as she licked the foam from her lips.

"Is that why you wanted to fly?" Rusty asked as he sipped his beer.

"At first it was," Blake admitted as she nibbled a chip. "Dad would take me out to the runway and let me watch the jets take off, and he would tell me that I'd be up there someday. But later, of course, I came to love flying because I love flying. Loved flying," she corrected herself quietly.

"Blake, it doesn't have to be over, you know," Rusty said cautiously as the waiter brought them steaming plates and cautioned them not to touch the plates, as they too were hot.

Blake picked up her fork and pointed to an item that looked like a crepe. "What's that?" she asked curiously.

"An enchilada," Rusty said as he cut into his with a fork. "Watch out, the cheese is runny."

"And hot," Blake said as she fanned her mouth from too large a bite.

"You have a way of doing that," Rusty teased her as she grabbed her beer and drank thirstily. "Seriously, Blake, what did you think of the meeting tonight?"

Blake shrugged her shoulders and pointed to another item of food on her plate, something wrapped in a corn shuck. "What is that?" she asked curiously.

"A tamale," Rusty replied. "Take off the corn shuck before you eat it."

Blake removed the shuck and took a bite of the spicy

tamale. "Tell me a little more about the organization," she invited him.

"Well, the C.A.P. is organized as a civilian volunteer organization that assists all government agencies in search-and-rescue work. Although most of the members join because it gives them an excuse to fly, the C.A.P. does perform a vital function whenever a private plane goes down. That's a taco you're staring at," Rusty added.

"So how do I eat it?" Blake asked in puzzlement.

"Pick it up and bite it off," he replied, laughing when Blake spilled most of the contents of the taco into her plate. "We also train teenage cadets so they can get their pilot's licenses. We hold practice search-and-rescues for both aerial and ground teams, and we hold flying clinics."

"Sounds good," Blake conceded. "What's that?" she asked, pointing to a concoction on the table in a small bowl.

"Hot sauce," Rusty replied. "Go light on it. It's easy for someone who already flies to become a member," Rusty continued as he spooned his refried beans into a tortilla and added a little hot sauce. "All you would need to do is to take a simple written exam and then demonstrate to one of the officers that you can indeed fly an airplane. Then they will submit your name to Maxwell—"

"Not so fast, Rusty," Blake admonished him quietly. "I never said I intended to join."

"And may I ask you why not?" Rusty demanded imperiously.

"That kind of flying—I'm just not sure that's what I want," Blake replied haltingly.

"Damn it, are we back to that again?" Rusty groaned. "You've seen the organization. You know they're good pilots—they aren't a bunch of incompetent snobs."

"I know all that," Blake said quietly. "It's just that, well, that isn't the kind of flying I can see myself doing."

"Well, that's the only kind of flying left open to you," Rusty pointed out harshly, ignoring Blake's indrawn breath at his brutal statement. "It seems to me that you can either join the C.A.P. or you can sit around and pout."

"I am not pouting," Blake said evenly through clenched teeth. "Those pilots are great, I've already told you that, and I have the deepest respect for what they are doing. Look, Rusty. I haven't flown a plane in three years. After the accident I learned to live without flying. I'm just not sure I want to go back into it at this point."

"Why not?" Rusty challenged her softly.

"Because I've learned to be reasonably content with my life as it is," Blake said quietly. "I've learned to live without it, like an alcoholic learns to live without booze. What happens if I start flying again and become more dissatisfied because I'm not flying professionally?"

Rusty shrugged. "I don't know, Blake, but it seems to me that if you were all that content with your life as it is, then you wouldn't resent every pilot you come in contact with. Honestly, I think that if you came and flew for us, that you would find yourself more contented with things the way they are, not less so. Now, admit it, Blake—has a day gone by in the last three years that you haven't wished you were up there somewhere, soaring above the clouds?"

"Of course there hasn't," Blake replied hotly. "I miss flying a great deal and you know it. But what if you're wrong and it makes it worse for me, wanting to fly jets again and not being able to?"

"Could it get much worse?" Rusty challenged her softly.

"Oh, yes, Rusty, it could get a lot worse," Blake replied

feelingly. "All right. I'll go back to the meeting next week and I'll think about flying again. But if I decide that I'd rather not fly again, you're going to have to accept that and get off my tail about it."

"Fair enough," Rusty said as he finished the last of the rice on his plate. Blake looked down in astonishment. In spite of their heated discussion, she had managed to clear her plate. "But Blake," Rusty added.

"Yes?" she replied.

"Are you ever going to be completely happy again if you aren't flying?" Rusty asked quietly.

"I just don't know, Rusty," she replied. "I really don't know."

Rusty shrugged his shoulders as the waiter handed him the check. He started to say something but changed his mind as he took a couple of bills from his wallet and tossed them on the table. He extended his hand to Blake and wordlessly they stood up and walked to the cashier. As they waited in line to pay the check, Blake spotted a bakery area around the corner from the cashier's desk with rows of interesting-looking breads and sweets. "Oh, Rusty, look at all this," she murmured as she wandered down the glass case and examined the various baked goods.

"How can you even think about those after all you just ate?" Rusty groaned.

"I can always make room for a sweet," Blake admitted.

"All right, pick out a few and I'll get them for you as soon as I pay the check," Rusty replied indulgently.

Blake walked along the case and looked at the various breads and rolls longingly. Hesitantly she asked the lady behind the counter what was good, and the lady suggested pan de huevos and empanadas and of course Blake wanted to get a few buñuelos, so by the time Rusty joined her she

129

had quite a sack of rolls. "Gonna share those with me?" he teased.

Blake dug down into the bag and broke off a piece of the empanada. "The lady said this one was made with pumpkin," she said as Rusty bit in. "Is it good?"

"Umm-hmm," Rusty nodded as he swallowed the tasty bread. "Give me another piece of that."

"I thought you said you weren't hungry anymore," Blake said dryly as she broke him off another bite.

Rusty shrugged. "I can always make the sacrifice," he said nobly as he popped it into his mouth and ate it quickly.

In spite of the huge meal they had just eaten, between them they ate nearly all of the sweets by the time they had gotten to her apartment. Blake brushed the crumbs off the truck's upholstery the best she could and Rusty said not to worry, that he would get it vacuumed the next day.

They laughed and talked casually as Rusty walked her up the stairs, but the tension between them was beginning to build, as it always did when they were together. It was like a fine steel lasso, binding them closer and closer almost against their wills, and in spite of her ambivalent feelings about becoming involved with him, Blake longed for the feel of his mouth on hers and to abandon herself in his arms and let him do with her what he would.

Solemnly she handed Rusty her keys and he unlocked the door to her apartment and followed her in, but did not immediately move to take her into his arms. Instead, he opened the curtain covering the sliding glass door onto the balcony and stared out at the full moon that was spilling light out over the warm spring night.

Blake followed Rusty over to the window and stood with him, staring up at the round moon high in the sky. "Good night for flying," she said softly.

"Yes, it would be," Rusty said softly. "Good night for some other things too." He slid his arm around Blake and drew her to his side, but made no move to kiss her. He just held her tightly to him, his arm casually around her waist.

"Can I get you anything?" Blake asked softly.

"No, I'm fine," Rusty said gently as he gazed into Blake's eyes, her face bathed in the soft moonlight. "Blake, I'm going to kiss you now," he added as he bent his head and touched her lips softly. Blake reached out with her mouth and met him willingly, her lips straining to capture his. Rusty groaned and pulled Blake even closer to him, his other hand anchoring her head as he nibbled the edges of her mouth, postponing the plundering of her sweetness for long agonizing moments as he sampled her lips and the soft skin above her upper lip, then pressed his lips firmly over hers, finding Blake's teeth a tantalizing barrier to his further possession. Blake let his tongue play along her lips for long moments, denying him the entrance that he wanted, knowing that when she finally did let him in that his touch would be just that much sweeter.

Finally, as Rusty thought he could stand no more of Blake's sensual torture, she opened her mouth to him and he possessed it fully, their tongues fencing back and forth in an erotic dance that Blake found incredibly thrilling. Darts of pleasure jolted through her body as Rusty tormented her lips and teeth with his tongue, groaning when she returned his caresses with gentle forays of her own. Ever so slowly Rusty pulled away from her lips and gently inspected her face with his lips and his tongue, softly caressing her eyelids with his warm touch as Blake put her wandering fingers up to the side of his face. "Rusty, we're right in front of an open window," she said softly.

Rusty reached over and yanked the curtain shut, immediately bathing the room in darkness. Blake reached out to turn on a light, but Rusty stopped her, leading her carefully to the couch and sitting down beside her. Then he reached over and turned on the small lamp beside the couch. "I do like to see you when I touch you," he explained softly as he reached out and unbuttoned her shirt, button by button, until it was open to the waist. He leaned down and touched her shoulders gently with his fingers. "I've carried the memory of how you look with me for the last week," he murmured as he ran his finger down her collarbone. "I think about you all the time—when I'm driving home, when I'm in the shower, when I'm trying to test those damn planes. I just can't get the sight of you out of my mind."

"I've thought about you too," Blake admitted as she reached out and pulled Rusty's shirt out of his jeans. Slowly she inched the shirt up his chest and over his head, exposing his entire muscular chest to her hungry gaze. "I've thought about the way your hair tickled my breasts." She reached out and ran her fingers through the soft, thick red hair. "Is it red everywhere?" she asked, blushing as she realized exactly what she had just asked him.

"Everywhere," Rusty confirmed as delighted amusement danced in his eyes. He bent his head to her shoulders and bathed them in warm, sweet kisses as Blake fingered the hard muscles in his back and sides, eagerly touching the warm velvety skin that covered a layer of lean, tough muscles. Although Rusty was not a big man, he was perfectly proportioned and Blake loved the way his broad shoulders tapered into a lean, hard waist.

Rusty reached around and unhooked her bra, eagerly pulling it away from her body as his eyes explored Blake's firm, generous breasts. Slowly he bent his head and touched her shoulder with the tip of his tongue, then his lips and his tongue caressed her body to where her breasts

132

swelled. Nibbling the outer edges of her breast, Rusty slowly worked his way to the tender center, nibbling and nuzzling in mind-spinning circles, working his way around and around until he had finally reached the tender center.

When his lips gently closed over the tip, Blake gasped audibly, the touch of his mouth driving her to arch her body closer to his, to give him further access to her sensitive peaks, hardened and darkened into rosy nubs of pleasure. Rusty tormented one breast until Blake was moaning, then turned his attention to the other, pushing Blake down into the cushions of the couch and tormenting her breasts and the soft skin below them until she was squirming beneath his touch.

"Let's trade places," she murmured as Rusty's erotic tongue painted pictures on her midriff.

"My pleasure," he admitted, his body sliding down as Blake raised herself and put her head on his chest. She found one hard nipple and tantalizingly enticed it with her tongue, then wove a path through the soft red hair to the other, teasing it into a hard pinnacle of desire. Slowly she trailed her mouth down Rusty's middle to where the soft red hair arrowed down into his jeans, then she explored the soft patches of skin on either side where there was only a light sprinkling of hair.

"You're beautiful, you know that?" she murmured as she slid back to survey Rusty lovingly. Unfortunately, her couch was not too wide, and the slight movement backward sent her sliding off the side of it. "Rusty, catch me!" she wailed as she tumbled onto the soft carpet.

Rusty peered over the edge of the couch, his eyes dancing with laughter. "We'd never make it on an army cot," he laughed as he rolled off the couch and joined her on the floor.

"Or in a single sleeping bag," Blake admitted as Rusty's passion-glazed eyes examined her bare skin.

"So what do you say we go try out your bed for size?" Rusty asked softly as Blake's eyes widened in astonishment.

"Uh, Rusty, I don't think so," Blake stammered as she scooted across the floor, putting a vital foot between them. "Rusty, I never meant for things to get this far tonight," she said quietly. "I'm not going to start an affair with you." She watched anxiously as Rusty's face reflected angry bewilderment.

"You mean that you're going to turn it off just like that?" Rusty asked angrily. "Just like that?" He snapped his fingers in her face. "I said once that you were cold, Blake, and, boy, I was right, wasn't I? You can turn it on and off like a faucet, can't you?"

"My God, do you think it's easy for me to pull away from you?" Blake demanded angrily. "Don't you think I'm tempted? Do you know what I'd give to take your hand and lead you into that bedroom? Do you know what I'd give to take you into my bed tonight and make love with you until morning?" She buried her head in her hands, her hair falling like a curtain around her face, hiding her anguish from Rusty's angry eyes.

Rusty reached over and tipped her face up to his. "So why don't you?" he asked softly.

"Because you're a pilot," she answered quietly.

Blake watched as hurt and astonishment played across Rusty's face, to be replaced swiftly by redfaced anger. "So we're back to that," he jeered as he let go of her chin and stood up angrily. "Poor little Blake, the thwarted pilot, is going to do everything she can to make herself and everybody else miserable, including turning me away because I just happen to be a pilot. Damn it, Blake, are you ever going to let it go? Are you ever going to be able to see me as a person? As a man, not a goddamned flyboy?"

"I don't know," Blake answered quietly, reaching over to the couch and finding her bra. She tugged it on as she spoke. "That's just it, Rusty. I don't know if that day will ever come. Yes, I see you as a pilot sometimes, and when I do I resent the hell out of you. Now, do you really want to start an affair with a woman who feels like that about you?"

Rusty grabbed his shirt and tugged it over his head with sharp, angry motions. "I don't know how I'd feel in the morning, but right now I sure wouldn't feel bad about starting an affair with her."

"It's morning I'm worried about," Blake admitted dryly. She looked up at Rusty, honest regret on her face. "I'm sorry, Rusty, if you think I led you on tonight. I really am. I should never have let the kissing get out of hand."

"Kissing, my foot," Rusty snapped. "If you hadn't fallen off the couch, we would have been lovers by now and we both know it."

"And we would have had a lot to face in the morning that I'm not ready to face yet," Blake retorted firmly. "I said I was sorry, but I'm not going to jump into anything that I can't handle, and, frankly, I can't handle an affair with a man who sometimes I'm so jealous of I could strangle."

Rusty looked at Blake slowly and disdainfully. "And I've shown you what you can do to get over that jealousy. If you ever decide to come out of that lovely cocoon of self-pity that you've constructed around yourself, you let me know." Very deliberately he walked to the front door and left.

Blake stared unseeingly at the closed door, a tension

headache splitting her head wide open. *No, Rusty, it isn't self-pity,* she thought as she sat back against the couch and rubbed her sore head with the heel of her hand. But she was jealous and resentful and it wouldn't be fair to either one of them to become involved in an affair with a man she resented as badly as she resented Rusty sometimes. *If I thought I could cope with the jealousy,* she thought, *I'd follow him to his house with my toothbrush and my fatigues and spend the night with him tonight!*

But what about emotional involvement? Blake groaned and sat with her knees drawn up and her head resting on them. She was becoming emotionally involved with Rusty in spite of her intentions to the contrary, and that was almost worse than physical involvement would have been. Shrugging her shoulders, she stripped off her jeans and took a quick shower, falling naked into bed only to stare at the ceiling, sleep far away. *I care about him and I would like to be his lover,* she thought, *but I'm afraid. I can't afford to let the relationship go any further until I can get over the resentment I feel every time the man flies an airplane.* Wondering if she would ever be able to do that, Blake turned over and fell into a troubled, restless sleep.

Blake squinted at the street map and read the sign carefully. Yes, this was it. She turned onto Mission Road and followed the winding old street until she saw the entrance to Stinson Field. She turned into the lot and parked her car, then wandered hesitantly toward the door.

Did I really want to come here tonight? Blake asked herself as she slipped into the meeting room. *Do I really want to get involved in this?* She was a little late and the meeting was already in progress, so she sat down in the back of the room and listened quietly as Commander Prescott reviewed a search-and-rescue that they had performed just this past weekend. A plane had gone down near Austin, and the C.A.P. had searched for nearly two days before finding the wreckage. Blake's heart went out to the families of the dead as she remembered the way she and her mother had felt when her father's plane had gone down and it had been two solid weeks before it was found.

She glanced around and spotted the familiar head of flaming hair in the first row. Rusty gave a report on the actual spotting of the plane, and Blake gathered from his comments that he had been the pilot who had finally spotted the wreckage.

So maybe that's why he didn't call me this weekend, Blake thought as the meeting droned on. Not that she had really expected him to, not after the way they had parted last week. No, Rusty had thrown the ball into her court and the next play was hers.

As the meeting adjourned, Blake slid out of her chair, intending to make a quick exit, but Rusty and Commander Prescott spotted her simultaneously and both rushed across the room to greet her. "You came!" Rusty said with almost boyish enthusiasm.

"I told you that I would," she reminded him quietly.

"Captain Warner!" Commander Prescott said as he reached out and shook her hand vigorously. "I'm so glad you came back tonight."

"I enjoyed coming, Commander," she said sincerely.

"Do I take it that you want to be a part of this illustrious organization?" he asked eagerly.

"Not—not yet," Blake said quietly, watching as both Rusty's and Commander Prescott's faces fell. "I'd like to visit a few more times before I make up my mind, if that's all right," she added.

"Of course," Commander Prescott said agreeably. "Be

sure to come next Sunday to the practice S.A.R.—that's a search-and-rescue—we're holding."

Blake nodded. "I'll try to make it," she said.

"How about you, Captain O'Gorman? Will you be flying it?" Commander Prescott asked.

"Sorry, I've got a cross-country coming up," Rusty said regretfully. "See you next week." Commander Prescott left them and Blake and Rusty wandered toward the door. "I can't believe you really came," he said as they walked together out into the warm May evening.

"I told you that I would," Blake reminded him softly as she walked swiftly to her car.

"Hey, would you like to go out for a meal?" Rusty asked as Blake hurriedly opened the door and got in.

Blake turned sincerely regretful eyes toward him. "I promised Mom I'd call her tonight," she said softly. "It's her birthday. Maybe some other time." She got into the car and pulled out of the parking lot, leaving Rusty staring at her disappearing taillights.

"You're making progress, Blake," he said softly as he walked toward his truck and got in. "Not as fast as I'd like, but the progress is there, honey." Rusty drove down Mission Road and got on the expressway, singing along with the car radio in his off-key baritone all the way home.

CHAPTER EIGHT

"Damn, this hangar's hot," Blake muttered as she wiped her forehead with her hand and climbed into the cockpit of the jet. "Now, Pat," she said as she leaned out of the window, "tell me again what the brakes are doing when you try to stop this thing."

"They're skipping," Pat replied, demonstrating with his hand the jerky motion that the brakes produced on the runway.

Blake worked the brakes for a minute and nodded. "Okay, I'll get the boys in the shop to work on it. I think I know what the problem is."

"Super," Pat replied. "Good grief, this place is hot," he griped as Blake climbed out of the cockpit and jumped to the floor.

"Aw, come on, you soft Yankees you. Can't you take a little heat?" Rusty teased as he poked his head around the door. "It's only ninety."

"That's here in the hangar. It'll be one hundred and twenty-five in the cockpit today," Pat complained.

"Well, maybe we don't like the heat down here, but I'd love to watch you cope with a six-foot snowdrift," Blake teased Rusty as the three of them walked toward her office.

"Today that sounds good," Pat said as he handed Blake

some release papers. "If it's this hot at the end of May, what's it going to be like in August? Denise is going to be big by then."

"Oh, is Denise going to have a baby?" Blake squealed. "Congratulations!"

"I don't know about that," Pat admitted. "This one was an oops, and she's not too thrilled with me," he added sheepishly.

"I think she'll get over it," Blake assured him as Rusty laughed out loud. "Once she gets a load of that little baby, she'll be fine."

"I hope so," Pat replied doubtfully. "In the meantime, do you know anywhere I can hide out on weekends?" He waved and strolled out the door, Blake and Rusty laughing as he went.

"I bet that poor guy has hell to pay," Rusty said. "Denise has a temper."

Blake shrugged. "If I remember that biology lecture they gave us in the tenth grade, I think it took both of them to accomplish something like that! Anyway, she'll love the baby."

"I bet you would, if it were you," Rusty said softly.

"Sure I would," Blake admitted, her eyes shining. "I'd love it to pieces. So, are you going to release any planes, or do I spend the entire meeting tonight worrying about my schedule?"

Rusty handed her two papers. "So you're coming back again?" he asked.

"I've come to the last four meetings," Blake reminded him. "I enjoy them."

"But you haven't joined yet," Rusty said as Blake took her purse out of her desk drawer.

"True," Blake replied as they left her office and she locked the door behind them.

"So why not?" he asked as they walked through the large, empty hangar.

Blake shrugged. "It's a long story," she admitted as they left the hangar and together headed toward the parking lot. "I don't have time to go into it right now."

"Okay, tell you what. I don't have to fly tomorrow, so after the meeting I'll take you out for a drink and you can tell Uncle Rusty all about it," he said as she unlocked the door of the Datsun. "Pick you up in an hour." He reached out and kissed Blake on the nose, then was gone before she could protest.

If that man gets much more high-handed, I'm going to wring his neck, Blake said to herself as she drove home through the heavy traffic and rushed through a shower and washed her sweaty hair. Not bothering to dry it, she toweled it as best she could and plaited a long wet braid down her back. In spite of her annoyance with Rusty, she made him a fat roast beef sandwich, and it was waiting for him when he rang her doorbell exactly one hour later.

"Thanks," Rusty said as he took the sandwich and ate it in three big bites.

They hurried out and climbed into Rusty's truck, both loathe to be late to the meeting. As he jockeyed his way through the heavy traffic, Blake admitted to herself that she was enjoying the meetings more and more every week. The pilots were great, every one of them, and Blake enjoyed the feeling of camaraderie with them that she no longer felt with the Air Force pilots. *So why don't I join?* she asked herself as Rusty parked in front of the small control tower and walked with her into the meeting. They were a little early, but they spent an enjoyable few minutes speaking with Bob Merrill, who was complaining hilariously about the new couch that his wife had picked out over the weekend.

* * *

When the meeting adjourned, Rusty drove them to a small, quiet pub that wasn't too far from Blake's apartment. Rusty ordered a daiquiri and Blake, feeling adventurous, ordered a Cuba libre. As the shapely barmaid waltzed to the bar, Rusty tore his eyes from the girl and sought Blake's. "So why haven't you joined up yet?" he asked quietly. "You go to the meetings every week and you obviously enjoy them a great deal, but you just won't commit yourself, Blake. Why?"

Blake nibbled her fingernail and shrugged. "I told you that I wasn't sure that I wanted to fly again," she reminded him. "I'm still not sure."

"But Blake," Rusty chided her gently. "You miss it so much!"

"Yes, I do," Blake admitted. "I didn't realize just how much until I started going to those meetings. But I'm still afraid that if I start flying with the C.A.P. that I'll become even more unhappy in the Air Force. I'm afraid that I'll get the bug to fly full-time, and we both know I can't do that. And there's something else," she added sheepishly.

"What's that?" Rusty asked.

"I'm scared," Blake admitted.

"Scared?" Rusty asked. "You?"

"Yes, me," Blake said crossly. The barmaid brought their drinks and Blake sipped hers cautiously. "This is delicious," she said with enthusiasm.

"Don't change the subject," Rusty said firmly. "What are you scared of?"

"Flying," Blake said. "Getting up in a cockpit and flying a plane. I haven't flown one in three years, you know."

"Oh, Blake, is that what's stopping you?" Rusty asked

as he sipped his drink. "Why didn't you tell me before now?"

"I felt stupid," Blake admitted. "I was the best, and now I'm nervous about even getting into a plane again."

"I don't think that's stupid," Rusty said firmly. "I think that's normal. So here's what we'll do. You'll need to make a check-flight before you can fly again anyway, so Saturday morning I'll rent a Cessna at the Kelly Aero Club and check you out. You'll have to go in for a physical before then, of course."

"Rusty!" Blake cried. "Hold on! I never said I'd do it! I sleep late on Saturdays!"

"All right then, I'll come over and sleep late with you," Rusty teased as Blake blushed. "Come on, Blake," he wheedled. "It'll be fun!"

"Oh, all right," Blake said, knowing that she couldn't refuse Rusty anything that he really wanted. She drank the last of her exotic drink and wrinkled her nose. "I've probably forgotten everything I ever knew about flying."

"Now, Blake, I'm sure you'll do just fine." Rusty smiled at her encouragingly as he drained his glass. "Saturday morning at seven. I'll pick you up, all right?"

"All right," Blake agreed.

Blake jumped nervously as Rusty's knock sounded on the front door. She ran to answer it and in her rush banged the door into her toes, slapping them smartly. "Ouch!" she snapped as Calico squawked in the bedroom. "Would you like a cup of coffee?" she asked as Rusty came into the apartment.

"Yes, we've got time," Rusty said as he checked his watch. He followed Blake into the kitchen and watched as she picked up the coffeepot and tried to pour a cup of coffee with hands that shook. Missing the cup, she poured

143

it straight onto her hand and called the coffee a very unladylike word. "Here, let me," Rusty said as he took the coffeepot from her trembling fingers and poured them each a cup. Blake sipped hers nervously as Rusty found the sugar bowl and poured in a little sugar. "You're really shook, aren't you?" he asked, observing her pale face and shadowed eyes.

"Wouldn't you be?" she snapped. "Oh, I'm sorry for snapping," she said repentantly. "Yes, I'm shook."

Rusty drank about half the coffee in his cup and set it on the counter. He took Blake's from her and set it beside his. "Then I guess the sooner we do this, the sooner you get over your nerves," he said as he took her arm and led her from the kitchen.

In spite of her nervousness, Blake enjoyed the ride out to Kelly. Traffic was sparse early on Saturday morning and the city sparkled in the morning sunlight. Kelly was a huge, sprawling base with, surprisingly, the same red-and-white motif that made Randolph so attractive. Rusty drove through the base and parked next to a hangar that had a number of small craft tied down next to it. "Are those the planes?" Blake asked, her stomach a pit of nerves.

Rusty nodded. They climbed out of the truck and Rusty took Blake's cold hand as they walked into the hangar and into a small office marked KELLY AERO CLUB. The office, littered with every kind of flying notice under the sun, was manned by a friendly man that Rusty introduced as the manager. Blake sat silently in one of the old swivel chairs as Rusty filed a flight plan and they both signed a release relieving the government of any responsibility in case of an accident.

They wandered over to another office to check the weather forecast and the wind velocity. "These winds are good," Blake admitted as they left the weather bureau and walked back toward the planes. "What-where-what flight plan did you file?" Blake stammered. "Where are we going?"

"Since I rented the plane for only two hours, I thought you might like to fly up north and west of the city, circle east to Canyon Lake, and then fly back across the city toward Kelly. All right with you?"

Blake nodded stiffly as they approached a Cessna 170. "All the two-seaters were taken," he apologized as he started to untie the plane.

"This is fine," Blake said as she untied the other side. In spite of her nerves, she automatically went into the ritual of checking out the airplane, the ritual she had performed so often so many years ago. She checked the flaps as Rusty checked the fuel for purity with his small drainer, then she checked the strut, wheels, and brake as Rusty visually examined the airplane and checked the oil. She checked the leading edge of the propellers for dents and birds' nests, although as often as these planes were flown a nest probably would never be a problem.

"Are you ready to get in?" Rusty asked as Blake nodded, her mouth dry.

She was really about to fly this plane. Her fingers fumbling, she climbed in the left side, the pilot's side, and locked the door. As Rusty climbed in the other side and hooked up the headsets, she checked the yoke and all the controls, finding them all satisfactory.

"We're flight 529," Rusty told her as she primed the engines.

Taking a deep breath, she put on her headset and switched on the engine. Her hands trembling, Blake taxied to the edge of the runway. "Flight 529, calling Kelly Tower," she said softly. Rusty reached over and switched on the radio, smiling as Blake blushed. "Flight 529, calling Kelly Tower."

"Flight 529, this is Kelly Tower," a voice crackled over the radio. A large cargo plane touched down and taxied down the runway.

"Flight 529 is ready for takeoff," Blake replied.

"Flight 529 cleared for takeoff," the friendly voice said. "Have a nice flight." Blake looked at the radio in surprise at the friendly greeting.

So this is it, she thought as she swung onto the runway and increased the speed of the small plane. *I'm really going to do it,* she thought as the little plane gathered the speed it would need to leave the ground. The propeller whirred faster and faster and the little plane whizzed down the runway. *Here we go,* Blake thought as she pulled forward on the yoke and the Cessna left the ground.

"Good takeoff," Rusty commented, his voice sounding scratchy through the headphones. "Now, if you'll circle around that subdivision and set your trim tab on ascend, we can see the sights."

Blake circled around over the subdivision and headed northwest, speaking a couple of times to the control tower as she left Kelly airspace. Gradually she relaxed and her death grip on the yoke eased as the old magic wove its spell over her. She was flying! She really was flying! She took a deep breath and set her trim tab on ascend. "What do you want me to do, since this is my check ride?" she asked Rusty, her excitement clearly revealed in her voice.

"Fly," came his succinct reply.

So fly Blake did. The wide sprawling hill country below her, Blake winged upward, leaving the earth far behind. Gradually, not pushing her plane, she climbed farther and farther from the ground, gasping with pleasure as they rose to meet the fleecy clouds that spotted the sky. Al-

146

though she could have flown through them, Blake chose to find a break in the clouds and fly through it, the topsides of the clouds dazzling her eyes with their brightness. "Oh, Rusty, I'd forgotten how beautiful it is up here," she breathed with delight.

Rusty smiled wordlessly as he glanced over at Blake, a smile of pure pleasure wreathing her face. Yes, he had done the right thing in bringing her today. He looked at the thermometer that was mounted by the window. "We've hit a temperature inversion," he commented.

"Yes, I'd noticed," Blake replied as the little plane purred through the sky. *I'd forgotten how close this is to heaven,* Blake thought as the sun sparkled on the topsides of the clouds. *I'm free—it's just me and my plane—and Rusty, of course.*

"How about we go down now and see a little of the countryside?" Rusty asked as Blake adjusted the trim tab for a slow descent. They flew through the clouds this time, emerging from the white cocoon to see the patchy green fields below, interspersed with grazing land.

"Am I headed the right way to get to Canyon Lake?" she asked.

"You're doing fine," Rusty assured her as she adjusted the trim tab to hold a steady altitude. They flew against a strong headwind, but after a few minutes the shimmering blue water of Canyon Lake sprawled below them. "Beautiful, isn't it?" Rusty asked.

"Sure is," Blake replied. "Want to see some fancy flying?" she asked wickedly.

"I had a feeling this was coming," Rusty said dryly as Blake swung into a lazy eight, a figure eight turn that involved both climbing and dipping and that required a good deal of skill. Blake moved her arms and her legs automatically, her eyes on the instrument panel and the

147

horizon simultaneously as she performed the maneuver flawlessly.

"Very good," Rusty replied sincerely. "What else can you do?"

"I'll do a Chandell," Blake said as she put the plane into the smooth climbing turn that appeared simple but required the utmost skill. Rusty watched with admiration as she skillfully applied additional power and turned the plane slowly in a 180-degree arc that left them five-hundred feet higher than they had been.

"Excellent," Rusty breathed. "But we better head back."

"Well, why do you think I did the Chandell?" Blake asked pertly. She flew back toward the city, talking with the controllers out of San Antonio International and receiving permission to fly across the city instead of around it. She and Rusty spotted several familiar landmarks as Blake flew across the north side of town and around the east side of downtown, the tall buildings of downtown appearing tiny from the plane.

Rusty gestured in the direction of Kelly, and Blake raised the Kelly Tower and asked permission to land. Permission was granted, and she lined the little plane up with the landing markers and zoomed down toward the runway. Grinning cheekily, she touched down on the runway with first her left wheel, coasting on it for a moment, then rising off the runway, only to lower the right side of the plane and coast on her right wheel for a moment before she touched both wheels to the ground. "Showoff," Rusty said dryly as Blake taxied down the runway, lowering her speed as she turned off the main runway to the large concrete slab in front of the hangars.

"Where can I refuel this thing?" she asked. Rusty gestured toward a gas pump on one side of the hangar. Blake taxied to the pump and killed her engine, then he hopped out and helped her pump fuel into the tanks. She then taxied the airplane to where they had found it parked. "I see that all the planes are in use today," she said as they tied down the Cessna. All of the other planes were gone.

"Yes, and this one will be gone in fifteen minutes," Rusty said. "I have to admit that you're a damn good pilot, Blake," he said frankly. "You probably are better than I am."

Blake shook her head. "Not anymore," she said as she unhooked Rusty's headphones and handed them to him.

"We'll have to agree to disagree on that," he replied. "Say," he said, changing the subject, "would you like me to call Suzanne and John and see if they would like to go out for dinner tonight?"

"Sure," Blake said. "If you pick someplace that's on our budget, not theirs!" she added wickedly.

Rusty turned in the keys to the plane and called the Parkses from the office. Suzanne and John were delighted with the plan, so Rusty drove Blake home and agreed to pick her up at seven.

Once home, Blake got the application to join the Civil Air Patrol out of her desk drawer and filled it out, answering question after question. She wanted to fly again. She was sure of it now. Even if it did stir up her dissatisfaction later, any flying was better than no flying at all. *I hope it doesn't take too long to process this application,* she thought as she rummaged around in her desk for an envelope and a stamp. She addressed the envelope and licked the stamp, then jogged to the mailbox and dropped the application in. *Come on, C.A.P.,* she thought as she jogged back to her apartment. She could hardly wait to fly again!

Blake jumped as the doorbell sounded, then pushed on her shoes and ran for the door. "Rusty, I'm coming!" she

149

called as she struggled into her dress, the back zipper gaping open as she flew into the living room.

"Are you alone?" she demanded, opening the door a crack and peeking out to find Rusty on the top step.

"Oh, boy, this sounds good," Rusty said as she let him in.

"Zip me," Blake demanded, turning her back to him.

"Glad to oblige," Rusty said as he ran his finger down Blake's back, the touch of his hand sending shivers down her spine. "Pretty dress," he said as he turned Blake around and kissed her lightly.

"I'm taller than you again," she said. "Are you sure you don't mind?"

"Are you kidding?" Rusty laughed. "When the guys look at me with you, they think I must be pretty hot stuff to hold on to a gorgeous Amazon like you!"

"I swear, you're good for my ego." Blake blushed as she put her arms around Rusty's shoulders and hugged him tightly. "Where are we going to eat?" she asked as she picked up her purse and keys.

"John gave me the name of a new French restaurant on Broadway," Rusty said as they locked her apartment and climbed into his truck.

"It's bound to be expensive," Blake murmured as Rusty started the engine.

"Oh, John knows what we can and can't afford," Rusty said blithely. "I'm sure it will be quite reasonable. How did you like flying this morning?"

"I mailed in my application to join the C.A.P. this afternoon," Blake said shyly. "I do want to fly again, now that I've done it once."

"Super!" Rusty said as he banged his hand on the steering wheel. "We'll be flying some together then."

"I'd like that," Blake admitted. "I've never really flown with you."

Rusty followed the directions that John had given him, and before too long they were pulling up in front of a swank-looking restaurant with a valet waiting to park the car. "Are you sure this place is on our budget?" Blake asked hesitantly.

For the first time Rusty looked unsure of himself. "I—I think so," he murmured as he drove up to the canopied entrance. "Surely John—well, it's too late now," he said as he climbed out of the truck.

He opened the door for Blake and together they walked into the plush restaurant. Blake looked around at the lavishly dressed diners and down at her own simple jersey dress, then over at Rusty's sport coat and open-necked shirt. He saw her glance and squeezed her hand reassuringly.

Suzanne and John were waiting for Rusty and Blake in the bar, every bit as elegantly dressed as the rest of the diners. *Oops,* Blake thought. *I have a feeling John and Suzy have both forgotten how the rest of us live!* Suzanne jumped up and hugged Blake's neck, and John shook hands with Rusty, but his greeting toward Blake was a very cool nod. Rusty noticed this and his eyes narrowed, but the waiter came to usher them to their table and Rusty was distracted for the moment. The waiter seated Blake and Suzanne as Rusty and John seated themselves, then handed them each a menu.

Blake opened hers and stifled a gasp. There were no entrees on the menu for less than thirty-five dollars! And that didn't include any of the rest of the meal or the wine. She glanced over at Rusty and saw his eyes widen in shock. *Oh, no, I bet he doesn't have the money for this tonight.* He never carried that much cash, and the restaurant had conspicuously posted a notice that said American Express only, and she knew that he carried only a Visa card. He had paid cash for the airplane this morning, and that probably took a chunk of what cash he did have. His face was turning a bright shade of crimson and his mouth tightened. Oh, how embarrassing for him! Men were always so hurt when they had to admit that they couldn't afford something.

Quickly Blake fumbled around on the floor for her purse. Reaching into her wallet, she grabbed the wad of bills that she had gotten at the bank yesterday. It was almost one hundred dollars and was supposed to be for her groceries and incidentals for the next month, but she would worry about that tomorrow. She slipped off her shoe and gently nudged Rusty's foot. As he looked over at her in annoyance, she reached under the table and shoved the wad of bills into his hand. "Wasn't the flying weather great today?" she asked Suzanne brightly.

"It was wonderful," Suzanne acknowledged with puzzlement as relief swept Rusty's face. "What would you like to order, John?"

John picked a fancy beef dish that was well over thirty-five dollars. Suzanne ordered the same, but Blake and Rusty both ordered the simplest thing on the menu. Blake didn't understand French and hoped that it was something she liked.

As the waiter walked away, Suzanne turned to Blake. "Were you at work today?" she asked. "Usually I don't worry about the weather unless I'm flying." John looked at Blake strangely but said nothing.

"No, I wasn't at work," Blake said simply. "I was flying."

Suzanne swallowed. "I thought you couldn't fly anymore," she said, baffled. "Oh, Blake, can you fly again?"

"Well, the Air Force still doesn't want me," Blake said lightly. "But the Civil Air Patrol isn't nearly so picky. I'm going to fly for them."

"Oh, Blake, that's wonderful!" Suzanne said. She smiled over at John. "Isn't that just great, John?"

"C.A.P.?" John asked with genuine interest. "I hear they're absolutely indispensable when it comes to search-and-rescues."

"We are," Rusty said. "John, you and Suzanne really ought to come out sometime and see what we do."

John and Suzanne looked at each other and slowly shook their heads. "We get enough flying during the week," John said. "We're not quite as fanatic about flying as you two seem to be," he added teasingly, winking at Blake. So he can be friendly, she thought.

"Yes, we have other things we like to do on Saturday morning," Suzanne piped up, then she and John both turned a bright shade of pink.

Blake and Rusty both laughed out loud at their embarrassment. The waiter brought their dishes to them, and Blake was relieved that she had ordered a simple chicken breast cooked in a wine sauce. The dish was delicious, although there wasn't too much of it! She looked over at Rusty and saw him shaking his head ever so slightly. *I hope he has something he can eat at home later,* she thought as she remembered her own empty cabinets. *I certainly can't offer him anything!*

Blake thoroughly enjoyed her dinner, what there was of it. John had let his guard down with her and the four of them chatted happily about all of the small-plane flying they had done over the years. Blake and Suzanne agreed to rent a Cessna and go flying, although Blake made a mental note that it would have to be after her next payday, and John and Rusty discussed whether John and Suzanne would get enough use out of a small Piper to buy one of their own. It was late when the waiter finally brought them their checks and the evening broke up. Rusty put her stack of bills on the little tray that the waiter gave him, and the man's eyes widened with new respect.

"Can you believe that place?" Rusty asked as they pulled out of the parking lot. "Thirty-five dollars for four ounces of meat! Listen, I appreciate your getting me out of that," he told Blake as he reached out and squeezed her hand. "You're a real sweetheart."

"Thanks," Blake said, warmed by the affection in his voice.

"And I will pay you back," he said. "Although it will have to be after my next paycheck," he added ruefully.

"That's all right," Blake said, thinking of her empty refrigerator and wincing a little. Oh, well, she could take a little out of savings to buy a few groceries.

"Say, do you think we could have a snack at your place?" Rusty asked as he got on the expressway. "I'm hungry!"

"So am I," Blake admitted. "But it will have to be at your place. That was my grocery money. I'm down to catsup and mold."

"Oh, no," Rusty groaned. "Sure, we can eat at my place, but you should never have given me your grocery money. We could have left. You really are a good sport, woman."

He got on the expressway and took the exit just before hers, driving through a quiet suburban subdivision to a roomy-looking ranch house. "Not quite on John and Suzanne's level, but it's a great tax shelter," he admitted as they pulled up in the driveway. Blake followed Rusty through the garage and openly admired his sleek skiing

154

boat, complete with a powerful outboard motor and fancy trailer.

"Another tax break?" Blake teased.

"No, that's *Rusty's Folly*," he said as he unlocked the door into the house. Inside, the house was furnished simply but comfortably in Early American, and Blake noted with amusement that Rusty proudly displayed several graceful models of the T-37 and T-38. "So what would you like to eat?" he asked as he wandered into the kitchen.

"Anything," Blake said sincerely as she followed him into the kitchen. Checking in the cabinet, he found a package of spaghetti and a bottle of instant sauce and got them out. He dumped the spaghetti into a saucepan and covered it with water, then as the spaghetti cooked he warmed the sauce in the microwave. Blake made them each a glass of iced tea and they sat down at Rusty's table with their second dinner of the evening.

"I'm surprised that John picked out such an expensive restaurant," Blake said as she expertly twirled the spaghetti around her fork. "He and Suzanne both know what we make."

"John forgot and did this to me one other time," Rusty acknowledged as he popped a forkful of spaghetti into his mouth. "But I guess he just wasn't thinking. I know he's been awfully worried about Suzanne lately."

"Why?" Blake demanded. "Is she sick? Pregnant? Is something wrong in her family?"

"No, nothing like that," Rusty reassured her. "Oh, Suzanne's apparently very upset over something that happened two or three years ago. She feels that she did something to someone that ruined that other person's life, and she just can't let go of it. John says she broods over it all the time."

"Oh, no," Blake whispered as she laid her fork on her

plate. "I thought she'd gotten over all that. Damn, I didn't think she was still blaming herself."

"For what?" Rusty asked. "What on earth did she do?"

"She was driving the car when I got hurt," Blake said quietly.

Rusty whistled under his breath. "No wonder she feels bad," he murmured.

"But she doesn't have any reason to," Blake declared firmly. "And I've told her so. I was distracting her from her driving, and then a carload of damn-fool teenagers tried to pass us on the right. That wreck was an accident, Rusty! Why can't she see that?"

"Because she loves you," Rusty replied quietly. "And she knows how much you loved flying and how much you miss it. In her shoes I'd feel exactly the same way."

"But she's letting it eat her up inside," Blake complained. "I'll try to talk to her again."

"You might wait until you feel better about your own life," Rusty suggested. "As long as you still feel bad about not flying, you're not going to be able to convince her of anything."

"I guess you're right," Blake replied as she ate the last of her spaghetti. "That's better," she admitted. "Thanks for the meal."

They carried their plates to the sink and Rusty got out a paper sack and started pulling things out of the cupboard. "I just went to the commissary yesterday, so I'll make you up a Care package to take with you and I'll feed you supper a few times until we're paid next," he volunteered as he put cans and packages into the sack. When that was full, he filled a second sack from the refrigerator.

"I'm not even going to be coy and protest," Blake said frankly. "I appreciate this and I'll take you up on those dinners! Got any eggs?" she asked.

156

Rusty put a carton of eggs into the top of the sack. "That should hold you for a while," he said as he took her hand and led her from the kitchen. He pushed her down on the couch and sat down beside her.

Blake turned to him and held out her arms, longing to have Rusty near her. "Hold me, Rusty," she whispered. "You gave my flying back to me today. I want to be near you tonight."

In response to her plea, Rusty reached out and took Blake into his arms, folding her close to him as he crushed her mouth against his. Blake melted willingly into his arms, pressing herself just as close to him as she could get, returning his embrace with an ardent one of her own. Eagerly, not willing to wait for subtleness, she thrust her tongue into Rusty's mouth and savored the sweetness there, lightly touched with the taste of the spicy spaghetti sauce. They kissed for long moments, loving the sensual communication between them as they lit the fire that had been smoldering between them all day.

"Oh, Blake, what you do to me," Rusty breathed as he drew back from her lips to gently feather soft kisses around her face. "I've never felt this way with anyone else in my arms."

"I haven't either," Blake admitted as she drew light circles on his ear with her tongue. "Why do you suppose we feel this way?"

"Hormones," Rusty teased as he nibbled his way down her neck. "Pheromones, that's what they call them now. I react to your pheromones." He reached the edge of her demure neckline and moved his hand to the back of her dress. Pulling down the zipper, he continued his erotic path down to where her lacy bra barely covered the salmon-colored tips of her breasts. "Yes, I think it's just the pheromones," he said as Blake giggled.

157

"Is that all it is?" she complained as she lovingly unbuttoned his shirt. "Do you suppose that's all it was for Romeo and Juliet?"

"Probably," Rusty teased, moving his arm under her and popping open her bra. "Why do you even bother with this?" he complained as he reached down with his mouth and curled his tongue over one breast, bathing it in the warm raspy texture of his touch.

"I wear it because I need it," Blake gasped as spasms of pleasure shot from her breast all the way to her toes.

"No, you don't," Rusty denied as his tongue traveled to her other breast and tormented it lovingly. "You're just as high and firm as you can be." His lips traveled lower, delighting the soft skin of her midriff.

Boldly Blake reached up and pushed the shirt off his shoulders. "Lay close to me, Rusty," she murmured. "I need that so much tonight."

Obligingly Rusty pressed his chest close to Blake's, returning his mouth to her own and sharing a deep, warm kiss with her as his warm chest pressed her into the couch. Not releasing her mouth, Rusty reached down and pushed her dress even lower, his fingers traveling under the waistline of her panties and rubbing her stomach in sensual circles. Blake moaned in pleasure and pushed her body closer to his questing fingers, willing him to seek out her hidden secrets and make them known to himself. Blake was past stopping or caring—she just knew that she wanted Rusty tonight. She wanted to be one with him, to explore the mysteries of love with him, and to make him her lover.

For long moments Rusty caressed Blake lovingly, but through a passion-glazed fog Blake could feel him withdraw from her. "What's wrong, Rusty?" she whispered. "Don't you want me?"

"Oh, God, Blake, yes, I want you!" Rusty ground out as he planted a sweet, harsh kiss on her lips. He sat up and reached for his shirt. "But I don't think we're ready for this yet."

"Why not?" Blake asked in bewilderment. "I want you."

"And I want you," Rusty replied honestly as he pulled on his shirt. "But last time, when you pulled away and I very selfishly got angry, I admitted to myself later that you were right. You weren't ready, and I was wrong to push you. And I'm still not sure you're ready," he said as Blake pulled on her bra and hooked it.

"But I want to make love to you," Blake protested. "And not just for the sex either," she added defiantly. "I want the commitment of lovemaking. I need that."

"And the next time I get into a cockpit and fly away, leaving you behind?" Rusty asked quietly. "Are you going to resent me when I have to do that?"

"I—I don't know," Blake stammered, pulling up her dress. Rusty reached around her and pulled up the zipper. "I wish I could say that I wouldn't care, but I don't know that for sure."

"That's what I mean," Rusty said as he put his arm around Blake. "If I honestly thought you were ready for me, to accept me, pilot and all, I'd have you flat on your back in that bed in there so fast it would make your head swim. But I'm scared, Blake. I don't want to get into that kind of relationship with you and then have you resenting me every time I fly."

"But I'm flying, too, now," Blake protested.

"Yes, you are," Rusty said, a hint of a smile around his mouth. "But you've just started. You don't know yet whether this will be enough for you. And until you're sure

159

you can come to me with no ambivalent feelings, I'd rather wait."

"I guess you're right," Blake sighed as she leaned her head on Rusty's shoulder. He leaned down and planted a kiss on her lips. "I'm sorry," she whispered.

"That's all right," Rusty said as he held her tightly. "You're worth the wait."

It won't be long, Rusty, she silently promised the man who held her so closely.

CHAPTER NINE

"This was a good idea, Blake," Rusty said as he raised his head slightly from the float and sipped his coffee carefully. "This is the first time I've been swimming this early in the morning."

"Well, it was the only time we can have the pool to ourselves," Blake admitted as she dangled her feet in the water and nibbled on a cinnamon doughnut. They had been out to a movie last night and Blake had invited Rusty over for an early Saturday morning swim and breakfast. She had made coffee and he had brought a sack of doughnuts, and they had played in the deserted swimming pool for the better part of an hour, laughing and splashing quietly so that they would not awaken the late sleepers in Blake's complex. The early morning June sun was warm, not hot as it would be later in the day, and Blake stretched her arms above her head and sighed with pleasure.

"Do you want another doughnut?" she asked as Rusty paddled his float closer to the edge of the pool. He nodded and she held a doughnut provocatively over his lips. "Here, take a bite," she said as she dangled the doughnut temptingly over his mouth.

As Rusty reached up to take a bite, Blake teasingly raised the doughnut high enough so that he could not reach it. "Kiss me first," she taunted as Rusty lost his balance and rolled off the float, splashing her with cool water. "That's the price you have to pay."

"No problem," Rusty said as he stood in the shallow water between Blake's dangling legs. He reached out with damp lips and kissed her lightly, then glanced around to make sure they were unobserved, and embraced her fully, drawing her against his wet naked chest and running his hands down her damp back. Blake slid her arms around his slick body and pressed herself against him, his wet chest rewetting the front of her swimsuit. "This is better than a doughnut any day," he murmured against her sugary lips. He let go of Blake and took the crumpled doughnut from her fingers. "Did a little number on it, didn't you?" he teased as he examined the mangled doughnut curiously.

Blake blushed, realizing that she had squeezed the doughnut while Rusty had been kissing her. *I think I'm ready,* she thought as Rusty flopped backward and swam across the pool on his back. *I'm ready to be his lover now.* She had watched him fly away every day for the last two weeks, and she could honestly say that it hadn't bothered her one bit. But then, she was now a full-fledged member of the C.A.P. and she knew that very soon she would be flying for them. And as soon as they had been paid, she and Rusty had gone back out to Kelly and rented the little Cessna again. They had taken turns flying this time, Rusty flying the controls on the right side and showing Blake some of the skilled maneuvers he could perform. *I simply don't resent him anymore,* she thought with wonder.

Should I tell him now, or wait until this evening? She looked over at the lithe, tanned body slicing through the water, and desire licked through her veins. *Wait, my foot. Why waste a day?*

"Rusty?" she called softly. "Rusty?"

"Is that your phone I hear?" Rusty asked as he raised his head out of the water.

Blake whirled around and listened for a moment. "Sure is," she sighed, getting up and running for the telephone. It was probably nothing, but Blake thought it might be her mother. She picked up the receiver and said "Good morning" cheerfully.

"Captain Warner? Commander Prescott here. We're doing an S.A.R. today. A plane's down near Corpus. Bring a bedroll and food for two days."

"Yes, sir," Blake said firmly. "Am I flying or am I an observer?"

"You're observing from Captain O'Gorman's plane."

"Fine, I'll tell him," Blake said crisply.

Commander Prescott was silent for a second. "He's with you?" he asked.

Blake looked at her kitchen clock which read eight thirty and smiled wickedly. "I'll tell him to get his pants on and we'll be right out there," she said, stifling a giggle at Commander Prescott's slight gasp. "We'll be there soon, sir."

"Whom did you just embarrass thoroughly?" Rusty asked from the door of the apartment.

"Commander Prescott." Blake giggled, then her face

162

sobered. "There's a plane down near Corpus. Bedrolls and food for two days. We better get a move on."

"I've got all my stuff in the truck," Rusty said as he slammed the door behind him and started pulling off his trunks, unmindful of the effect that his casual nudity was having on Blake's power of concentration. "Get your clothes changed and let's get moving."

Blake threw on her jeans and a top and got out her sleeping bag while Rusty packed enough quick foods to last them two days, and she plaited her wet hair on the way out to Stinson. The small airport was a beehive of activity, with pilots and observers climbing into planes and waiting for permission to take off. Blake and Rusty gave their gear to one of the ground crews that would follow them down by car, and before long Rusty, Blake, and two teenage cadets were airborne.

The flight to Corpus took only about an hour, and soon they were landing at a small airport just outside Corpus Christi and were refueling. Rusty made sure everybody visited a restroom because once they were in the air, he would fly for four hours or more, until he was forced to land for more fuel. Blake returned to the plane and got in the back with one of the cadets, who was an experienced observer in spite of his youth. The Corpus Christi commander assigned their plane a particular grid to fly, and almost immediately they were back in the air, flying the short distance to their assigned grid, ready to begin the tedious process of searching for the downed plane.

"Okay, folks, this is it," Rusty shouted over the roar of the engine. He descended to about one hundred and fifty feet off the ground and started the painstaking process of flying back and forth, combing the grid as Blake and the other two observers peered down, searching valiantly for anything that might be a downed plane.

This is not good terrain for finding a plane, Blake thought with dismay as she peered out of the window for hour after hour, straining to see any little thing that might indicate that a plane had gone down here. The farmland was all right, but the wooded areas could be sheltering a downed plane so easily. Blake mentally reviewed the photos she had been shown during her observer training sessions and searched for something, anything, that looked like aerial photos of crashes. At this low altitude the cockpit was unbearably hot, and Blake and the cadet next to her used up half a box of Kleenex wiping the sweat out of their eyes. Back and forth, over and over, each time searching only a narrow strip of the land's surface. They flew for the four hours that Rusty had predicted and returned to the base for more fuel.

Rusty landed at the small airport and Blake and the two cadets crawled out stiffly. She made sandwiches for the four of them and accepted cold soft drinks from the ground crew while Rusty refueled the plane. They ate quickly on a folding table set up in the hangar and visited the restrooms again, then once more they were up in the air, flying back and forth in the sweltering heat, Rusty flying and turning and flying again, Blake and the cadets searching the ground for some sign of the plane.

Blake's shirt was sweated through and her long braid hung damp at her neck. The glare was intense even through her dark sunglasses, and she thought that Rusty's eyes were bound to be burning by now. By late afternoon Rusty's second fuel supply was beginning to run low and he shouted that they would make one more swing down their grid and then go back for a refueling.

Blake glanced at her watch and figured that they probably would not be going back out today since it was close to seven. *Oh well, so much for telling Rusty I wanted to be his lover,* she thought as she looked down at her sweaty, grubby body. Since they would have to stay until the wreakage was found, and a hotel room in Corpus Christi would be hard to come by on Saturday night in June, they would probably have to camp out without showers. He wouldn't want her like this!

Rusty swung the plane around and flew over what appeared to be a field of sugar beets. "My God, there it is!" Blake squealed suddenly as they loomed over the mangled wreckage of what was once a small plane. It appeared to have crashed nosedown and exploded on impact, and there was not much left now but torn shards of metal.

Rusty flew in an arc around the wreckage, radioing the exact location to a ground crew. He circled once more and headed back to the Corpus Christi airport. By the time they returned to the airport, it was crowded with small C.A.P. planes trying to refuel and fly back to San Antonio or Houston, and they had to wait for nearly half an hour before they could refuel and fly back to Stinson. The two cadets volunteered to drive back with their fathers, who were in the ground crew, so a tired Rusty and Blake got their gear from the ground crew and walked toward the little Piper they had been in all day. "Here, you fly," Rusty said wearily as he handed Blake the keys to the plane and threw their stuff in the back. Blake's brow creased with confusion as she noted the despondent look on his face.

Rusty put on the headphones but said very little on the flight back to San Antonio. Blake, delighted that they had found the plane on their first day out, grew increasingly concerned by Rusty's depressed expression. What was the matter? They had found the plane! He should have been delighted. His mood did not appear to lighten at Stinson, where they tied down the plane and crawled tiredly into

165

Rusty's truck. "Take me home and I'll fix you some supper," Blake volunteered.

Rusty smiled faintly in the fading twilight. "I'll take you up on that," he agreed as he started the engine and drove home through the heavy Saturday-night traffic. Blake's eyes ached and her body was stiff and tired, but it was a satisfying kind of tired. They had accomplished something important today, and it was a good feeling.

Blake laid claim to a quick shower while Rusty unloaded the truck, rewashing her hair and letting it fall in a wet cascade down her back. She pulled on a pair of cutoffs and a tube top and pointed Rusty toward the bathroom while she poked around in her kitchen. She found a large can of pork and beans which she warmed while she fried a whole package of bacon and made a salad. She got out bread and butter and fed a piece of the bread to her chattering bird. Calico picked at the bread, squawking in protest when Rusty, clad only in a pair of shorts, came into the kitchen and accidentally banged into the cage.

"Sorry, birdie," he murmured, leaning down to peek into the cage.

"That's Calico," Blake said.

"Why haven't I ever seen Calico before tonight?" Rusty asked.

"Oh, the other times you've been here he's been in the bedroom," Blake said as she took knives and forks out to the coffee table, passing up the dining room table as being too formal. Besides, how could she seduce Rusty if she were sitting across from him?

"Okay, Calico, talk to me," Rusty said. The little bird stopped eating and looked at the stranger with beady black eyes. "Come on, talk to me," he wheedled. The little bird stared at him silently.

166

"All right, don't talk to me then," Rusty said as he turned away from the cage.

"Squawk!" called Calico loudly.

"Smart-ass bird," Blake murmured as she handed Rusty a plate and got two beers out of the refrigerator. "This is serve-it-in-the-kitchen night. I'll feed you formally some other time."

"This is fine," Rusty murmured, filling his plate and wandering out to the living room. Blake followed him with the two beers, then returned to the kitchen and piled her own plate as full as his.

Blake sat down beside Rusty on the floor beside the coffee table and leaned her back against the couch. "Want to talk about it?" she asked quietly.

"Yeah," Rusty replied, not pretending to misunderstand. He swallowed a big forkful of beans and looked at Blake sadly. "There weren't any survivors," he said.

"We knew that the minute we saw the plane," Blake said, her tone matter-of-fact. "There was no way that anyone could have survived that crash, unless they bailed out beforehand."

"Yeah, I know," Rusty said as he sampled the bacon and the salad. "But it always makes me feel bad when we have to radio back that there isn't anybody left down there." He swallowed a healthy swig of his beer. "I keep hoping, Blake, that there will be somebody alive down there. I keep hoping to save a life."

Blake slid her left hand around and rubbed Rusty in the middle of his back, scooping up her beans with the fork in her right hand. "And I have every confidence that you will someday," she said. "But Rusty, you have to remember that we performed a valuable service today even though there were no survivors."

"What service was that?" Rusty asked, his mouth full of food.

"We spared a family the agony of not knowing," Blake said firmly. "Believe me, that alone made today worthwhile."

Rusty looked at her with dawning perception. "How long did you have to wait for news of your father?" he asked.

"Two whole weeks," Blake replied. "And it was almost a welcome relief to hear that he was indeed gone, and not laying out there somewhere, exposed and in pain, or, worse, a POW in the hands of the Viet Cong."

"Then I won't feel bad anymore," Rusty said quietly. "I honestly never thought about it from that angle. I guess we did accomplish something valuable today."

"Yes, we did," Blake said as she turned to her meal, their conversation sparse. Their flying today had meant something. It wasn't like Air Force flying, but they had spared a family days of misery waiting to hear what had actually happened to their loved ones, and Blake felt that certainly counted for something. Blake enjoyed a definite feeling of accomplishment as she carried their plates into the kitchen and dished them each up a second serving of beans. "Feel better?" she asked Rusty as she handed him his plate.

"Yes, I do," he said with the return of his outrageous grin.

That's more like it, Blake thought with relief as she ate her beans. *I like it so much better when he's smiling!* Smiling tenderly into his eyes, she cleared the small coffee table and dumped the dishes into the sink, promising herself that she would tackle them in the morning.

Rusty was stretched out on the couch facedown with his hand trailing on the floor when Blake returned to the room, the sight of his tired, briefly clad body stirring her more than she had ever thought possible. *I want him,* she thought. *I'm sure of it. I couldn't care less if he's the busiest pilot in the Air Force. I just want him.*

Biting her lip, she sat down on the edge of the couch, Rusty obligingly scooting over to make room for her. "Back stiff?" she asked.

"How did you know?" Rusty groaned.

"Because mine is too," Blake admitted. She reached out and pushed the heels of her hands into the small of his back. "I'll do something about it," she volunteered as she gently but firmly kneaded the tired, achy muscles. His firm flesh, lightly covered with soft red down, felt warm and velvety to her fingers. *Oh, Rusty, do you still want me?* she asked herself as her fingers worked magic to his sore back muscles. She worked her fingers up his spine and over his shoulders, taking out the tightness and the tenseness there, then her hands crept back down his back and even lower, tantalizing the hard firm muscles of his buttocks.

Rusty stiffened at the intimacy of her touch. "Blake, you better watch it," he warned her from his facedown position. "You're getting pretty intimate down there for a lady who still isn't sure she wants to make love to me."

Blake let her fingers crawl back up his back, then she knelt by the side of the couch and whispered into his ear. "But now I'm sure," she whispered, her eyes shining.

Rusty looked up at her, astonishment warring with delight. "You're sure?" he asked.

Blake nodded. "You've flown off and left me behind every day for the last two weeks. And all I ever thought was how soon would you be back."

"Oh, Blake, you don't know how that makes me feel," Rusty murmured as he reached out and drew her face close to his. Blake saw the sheen of happy tears in his eyes, and she knew she had tears in her own. He kissed her long and passionately, then slid off the couch and sat on the floor, pushing Blake into the soft carpet. "Turn over," he commanded her quietly. "It's your turn. No, wait," he added as Blake turned to obey. "Take off the top and the shorts, all right? I want to do this right."

"Do what right?" Blake asked as she obediently stripped off the shorts. She hesitated for a moment on the top, suddenly feeling shy, but Rusty reached over and pulled the tube up over her arms, leaving her breasts free to his gaze.

"Why, I'm going to give you the same kind of massage that you gave me," Rusty replied as he pointed to the carpet. "Lay on your tummy."

Blake lay down on the carpet with a pillow from the couch under her head. Rusty knelt over her, one leg on either side of her, and placed his strong fingers in the middle of her back. Slowly but with controlled strength in his fingers he kneaded the sore, tired muscles in Blake's back, his soothing touch removing the stiffness and replacing it with a tingling awareness of his touch.

With not even so much as a hint of rushing, Rusty worked his fingers up her spine, pushing her heavy swath of hair out of the way and finding each and every kinked muscle and joint in her back. Then his fingers traveled upward, seeking out the soreness in the neck that was bent awkwardly all day, soothing away the tightness and the tiredness, bringing Blake to a gentle state of relaxed anticipation.

Rusty's hands traveled back down her back and below her waist, kneading her firm bottom and traveling lower, down her thighs and calves, his touch becoming less therapeutic and more sensual as he let himself have free reign exploring Blake's shapely legs. He gradually brought his hands upward, crossing over from her legs to her bottom and caressing it sensually, then sliding his arms around her waist and stroking it lightly. "Blake, turn over," he whispered.

Blake rolled over and away from Rusty, her eyes grinning wickedly. "Let's play catch," she teased as she rolled across the floor. Rusty lunged across the carpet and reached for Blake, but she quickly darted from his grasp and rolled back toward the couch. "You missed," she taunted as Rusty followed her back across the carpet and grabbed her ankle in his firm grip.

"Gotcha!" He held her leg firmly, scooting up beside her and trapping her neatly between the couch and his body. "Somehow I have the feeling that you weren't trying all that hard to get away," he murmured as he pushed her into the carpet and followed her down, covering her body with his own and capturing her mouth in a sensuous kiss.

Blake moaned as Rusty plundered her mouth, writhing beneath him to try to wiggle her body closer to his. This close, separated by only a couple of layers of clothing, Blake could feel the evidence of his desire for her, and she felt her desire for him spiral to meet him more than halfway. Groaning in frustration, she reached down and fumbled with the zipper of his shorts, breathing a sigh of relief when Rusty pulled away from her and yanked off the shorts and the briefs under them, baring his body to her eager gaze. "Good grief, you are red all over," she exclaimed as Rusty hooked his thumbs under the elastic in her panties and pulled them off her hips and down her legs. Blake kicked them off her toes, sending them sailing through the air to land on top of the television set.

"And you're a real blonde," Rusty said as he dipped his head and kissed one breast tenderly. "And beautiful," he breathed. "Even more beautiful than I imagined." His gaze traveled down her naked body, examining the tanned flesh where she was exposed to the sun and the creamy flesh where she was not, taking in her flat stomach, her shapely hips, and her long legs. "Let me love you, Blake, in every way imaginable."

"Oh, yes, Rusty," Blake breathed, her arms reaching for him and holding him to her. Rusty bent his head and captured one breast in his mouth, plundering it for its sweetness until Blake was writhing with pleasure. He bathed the other one in his touch as Blake cooed with delight, then his lips traveled lower, nibbling at the soft skin of her trim waist and flat stomach until she thought she would scream with pleasure. As his lips traveled lower Blake shifted her legs slightly, straining with the anticipated pleasure of Rusty's touch.

Rusty looked up at Blake with a dazed expression. "Blake, are you protected?" he asked.

"Am I what?" Blake asked, her mind in a sensual fog.

"Are you protected?" Rusty asked again. "You know. Protected."

"Oh my God!" Blake cried as she sat up, her hair flying out in every direction. "No—yes—I can be in a minute!" she said as she jumped up and ran for the bathroom. Protection! Good grief, she was so eager to make love to Rusty that she had forgotten that completely. Now, where was that damned thing? Blake hadn't needed it in a long time, and she didn't even remember where she had put it when she had moved from Ohio. She fumbled through the medicine cabinet in her bathroom and the drawers in the vanity, but it wasn't there, although she did find the cream that went with it. Slamming that down on the counter, she left the bathroom and fumbled through her drawers, flinging her underwear and nightgowns aside in frantic haste.

"You might have better luck if you slowed down,"

Rusty teased from the door. He leaned against the door-jamb, one leg casually crossed over the other, only the arousal of his body giving away his true state.

"Very funny," Blake snapped. "I haven't used it in so long I forgot where I put it."

"I have to admit that pleases me," Rusty said as he crossed over to the bed and turned back the covers.

Blake pawed through two more drawers, turning up nothing. "Don't you have something . . . in your wallet?" she wailed.

"Who, me?" Rusty asked. "I haven't carried one in years." He reached out and touched Blake's cheek tenderly. "Really, I take making love much more seriously than that."

"I'm glad," Blake whispered, rubbing her cheek against her hand. "Got it!" she cried, unearthing the small blue case from the bottom of the last drawer.

"Well, get a move on, woman," Rusty teased as he swatted her bare bottom. Blake ran into the bathroom and snapped open the case. She applied the cream with trembling fingers, but the slippery circle tumbled off her fingers onto the floor.

"Damn!" Blake snapped as she picked it up and washed it off and tried again. She forced herself to be calm and in just a few moments she was ready. Grinning sheepishly, she joined Rusty in the bedroom.

"Have a little trouble?" Rusty asked innocently.

"I dropped it," Blake replied frankly. "I had to start over."

"Why, Blake, anyone would think you were nervous," Rusty teased as he threw back the covers and bent over Blake.

"Not nervous," she admitted. "Eager."

"Then let's see what I can do to hurry things along,"

173

Rusty said as he bent his head to her breasts. He lovingly retraced the path that his mouth had taken, only this time his lips did not hesitate as they reached her secret places, but boldly explored her mysteries as Blake moaned beneath him, the flames of her desire licking her body.

Eagerly she opened herself to him, savoring every touch that Rusty gave her. As his mouth roamed back up her body, Blake twisted and turned beneath him, knowing that the ultimate possession was near. Rusty moved over her and bore her down into the pillows, taking her mouth and her body at the same time. The kiss stifled Blake's gasp of pleasure at the touch of his body in hers, the delight of his possession. Their lips mingled only momentarily as the demands of their bodies took over and they moved in a synchronized rhythm of sensual harmony.

They moved together for long moments, an erotic spiral taking Blake's breath away as she climbed closer and closer to the ultimate heights with Rusty. She could sense that he was holding back, but rather than intimidate her the thought gave her pleasure, for Rusty was holding back his own release to savor hers with her. Faster and faster, harder and harder, their bodies moved in harmony, and when the ultimate came Blake cried Rusty's name over and over. Blake's release triggering his own, Rusty moaned and pressed even closer to Blake, her name a hoarse whisper on his lips. They lay together for long moments, too spent even to move apart, as their breathing returned to normal.

"You're dynamite, woman," Rusty murmured as he finally built up the energy to move away from her.

"So are you," Blake said as she snuggled close to Rusty and laid her head on his chest. "I've never—it's never . . ." She trailed off and shrugged helplessly.

"I know," Rusty admitted as he pulled her close.

"Would you believe that it's never been like that for me either?"

Blake nodded, holding him close as she closed her eyes. She fully intended to rest for a moment and seduce Rusty again, but barely seconds later the even rise and fall of Rusty's chest told her that he had fallen asleep. Probably all that flying wore him out, Blake thought as she closed her eyes and slept, secure in Rusty's strong embrace.

Blake blinked her eyes as she stared out the window at the paling sky, Rusty's arm anchoring her firmly to him. *I could stay here for the rest of my life,* she thought as she savored the warmth of Rusty's chest against her back, the curling hair tickling her sensitive skin. Rusty had awakened her sometime in the wee hours of the morning for another time of love, a slow and gentle one, and they had again fallen asleep in each other's arms. *And I'm so glad,* Blake thought as Rusty's chest rose and fell in rhythmic slumber. *I need him. I need to make love to him, to have him hold me and to make my body come alive.*

But she needed more from him than that, Blake acknowledged to herself as the sky grew gradually pinker. She needed his outrageous grin, his dancing blue eyes, his silly pranks. She needed him to jolt her out of her self-pity when she fell into it and his tender touch when she was low. She needed to fly with him.

We can risk a relationship, Blake thought as Calico started his usual early morning chirping. *I don't care anymore if he's a pilot. I'm flying again, and it won't matter about his job.* Blake felt a sudden stab of apprehension about Rusty's career, but as she remembered the embraces that they had shared, her apprehension faded. After all, two people who could share what they had shared last night could overcome anything. *Yes, I want to take this relationship to wherever it goes,* Blake thought as Rusty shifted beside her.

"What is that godawful squawking?" Rusty murmured as his arm tightened around her.

"Oh, that's Calico," Blake said sleepily as she shifted to get closer to Rusty's hard warmth. In spite of the lovemaking they had shared just a few hours ago, Blake could feel desire tighten in her body. "He wakes me up every morning."

"Ugh," Rusty groaned, turning his face into the pillow.

Uh-oh, a night person, Blake thought as Rusty buried his head under the pillow. *Probably can't do a thing without a cup of coffee.* Kissing Rusty's exposed shoulder, she slid out of bed and threw her lacy pink robe around her and padded into the kitchen. Humming softly, she plugged in the coffeemaker, measured out enough coffee for several cups, and in just a few minutes the aroma of freshly brewed coffee permeated the small apartment. Blake put the sugar bowl and spoon, a small pitcher of cream, and two cups of coffee on a silver tray and carried the tray into the bedroom.

Rusty raised a bleary face to her. "Whas that?" he mumbled.

"A cup of coffee," Blake said as she set the tray between them on the bed. Rusty sat up, the covers hunched around his hips as he spooned sugar into one cup. Blake picked up the other and sipped it, watching Rusty gradually come awake before her eyes.

"That's better," he said as he finished his cup and set it on the night table beside him. Blake moved the tray onto the dresser and sat cross-legged beside Rusty. "Do you want to talk about last night?" he asked quietly. His blue eyes searched hers. "Are you sorry?"

176

"Oh, no," Blake breathed as she reached out and took his hand in hers. "I'm glad, and I want this to go on."

"Good," Rusty replied, relief evident in his voice. "I was afraid you might have regrets this morning."

"The only regret I have this morning is that I got out of bed before we had a chance to do it again," Blake admitted. "But if you're not a morning person . . ."

"Oh, I think I can rise early when the occasion calls for it," Rusty said as he reached out and pushed Blake's robe from her shoulders, drinking in the sight of her naked femininity for a moment before she pushed him back into the covers.

"I wouldn't want you to have to exert yourself so early in the morning," she teased as she ran her hands across Rusty's body lightly, feeling rather than hearing his delighted gasp. "You just lay back and let Blake have her fun."

Rusty complied willingly as Blake teased and tormented him with sensual abandon. Her fingers and her mouth knew no limits. She nibbled his face, his neck, his ears, his shoulders, trailing her moist kisses through the soft hair on his chest as Rusty moaned quietly. Her lips tormented the soft skin of his waist as her fingers moved even lower, delighting his masculine form with their delicate inspection. "Oh, Blake, what you do to me!" he moaned as her lips touched him intimately, exciting him and herself unbearably with her sensual touch.

Blake looked up with passion-glazed eyes. "Am I doing this right?" she asked shyly.

"Perfectly," Rusty gasped as she touched him again and again. Finally, when Rusty thought he could stand no more, Blake shifted her body and made them one, her body fitting over his in a new variation of the rhythmic harmony they had shared last night. She moved over him, her legs along his sides, in control of the lovemaking yet tempering her every move to bring him pleasure. Finally, as shooting stars began to go off behind her eyes, she felt him arch into her and knew that he had reached the pinnacle again with her. Her energy spent, Blake slid down slowly and pillowed her head on his shoulder.

"Better?" Rusty teased as Blake's breathing slowly returned to normal.

"Much," Blake admitted. She moved off Rusty and stretched luxuriously. "Want to spend the day with me?" she asked.

A rueful expression crossed Rusty's face. "I promised Bob Merrill I'd go fishing with him and his kids around noon today," he explained.

"You're not going to catch many fish at that time of day," Blake teased.

"Bob and I know that, but he wants to take his little boys and get them to like it," Rusty said as he cupped Blake's breast in his hand. "Tonight?" he asked as he bent his head and sampled the sweetness of her breasts.

"I'll be waiting," Blake murmured. "And I'll be ready."

Rusty lay back and laughed out loud. "You're going to get awfully tired of fooling with that thing," he teased as Blake blushed. "Why don't you go on out to Wilford Hall and get the pill?"

"You really think I'm gonna need them?" Blake asked as she sat up and looked down at Rusty.

"Oh, yes, Blake," Rusty said, his eyes bright in his face. "I can guarantee that you're gonna need them."

"Then all right," Blake whispered as she reached down and kissed Rusty's lips.

CHAPTER TEN

Blake took the exit to Randolph and drove her Datsun through Universal City and onto the base, humming softly through her teeth as she blinked sleepily in the early morning sunlight. What a beautiful morning! She parked her car and got out of it, stretching a little to overcome the slight stiffness she always felt after Rusty had stayed the night with her. What a perfect night, Blake thought as she wandered into the hangar and into her office, suppressing a giggle as she caught sight of the new test pilot patiently showing Sally how to make coffee. Blake and the others all missed Tommy Ochoa, who had been transferred to Travis, but Roger Catalani was a top pilot and cheerfully took a lot of ribbing about his prematurely bald head. Blake bit her lip to keep from laughing out loud as Sally obediently nodded her head and mimicked Roger's motions. A lot of good that is going to do, Roger!

Roger wandered out and Sally looked at the coffeemaker doubtfully. "Do you think you can do it that way next time?" Blake asked.

"I'm not sure, Captain Warner," Sally said frankly. "You know, every time a new officer gets transferred here, they stop and show me how to make the coffee just the way they want it. What if the rest of the officers don't like it the new way?"

"I guess we all have to adjust," Blake said, deadpan. "Here, Sally, run these papers over to the Taj Mahal for me."

"Yes, Captain Warner," Sally said as she picked up the papers and scooted for the door. Blake waited until Sally had time to get across the hangar, then bent over in her chair and whooped with laughter. *I love that girl,* she thought as she wiped tears from her eyes.

Blake composed herself and stretched again, the pleasant tiredness from last night returning. She and Rusty had been lovers for a month now, and it had been the most wonderful month of her life. They spent most of their evenings together and Rusty kept a clean flight suit in her closet so he could stay the night if the spirit moved them, as it usually did. Under Rusty's tender caresses Blake had blossomed as a woman, and if Rusty's step was even jauntier and the twinkle in his eye brighter, who was she to be modest? *We're good together,* Blake thought for the hundredth time as she poured herself a cup of Roger's coffee, grimacing a little as she tasted the first sip. This was worse than Sally's!

She dumped the coffee and started over, then sat back down and tried to concentrate on her paperwork, but a pair of dancing blue eyes kept interrupting her train of thought. *I'm already in love with him but could we have a future together?* Blake asked herself as she watched the newly prepared pot of coffee drip through the maker. Rusty had said nothing about the future and neither had she, but she realized that if they continued to experience the wonderful relationship they were presently sharing, the question of the future was bound to come up sooner or later.

Blake waded through paperwork for the better part of an hour, then decided that she needed to run an errand to one of the shops. She was just coming out of her office when Pat Gordon ran up, his face slightly strained. "Rusty's just contacted S.O.F. for help. The landing gear on his plane won't come down."

"What?" Blake asked, paling.

"Rusty's in trouble up there," Pat said grimly.

Blake uttered a crude word. "Let's get over to the squadron building and find out what's happening," she said. She fought not to think about the way he had looked when he had stepped out of her shower this morning, naked and vulnerable and so appealing, and ran beside Pat for the squadron building. They crowded into the small radio room, full of brass from all over the base, and asked Colonel Alda what was going on.

In muted whispers Colonel Alda explained that Rusty's landing gear wouldn't lower by either the regular or the alternate controls, and that he had done a number of checks and tried several things, but the gear simply would not come down. He had contacted the supervisor of flying and declared an emergency, and they were trying to help him from the ground in any way they could.

"Is he in any actual danger?" Blake whispered, her cheeks chalky.

"He's not going to die in a crash, Blake, if that's what you're thinking," Colonel Alda said comfortingly. He had noticed the growing relationship between his test pilot and his maintenance officer and privately thought it was a good thing for both of them. "The worst that could happen would be that Rusty would have to take the plane off somewhere and dump it."

"And eject," Blake said. Even that held a certain amount of danger. "So what can he do?"

"You know the answer to that as well as I do," Colonel

181

Alda chided her. "There are a number of things he can try."

"Shh, I have Northrop on the phone," a voice from across the room called impatiently. The officer listened as a manufacturer's representative gave him advice. Then he moved to the radio and picked up the mike. "Captain O'Gorman, we just talked to Northrop. How much gas do you have left?"

"Less than an hour," Rusty radioed back. "I've been up here awhile," he reminded them.

The officer then repeated the instructions Northrop's representative had given.

"Call a couple of bases," Colonel Alda ordered the officer. "See if any of them have had anything like this happen."

Blake wiped her sweaty palms on her fatigues and watched with hopeful eyes as the phone calls were made. When the calls turned up nothing more than the same advice to keep trying, she turned to Colonel Alda anxiously. "Is there anything I can do?" she whispered.

Colonel Alda shook his head. She listened to the radio transmissions, assuring herself that Rusty was really in no immediate danger, that if worse came to worst he could always dump the plane and eject. Mentally Blake reviewed the checks he would be making, going over them in her mind, straining to think of something Rusty had missed.

"Thirty minutes of fuel left," Rusty's voice called over the radio. "And nothing's working. Did Northrop say anything about pulling some G's?" he asked.

"Let me call them and see what they think," the officer who had called them before said.

Rusty, you can't do that! Blake thought as the officer made his call. *That's dangerous, and you could ruin the plane as well as kill yourself!* The officer left the telephone and returned to the radio. "Northrop says that it's risky, but if you want to try it, you may as well go ahead, if we're going to lose the plane anyway."

That's all the Air Force is worried about, Blake fumed to herself, anger joining her anxiety as she listened to the transmissions. They couldn't care less about Rusty. They just want their jet back! *Damn you, Rusty, recycle those gears again!* Biting her lip, Blake pictured Rusty up in the plane, exceeding the landing gear speed until he was in an excess of four G's, or four times the force of gravity, and then pulling down on the airplane and letting the extra gravity pull down the landing gear. The maneuver might be successful, or it might break off the landing gear, which would necessitate an ejection. He should have recycled that gear again before doing that, she fumed as she waited impatiently for word from the troubled plane. He should have tried everything else before trying the tricky flyboy stuff.

The room was silent, twenty anxious pairs of eyes staring at the radio. "S.O.F., this is Captain O'Gorman. It didn't come down this time—I'm going to try again." *Rusty, you reckless idiot,* she thought.

Blake waited what was only a few minutes but felt like an eternity. Finally the radio crackled once more. "S.O.F., this is Captain O'Gorman. The gear's down. I'm coming in."

A cheer went up in the small radio room. "Good for O'Gorman!" one pilot called.

"I swear that man can fly!" another said. "Wasn't that the best piece of flying you ever heard of, Captain Warner?"

"Sure," Blake said through stiff lips. *Good for you, Rusty! Risk your own life for a damned hunk of Air Force metal!* Her teeth chattering in anger, Blake marched back

183

to her office and shut the door, willing herself to stop trembling as she thought about what Rusty had just done. He had no business pulling a stunt like that! She ignored the sound of a landing jet and was filling out a set of request papers when Rusty and the other pilots walked by, their arms around Rusty's shoulders, singing his praises to the skies. *Everyone on base will be singing his praises for months for acting like a fool,* she thought bitterly. Slamming down her pen, she walked out of her office and ordered a hamburger in the Officer's Club, but was too upset to even eat it. He could have been killed out there!

Blake walked back to her office and was in the middle of scheduling planes for tomorrow when Rusty walked in, his flight suit ringed with sweat and the freckles standing out on his unusually pale nose. "Blake?" he called softly.

Blake looked up, her eyes narrowing. "What the hell do you think you were trying to pull this morning?" she asked evenly.

Rusty blinked at her frontal attack. "What do you mean, what was I trying to do? I was trying to save a plane this morning."

"By trying some half-baked glamor routine that only works one time out of five? Rusty, you must be out of your mind!"

"Out of my mind? Blake, what on earth has gotten into you? I was up there with a set of damn landing gear that was stuck. Stuck, damn it! Wouldn't come down! What was I supposed to do?"

"Anything but what you did!" Blake snapped back. "You could have recycled that gear again or something. Anything. But for heaven's sake, Rusty, to pull G's when the whole damn landing gear could have fallen off? Couldn't you restrain yourself from being a showoff pilot even when your own life was in danger?"

"What would you suggest?" Rusty asked angrily. "Dumping the plane without even trying anything?"

"Yes—no—I don't know!" Blake admitted. "But not pulling G's. Anything but pulling G's."

"Blake, I tried something and it worked. I saved the plane. That's what matters, isn't it?" His eyes narrowed and he looked at her thoughtfully. "Or are you resenting me again for being the pilot? You're jealous because I made it, aren't you?"

Blake's face paled. "Get out of here and go on home," she said. "I believe they gave you the rest of the day off, didn't they?"

Rusty turned on his heel and marched out of the office, inwardly shattered. *How could she have attacked me like that?* he asked himself as he drove his truck home in the hot July sun. Damn it, hadn't she known how scared he was up there? Didn't she realize that if it were not for his loyalty to the Air Force that he would have gladly ditched the plane and ejected to safety? He dragged himself into the house and showered away the sweaty fright from this morning, but although he tried he could not shower away Blake's cruel attack.

How could you have been so cruel? Blake asked herself hours later as she sat in front of her silent television, a glass of calming wine in her hand. She had verbally ripped poor Rusty to shreds! And after the terror he must have felt, knowing he might have to eject! Swirling the wine around in the glass, she relived the argument in her office. Was Rusty right? Was a part of her anger with him actually her resentment over his flying coming back out in a different form? *Oh, it can't be,* she thought. *I was worried about him; I really was.*

But the slow truth began to dawn on Blake, leaving her

miserably chagrined. Sure, she had been worried, but a part of her had been jealous too. Rusty had been in the cockpit, and he had been in control. He had been the one to bring the plane down safely, and he had been the one to get all the praise. *You are not a very nice person, Blake Warner,* she thought as she gulped down the rest of the wine and picked up her car keys. *You owe that man an apology, even if you have irreparably damaged your relationship with him.*

Grabbing her car keys, she ran out of the apartment and drove the short distance to Rusty's house. *Good, if the truck's here, then he's home,* she thought as she parked in front of his house and tentatively rang his bell. After this afternoon, he would be justified if he never spoke to her again!

A wary-looking Rusty opened the door. "Can I come in?" Blake asked in a quiet voice.

Wordlessly Rusty moved aside and let her in. Nervously she walked into the den and sat down on the couch, then when she felt the warm spot where he had been sitting she moved to an easy chair. Rusty sat back down on the couch. "Rusty, I'm sorry," she blurted out. "If you never speak to me again, I understand, and I won't blame you, but I'm so sorry and I would do anything to take back all those mean things I said to you this morning." Rusty stared at her impassively. So he wasn't going to forgive her. She'd better go. She stood up and picked up her car keys. "See you tomorrow," she mumbled.

"Oh, sit back down, woman," Rusty snapped impatiently. "Of course I'll speak to you again, you silly idiot."

"You will?" Blake asked.

"Of course," Rusty repeated with exasperation. "But I suggest that you explain to me just what prompted that

186

outburst this afternoon, so I can be out of the state the next time you feel one coming on."

An unwilling smile lifted a corner of Blake's mouth. "When I first heard that you were in trouble, all I could think about was that you were in danger, that you could be hurt. Yes, I know that you could always eject, but that's still not too safe. And then, well, you started doing things differently than I would have up there, and you risked your life doing them. That made me angry."

She stopped and twisted her hands together. "You scared the living daylights out of me. There wasn't a thing I could do to help you get down safely. And then I had to listen to them brag on your fabulous flying. Yes, Rusty, I wish I had been in that plane today, and not entirely to spare you from danger. I wish I could have had a go at getting it down. Hell, I don't know, maybe I would have done exactly what you did. So when you came back I took it all out on you."

A sheen of tears covered her eyes. "I'm a rotten person, you know that?" she asked as a tear rolled out of her eye and down her cheek. One tear followed another and the tensions of the day were released in a storm of quiet weeping. Blake buried her head in her hands and sobbed out both her fear for Rusty and her frustration at having to listen helplessly while Rusty landed the plane.

Blake felt a gentle hand on the back of her neck, then Rusty knelt on the floor in front of her and gathered her into his arms, letting her cry all over the front of his checked shirt. "Blake, honey, it's all right," he whispered as he cradled her head close to his chest.

"It's not all right!" Blake sobbed. "I was awful!"

Rusty held her until her crying was down to an occasional sob, then he pulled her down on the rug beside him, holding her hand as she wiped her eyes with the back of her other hand. "You weren't awful," he said as he rubbed his finger up and down her arm. "I didn't know you were worried about me," he volunteered. "I thought you were just jealous about the flying."

"I was, in a way," Blake reminded him. "But mostly I kept thinking that you were risking your life for a piece of metal. But afterward I was jealous and I feel so bad about that!"

"Blake, every pilot in the room was jealous of me after I brought the jet down," Rusty said. "That's only natural —every pilot, you included, has daydreamed at one time or another of being in danger and doing the perfect thing to save the day. Today I happened to get my chance to live out that fantasy."

"So how was it?" Blake asked.

"It was awful," Rusty stated baldly. "I was scared as hell, and if I hadn't felt a whole lot of responsibility toward dear old Uncle Sam, I would have dumped and ejected. I swear, I'll never daydream again about being the hero. It's no fun at all!"

"I'm sorry," Blake said quietly. "I had no idea it was so bad for you."

"And I hope you never find out firsthand," Rusty said as he slid his arm around her and held her close. "Would you kiss away all those things you said this afternoon?" he asked.

"My pleasure," Blake agreed as she leaned forward and held Rusty in her arms, gently placing her lips against his. She nibbled his lips lightly, kissing him all around the edges, then pressed her lips closer to his and gathered him closer to her, the warmth of his body reminding her that something very easily could have happened to him today. "Oh, Rusty, I was so scared today," she whispered as she withdrew her lips from his and kissed his cheek. "I was so afraid that something would happen to you." Fresh tears filled her eyes and ran down her cheeks. "Please love me, Rusty. I need to hold you to know that you're all right."

"I need you too," Rusty admitted as he stood up and extended his hand to her. He led her into his bedroom and turned back the sheets of the big bed that Blake had learned to love. "No, wait," he said as Blake started to unbutton her blouse. "I want to unveil the rose myself tonight."

Rusty reached out and slowly unbuttoned Blake's blouse, button by button, until it was free and he could push it off her shoulders. Then he unhooked her bra and removed it from her body. With trembling fingers he unzipped the jeans and pulled them down her legs, Blake stepping out of them when he had lowered them to her calves. Finally, he pulled her lacy panties down her legs and off her body, leaving Blake naked and proud to his gaze. "I've seen you naked nearly every day for a month, and you just seem to get more beautiful to me," he breathed as he stepped back to survey her shapely body.

"My turn," Blake said as she reached out and pulled Rusty's T-shirt over his head. She tossed it on the carpet and unzipped his jeans, pulling the jeans and his briefs down together, exposing his proud masculinity to her view. She had been with him many times by now, but the sight of his strong manly body stirred her more each time she saw it.

Rusty stepped out of his jeans and gently pushed Blake back on the bed, pinning her to the mattress by the weight of his body, and cradled her head in his hands. "Please, don't ever attack me like you did today," he pleaded as he rained soft kisses on her lips. "You don't know it, but I have no defenses where you're concerned."

"Never again," Blake promised, and she meant it. "I'll never talk to you like that again."

"I guess this means we've had our first argument," Rusty said musingly as he nibbled the soft skin on her neck.

"And now we get to make up," Blake said as she wrapped her long legs around his slim hips and pulled him close.

"So let's make up, woman," Rusty groaned as his mouth traveled down one silky shoulder.

Slowly holding and kissing and caressing each other, they brought the forgiveness that was needed, and the hurt was kissed away. Blake held and caressed Rusty, kissing away all the cruel things she had said to him. Starting with his mouth, she nibbled, then lowered to his neck, his shoulders, and the hard nipples nestled in the soft hair of his chest, his quivering stomach, and the intimate parts of his body that by now she knew as well as she knew her own. She gave Rusty physical pleasure but emotional pleasure also, conveying in her sensual touch just how much he meant to her, and her regret over the way she had lashed out at him earlier.

Rusty lay back and let Blake touch him until he was nearly at the brink, then he sat up and pushed Blake down into the sheets. "Let me love you," he said simply as he stroked the sensitive skin at her waist, her stomach muscles tightening at his seductive stroke. "You look even more beautiful than you did before we became lovers, if that's possible," he said as his eyes traveled down the womanly body that had given him so much pleasure in the last month. "So feminine and so sweet," he breathed as he tormented her breasts with his tongue, then he dipped his head lower, running his tongue around her navel, knowing that Blake would be reduced to a quivering mass of desire in seconds.

"Ooh, Rusty, you know what that does to me," Blake moaned as his mouth dipped lower. Rusty sampled her sweetness, then shifted his body to nudge her knees open and joined their bodies together. Groaning with delight, Rusty set a sensual pace for their pleasure together, Blake twisting and turning under him so as to make both of them experience the ultimate. They had become accustomed to each other's needs in the last month, knew just what the other liked and needed, and tonight they applied every bit of that knowledge to their union. They twisted and turned, rocked and writhed, as their mutual excitement spiraled upward. When the explosion came, both of them were ready, cascading together from the edge of the cliff and plunging together into a spiraling abyss.

"Maybe we should fight more often," Rusty teased as he nestled Blake in his arms. "Making up was such fun."

"That's not even funny," Blake said as she sat up and pulled away from him, sitting with her knees hunched up and her chin resting on them.

"Hey, I was only kidding," Rusty protested as he ran a soft finger down Blake's spine, sending a shiver down her back.

"A few more fights like this afternoon and they're won't be any making up," she replied.

Rusty sat up beside Blake and took her face in his hands. "It wasn't that bad, you know," he said as he kissed her lips. "I think the things you said to me hurt you a lot more in the long run than they did me."

"You're probably right," Blake acknowledged. "But we had our first fight about flying, and that scares me."

"Our first fight was as much about fear as it was about flying," Rusty corrected her. "If you hadn't been scared

191

out of your wits, you wouldn't have been thinking about being up in the cockpit, and you wouldn't have been angry with me for taking a risk."

Blake nodded as her stomach growled under the blankets. "Couldn't eat your supper either, huh?" Rusty teased as he pulled Blake close and kissed her gently. "How would you like me to get up out of this bed and cook us a steak?" He climbed out of the bed and threw Blake a velour robe of his, then found an old terry one in the closet for himself.

"Sounds good," Blake admitted.

In just a very few minutes they were sitting close together in front of Rusty's television, steak and salad in front of them, watching a rerun of *Superman* on cable TV. When the movie was over, Rusty switched off the set while Blake loaded the dishwasher. He sat back down on the couch and motioned her to his side.

"What do you say we take off for a few days at the lake?" he asked as Blake snuggled down beside him. "Maybe we can borrow Bob's boat."

"When?" Blake asked.

"Just as soon as we can get some time off together," Rusty said as he stroked Blake's hair.

"Let's ask Colonel Alda tomorrow," Blake said eagerly.

A faint smile touched Rusty's mouth. "You're certainly not shy about making our relationship known publicly," he said musingly. "Does it bother you that virtually everyone at Randolph knows we're lovers?"

Blake's eyes widened in surprise. "Lord, no," she said. She turned shining eyes on him. "I'm so proud to be your lover, it's all I can do to keep myself from renting a plane and putting it into skywriting right over the base."

"Oh, Blake, I don't know what I ever did to inspire that

kind of feeling in you," Rusty said. "Come on back to bed, woman. I feel like making love to you again!"

Later, much later, after they had made love again and again, Blake stared out the window, Rusty fast asleep beside her, his head cradled between her breasts. *I love this man so much*, she thought. *He's become so precious to me.* Blake lay still as the even rise and fall of Rusty's chest tickled her stomach. *And I'm scared. So scared!*

Blake suppressed a sigh. Yes, the emotion that was uppermost in her mind tonight was fear, not the joy that she wished it could be. She was frightened of being in love with Rusty. Not because she thought that he didn't love her in return. He did return her love, or he was extremely close to doing so. It was the flying that was still bothering her.

Blake felt two large tears escape from her eyes and run down onto the pillow. Even though Rusty tried to blow off today's quarrel as being about fear, Blake knew that the real issue today hadn't been fear, but flying. In spite of her fear for Rusty's safety, she had wanted to be up in that cockpit herself today, and not just an observer on the ground. The old resentment had surfaced once again, and Blake had been jealous of Rusty, the ace pilot.

And today wasn't just an isolated incident, Blake thought to herself as she cradled the man whom she loved so much in her arms. There would be other times when she would react to something as a frustrated pilot, no matter how hard she tried not to let it happen, and she would say or do something that was bound to affect Rusty. And it would hurt him every time it happened. Did their fragile new love have a chance under those circumstances?

CHAPTER ELEVEN

"You know, this was a good idea," Blake said as Rusty took the turnoff that would lead them to the marina on Lake LBJ. "I feel more relaxed already."

"Let's face it—the Air Force can get to you sometimes," Rusty replied as he checked the wide rearview mirror on the side of the truck. There was no one behind them, so Rusty eased the truck into the right lane. "Last week was a killer."

"Let's not even think about it," Blake said as she made a face. There had been constant problems with the fleet, and the machinists seemed to have suddenly turned all thumbs, causing the test pilots to have to reject plane after plane and Blake to have to struggle frantically with her schedule. But Colonel Alda had been more than willing to let them take a week off together, and late this afternoon they had rushed off base and packed the truck and were now almost to their destination.

The glowing sunset stung Blake's eyes as she stared into it, searching for the small ranch road that would lead them to the marina where Bob's cruiser was docked. She squinted into the red brightness and pointed to a numbered road. "Is that it?" she asked.

"Looks like it," Rusty replied as he put on his blinker and turned into the little country road. *I love this man so much,* Blake thought as Rusty drove through the hilly terrain, the light from the sun turning his hair into fire. *I love him like I never thought I could love.* And as always, that thought was followed by a swift stab of apprehension. Did they have a future together, or would her feelings about his flying always get in the way?

Rusty turned off onto a gravel road, leaving a trail of dust behind him as he followed the narrow road through the rocky hill country. Although the spring wildflowers were long gone and the ground was arid and dusty, Blake could appreciate the stark beauty of the landscape. They rounded a curve and the lake and the marina appeared, the lake shimmering in the light of the setting sun. "Oh, this is beautiful!" Blake breathed.

"Bob said it would be," Rusty said as he reached out and squeezed Blake's hand.

"Is that Bob's boat?" she asked, pointing to a long, luxurious cruiser that was docked at the end of the marina.

"Yes, he said we were more than welcome to use it for as long as we liked," he replied.

"That was certainly gracious of him," she said.

"He said that we would enjoy the way Margie had decorated the cabin," Rusty said as he turned by a sign that said STARLIGHT ESTATES and took the second gravel road that veered to the left. "I wonder what's so special about the way she's done it?"

"Oh, it's probably very nautical and informal—you know, a place where they can entertain their friends for the weekend."

They drove up to the marina and parked the truck, then Rusty and Blake each got a load out of the back of the truck and trudged down the walkway of the marina. He climbed onto the boat, and unlocked the door, then pushed it open cautiously and peeked in. Rusty wandered inside, grinning from ear to ear as Blake followed him with her mouth hanging open in astonishment. "I—I hope Margie doesn't entertain anybody but Bob up here," she stammered as she took in the opulent, almost decadent decor of the tiny cabin. The cabin was dominated by a wide bunk with a white fur bedspread, and the floor, except for the galley, was carpeted in baby blue ankle-deep shag. A huge mirror was bolted to the ceiling right above the bed, and the walls of the cabin were covered with baby blue velvet.

"No wonder Bob's always complaining about her decorating," Rusty whistled through his teeth. "This must have cost him a fortune."

"How many kids did you say they have?" Blake asked.

"Four," Rusty replied.

"No wonder!" Blake laughed.

"Well, are we going to gape at our love nest all night, or are we going to unload the truck?" Rusty asked as he dumped his load on the elegant kitchen table.

"To hell with the truck," Blake said as she unbuttoned her shirt and threw it across the room. "We can unload it anytime."

"Blake? What are you doing?"

"I've never done it with a mirror," she explained as she unzipped her jeans and kicked them across the floor.

"But Blake, I'm hungry!" Rusty protested, but he shut the door and started unbuttoning his shirt also and soon they were sprawled naked on the fur bedspread, a small bedside light bathing their bodies in its soft glow.

Blake flopped down on her back and stared up at their unclothed images. "I'm getting saddlebags," she complained as she surveyed her reclining body carefully. "You look just perfect."

"That's because from this angle you can't see the little tummy I've grown in the last six weeks," Rusty said as he ran his hand down his stomach.

"My cooking?" Blake asked, leaning over and dropping a kiss on Rusty's imaginary bulge.

"My contentment," Rusty replied, gently caressing Blake's bent head.

She nibbled at Rusty's stomach with her tender mouth, then as his muscles tensed in delightful anticipation she let her lips drift lower and caressed him in the way that he loved so much, Rusty writhing below her in delighted abandon. When she had brought him beyond the point of control, he pushed her back into the pillows and proceeded to do the same to her, touching her in all the ways that he knew would send the blood singing through her veins. Her eyes clenched tightly shut, she let Rusty caress her, the raging fire licking through her senses as he stroked her body with knowing hands. Blake had never dreamed, on the first night that Rusty made love to her, that it could actually get any better than it was that night, but in the last six weeks she had learned how much better it could really be. Her eyes closed, she let Rusty explore her body, knowing that when she was fully aroused he would possess her completely and take her soaring.

"Are you ready?" Rusty whispered when Blake shifted restlessly beneath him.

"Oh, yes," she assured him.

"Then open your eyes," he commanded her. "I want you to see me when I make love to you."

Blake opened her eyes as Rusty possessed her completely, staring up at the ceiling mirror as their bodies joined together. Blake's first thought was *How erotic,* but as Rusty began to move over her, the sight of them together struck her as unbelievably silly, and amusement warred with the sensual feelings Rusty was arousing in her. She clenched her teeth and tried to concentrate on Rusty's divine lovemaking, but the more she saw, the funnier it seemed, and involuntarily her chest started to heave.

Rusty looked down in confusion. "Surely not already?" he asked softly.

Blake shook her head, finally giving up and laughing out loud. "No, of course not," she sputtered as Rusty looked at her as though she were crazy. "It's just that we look so funny!"

"Some people sure pick a great time to get tickled," Rusty muttered as he rolled them over with one swift motion. "Here, now maybe you'll stop laughing and make love to me."

Now that she could no longer see in the mirror, Blake's sensual feelings returned with even more strength than before, and she moved over Rusty with uninhibited abandon, pouring her love into every stroke. Caught up in the force of her lovemaking, she did not notice Rusty's withdrawal until his chest started to heave quietly beneath her. "Rusty, are you all right?" she asked in alarm, looking down into two dancing eyes.

"You're right, it does look funny," Rusty snickered.

"I don't think either one of us were cut out to be swingers," Blake said as she reached over and turned off the small light.

As soon as they were plunged into darkness, Rusty pushed Blake back into the lush fur and made love to her with gentle fierceness, holding sway over her with tender abandon until she was moaning. *Oh, Rusty, we have something so special,* she thought as her body whirled higher and higher with his, soaring with him to the ultimate as she softly called out his name. As their passion burst in great shuddering pulses, they held each other tightly, loathe to let go long after their bodies had calmed.

"That was so wonderful," Blake said as Rusty switched on the light. "What are you doing?"

"Trying to figure out what makes you so incredibly wonderful," he replied, laying back and studying her body critically in the mirror as they relaxed together side by side on the bed. "You're so beautiful, it's unbelievable," he said as he stroked her body lovingly. "And you give such pleasure to a man."

"Not to just any man," Blake smiled. "Only to you."

"So what are we going to do today?" Blake asked the next morning as she and Rusty shared a late breakfast. The night before they had eaten a late supper of steaks grilled on Bob's small hibachi and then had curled up together in the wide berth for another session of lovemaking, falling asleep in each other's arms. They had awakened early this morning in the cool gray dawn, delighting in the giving and the receiving of each other's love. For although Rusty had not come out and declared his love for her, he showed it to her in each and every touch.

"Well, we can go swimming, or we can go fishing, or we can go water-skiing," he said. "Or we can go back to bed and make love again," he added hopefully.

Blake groaned. "The spirit's willing but I don't think the body's able," she explained. "Give me a couple of hours. Oh, stop laughing!" she added crossly as Rusty snickered out loud.

"All right then, if you really would rather not go back to bed, let's go water-skiing."

"Are you willing to teach me?" Blake asked eagerly. She had never learned to water-ski, but it had always looked like fun to her.

Rusty nodded. "Let's go, then," he said as they dumped the dishes into the sink.

Before long, clad in only their swimsuits, Rusty and Blake were up on deck, carefully easing Bob's boat out of the dock. She watched anxiously as Rusty skillfully backed the boat out of the narrow confines and steered it into the main body of the lake. Then they motored to a calm cove and Blake sat on the edge of the boat and listened carefully to Rusty's instructions to bend her knees with the motion of the water but to hold her arms rigid.

She put on the skis and climbed out of the boat, half-floating in the waist-deep water as the awkward skis floated in front of her. Rusty handed her the tow rope and gently eased the boat away from her, then when she nodded her head he pushed down on the throttle and the tow rope suddenly tightened. Blake got halfway out of the water when one of the skis twisted beneath her and she pitched forward, letting go of the tow rope and landing facedown in the water.

"Sorry about that," Rusty said as he came back to within fifteen feet of her and threw her the rope. "Are you all right?"

"Fine," Blake replied, spitting out a mouthful of lake water.

"Ready to try again?"

Blake nodded and picked up the tow rope. This time she got almost all the way out of the water when she forgot and stiffened her knees, toppling forward and getting another mouthful of water. Skiing was harder than it looked!

"Now, remember, Blake, let your knees give," Rusty said as he threw her the rope for the third time. Blake nodded and at her signal he pushed down the throttle. This time Blake rose up out of the water with the grace of a professional, holding tightly to the tow rope as Rusty motored across the quiet cove, turning in a gentle circle when he reached the main body of the lake. The wind whistled in Blake's ears as the stinging spray pelted her arms and her legs. The houses along the shore whizzed by, slightly blurred at the speed at which they were traveling.

This is great! Blake thought as Rusty whirred back into the cove. This is almost as good as flying! She skied until a large wave from a passing cruiser upset her balance and she fell, and she waited patiently in the water until Rusty came to get her.

"You did great for a beginner!" Rusty enthused as he pulled her over the side into the boat. "Want to have another go at it?"

"In a minute," Blake said, rubbing her sore arms. "Would you like me to drive the boat for you?"

Rusty showed her how to drive the boat fast and steady for a skier, and after she had practiced a little she drove the boat while he skied around the cove. They took turns for most of the day, donning T-shirts when their backs and shoulders started to sunburn. The tension of the Air Force melted away for both of them, and they relaxed and played together like two children.

"Would you like to walk on the beach tonight?" Blake asked as Rusty dried the last dish and stacked it in the cupboard. "It's beautiful out there."

"I know," Rusty said as he took Blake's hand and helped her up to the deck. "Somehow, Margie's boudoir doesn't quite fit in with my concept of how a boat should be decorated," he laughed. "It doesn't fit in with the environment."

"I know," Blake said as they shut the door behind her. Outside it was still quite warm, but the sun would be going down soon and the gentle breeze from the lake was cooling. "I would have done it in simple woods and rustic paneling."

"Sounds like Mom and Dad's house," Rusty said musingly. "They always have liked things understated and simple." He grinned as a thought struck him. "I bet I was a shock with this hair," he said as he and Blake followed the curve of the shoreline, their sandals crunching in the sand. "They probably always thought they would have understated kids, too, but then I came to them. I bet they were surprised."

"But isn't there usually some red hair somewhere in preceding generations?" Blake asked.

Rusty shrugged. "I don't know," he replied. "The adoption agency never told them one way or the other."

"You're adopted?" Blake asked.

Rusty nodded. "And after they had four boys of their own too. But that's just the kind of people they are. And it never made one whit's worth of difference between me and the others," he added fondly. "I guess that's why I've never felt the need to find my biological parents. I'm so completely Mom and Dad's that it's never occurred to me to wonder about my heredity, except when I joined the Air Force to fly. None of the others had wanderlust. All of my brothers stayed in Alabama."

"Are your parents still alive?" Blake asked.

"Oh, yes, and I go home to see them whenever I can. I'd love for you to meet them, Blake."

"I'd love to meet them too," Blake replied. She looked at him mischievously. "And I thought all this time you were redheaded Irish!"

Rusty bent his head back and laughed out loud. "No, the O'Gormans were black Irish. Black hair and the darkest eyes you ever saw. And every one of them six feet or better. I stuck out like a Christmas tree light."

Oh, but you knew they loved you, Blake thought as they walked hand in hand in the red-hued dusk and Blake plied Rusty with questions about his family. His father and one brother were farmers and the other three brothers had jobs in Mobile. They had to be loving people, Blake thought, to raise a man to be as loving as Rusty was. She was suddenly seized by a desire to meet these people and tell them how much she loved their son. And she wished that Rusty could meet her mother, and see the house in Chicago where she had grown up. *I want to share roots with you, Rusty. I want to know your background and you know mine. I want to know who you were and what you did before you came into my life, and I want you to know the same about me. I want to share everything with you—including your future.*

Blake and Rusty spent a delightful week at the lake, relaxing together and getting to know each other better on every level. They spent hours speeding around the lake, taking turns driving and water-skiing, and before long Blake was an excellent skier. On other mornings they fished, Blake waking up with Rusty at the crack of dawn while he sought out the hidden coves where the older, bigger fish congregated. They would drop a line at each end of the boat, and Rusty would glower in exasperation as Blake squealed in delight every time she caught a fish, although he was always good-natured when she caught more fish than he did, which she usually managed to do.

In the afternoons, after they had cleaned and fried the fish for lunch, Rusty would sack out on the big berth and Blake would slip on a very brief bikini and take a book and wade to the shore of the lake and read, catching up on all of her beloved espionage stories that she so seldom had time to read at home. She would bury herself in the story, emerging only to wet herself in the cool lake water as she dried out and became uncomfortably hot. Rusty would join her about the time she was at the most exciting part of the book, and he would sit patiently while she whizzed through the story to the inevitable mind-twisting climax.

Then they would sun together, taking turns rubbing suntan lotion into their browning limbs. The freckles on Rusty's nose grew even more prominent and Blake's face and body turned a deep golden brown, white only under the small patches that the bikini covered, and her hair bleached to a glorious mane of gold. They would intersperse the relaxing sunning with vigorous swims in the cool lake water, racing and ducking and playing with each other until the sun was low in the sky. Then, famished, they would go back to the boat and prepare a simple supper, which they ate with relish.

Most evenings found them back on the shore of the lake, hand in hand, talking about everything under the sun. They told each other everything about themselves, comparing thoughts and views on everything that really mattered and a whole lot that didn't. Not by any means did they agree on everything, but the conversations were always lively and they developed a deep mutual respect for each other's thoughts and ideals. Then, as the daylight faded and the night descended upon them, they would return hand in hand to the cabin of the boat and continue with their bodies what they had started with their minds, that vital reaching out and sharing that two people in love always needed. Then they would rest in each other's arms, drifting off to sleep as the waves pounded the shore of the lake and rocked them in their slumber.

One day she and Rusty broke their pleasant routine and drove into Kingsland to wash their clothes. After their clothes were clean and folded they explored the area, touring Longhorn Caverns and stopping by a small antique store that was on the highway in front of Lake Buchanan. Blake honestly didn't expect much when she walked in, and was frankly amazed by the quality of the merchandise. She liked one old pitcher and bowl so much that Rusty bought them for her, and then bought himself an old pocket watch that actually still ran. They had dinner at a restaurant that overlooked Lake Buchanan, staring mesmerized as the rougher waves of the huge lake pounded the shore and the sides of the dam.

As the week went by, Blake became so caught up in the delightful world that she and Rusty were sharing that the real world they had left behind became a misty haze in the recesses of her mind. To her the conflicts that had plagued them there simply no longer existed. There were two people in her existence, she and Rusty. They were in love, and that was absolutely all that mattered to her anymore. She never even gave flying a thought.

"I wish we didn't have to go," Blake said a little wistfully as they walked together on the shore on the last night of their stay. They had planned to drive back to San Antonio late the next afternoon so they would be able to go fishing one more time, but this would be the last night they spent together in Margie's ridiculous berth.

"So do I," Rusty admitted as he squeezed her hand. "This week has been great."

"Yes, it has," Blake said, a small smile lifting the corners of her mouth as she thought of all they had shared and of the physical heights they had brought each other to.

"So what do you say we make this last night special?" Rusty asked. "Would you like to take the boat out for a nighttime ride?"

"Oh, that sounds great!" Blake said excitedly. "Let's go."

They went back to the marina where the boat was docked, and Rusty once again steered it away from the narrow dock, Blake guiding it from the wooden walkway. Then she hopped on as Rusty started the motor and soon they were motoring slowly up the middle of the lake. The sun was completely gone by now and the lights from shore winked brightly through the purple shadows of the coming night. A warm breeze caressed Blake's face and flung her hair out behind her as the first stars of the night twinkled tentatively in the sky. "Look," Blake said, pointing to the southwestern sky. "Venus." The planet of beauty shone brightly in the cloudless night sky.

"It won't seem nearly so bright once the moon comes out," Rusty said as he brushed a strand of Blake's hair out of his face. Sure enough, in just moments the full moon rose over the horizon, bathing the lake in its milky white glow, dimming everything else in the heavens by comparison.

Rusty motored to one of the better fishing coves and cut the motor. "Are we going fishing?" Blake asked. It wasn't the most romantic thing she could think of to do tonight, but if Rusty wanted to fish, then fish they would.

"That isn't exactly what I had in mind," Rusty admitted. "I'd like to share the water with the fish tonight."

"Oh," Blake said, finally understanding. She and Rusty could have gone swimming on the beach in front of the marina, but that beach was a little public for what he had in mind. But here in the deserted cove, they would be able to swim together with only the moon for company. "I assume we don't need our suits either," she added.

"Only towels and a blanket," Rusty replied as he tied the boat to a tree trunk and got out, taking the towels and the blanket and laying them on the soft grass just beyond the sandy beach. Realizing that Rusty had more in mind for them than just a swim, Blake smiled into the darkness and unbuttoned her blouse and slipped out of it. She neatly folded it and then removed her jeans and her panties and piled them carefully on the boat cushion. Then she flipped over the side of the boat and into the lake while Rusty shed his clothes on shore and waded into the warm, shallow water.

"This is lovely," Blake said as she flipped over and floated on her back, staring up at the full moon shining down on her nude body. Rusty waded out to where she was floating and leaned over her, kissing her lips with a light touch, careful not to force her down into the water. Blake opened her mouth fully and let her tongue fence with his, darting and retreating as Rusty's wove a magic spell around hers. As the pressure of his mouth increased, he reached under her neck and her waist and held her, supporting her so that she would not be forced beneath the surface of the water. Floating weightlessly in the lapping water, Blake returned the passion of Rusty's kiss, her hands unable to caress him but her sensitive mouth conveying all the passion for him that her body felt.

Rusty released her mouth and then let go of her body, flipping over on his back and staring with her up at the stars, paddling a little with his hands. "Doesn't it give you a funny feeling every time you think of how big the universe is and how little we are?" he asked as his eyes surveyed the bright night sky.

"A little," Blake agreed. She put her feet down and stood in the chest-high water, staring down at the naked body of her lover. "You look like a Greek statue with the moonlight shining on you like that," she volunteered as she reached down and nuzzled his chest with her warm wet lips. "But you feel like a man," she added. "My man."

Rusty twisted and stood in the water. "I am your man," he said as he reached out and took her in his arms, pulling their wet, naked bodies together. He captured her mouth as he slid one hand to her breast, lightly punishing it into a hard wet button. Blake could feel every inch of his bare body against hers, his desire pressed against her. Then suddenly he pushed her away and splashed water on her chest. "We have all night for that," he teased as he swam away from her. "I brought you here to swim, and swim we will."

Sure, thought Blake as she watched him cut cleanly through the water, swimming out toward the main body of the lake. But she knew what he was doing, and why he was doing it. He was teasing her and tempting her now, long before he had any intention of making love to her, so that when he did make love to her later she would be on fire for him.

Well, two could play at that game, she thought as she struck out and swam slowly toward Rusty. He was swimming on his back, staring up at the sky by the time she reached him, and she reached out and slowly ran her fingers down the length of his body, tormenting every inch of him with her tender caress. Before he could right himself to touch her, she had dived below the surface of the water and with several powerful strokes taken herself away from him. Surfacing several yards away, she swam in lazy circles while Rusty swam slowly toward her.

"Did you want something, Blake?" he asked innocently.

"Oh, not a thing, Rusty," she assured him as he swam toward her. As he approached her she ducked under the water suddenly, surfacing a couple of yards away. "Looking for something?" she teased.

"So we're playing catch now, are we?" Rusty leered, his gaze softening to genuine passion when he caught sight of the moonlight gleaming white on her breasts. The game of catch forgotten, Blake reached out and extended her hand to Rusty. He drew it to his mouth and kissed it tenderly, his lips warm on the back of her hand.

Still holding hands, they swam through the water, using the powerful muscles in their legs to propel them through the warm lake. They would stop every so often and kiss in the moonlight, sinking below the surface of the water as they forgot to kick and then surfacing together when their breath had given out.

They swam and kissed and played for a long time. Blake was not conscious of time passing, but when she finally looked up into the still night, Venus was gone and the moon was much higher in the sky. Rusty swam to where Blake was floating and bent over her again, taking her lips in a sensual caress that left Blake reeling. Slipping his arms under her, he lifted her up and carried her out of the lake, standing her beside the pile of towels. He picked up a towel and dried her with it, rubbing her gently but with tender, knowing fingers. Blake picked up another towel and dried Rusty's body as he had hers, then together they spread the blanket out on the soft grass and sank down on it together, the moon dappling their naked bodies in its warm white glow.

"Come here, Blake," Rusty said tenderly as he pulled her to him. He dipped his head down and sampled her nipple with his tender tongue. "I'm going to make love to you tonight like I've never made love to you before." His tongue circled her other breast, and Blake thrust herself closer to Rusty's plundering lips.

"And you know why I'm going to make love to you like this tonight?" he added.

"I think I do, Rusty," Blake rasped at him.

"You do?" he asked, breaking off his tender caress to stare at her in astonishment. "You know that I love you?"

Blake sat up and pushed Rusty back on the blanket, snuggling down beside him and tormenting his face and his neck with her sensuous caresses. "Of course I know it," she chided him as she feathered light kisses across his face. "You've told me in a thousand ways." She let her lips crawl down his chest and found one taut nipple. "You've told me every time you've looked at me, every time you've smiled at me, every time you've taken me into your arms and made love to me." She trailed her mouth down his stomach to his navel, where she ran her tongue lightly around the inside. "But have I told you that I love you?" she asked anxiously.

"Yes, oh, yes," Rusty whispered as he sat up and took her face between her hands. "I've known how you feel about me for a long time." He pushed her down into the blanket and covered her body with his own, his knowing fingers finding her welcoming femininity. Blake gasped at the eroticism of his touch, and Rusty once again made them one.

Blake marveled at the sensual feelings that Rusty aroused in her time and time again. They would be almost at the moment of surrender when he would retreat, tormenting her body with his lips and his hands until she was writhing and then he would claim her again, building the tension higher and higher. Her fingers sought out all of his sensitive points and tormented them lovingly, driving him closer and closer to the brink. Their minds spinning, their bodies entwined, Rusty's motions were controlled yet tinged with a touch of tender savagery. When the explosion came, Blake was ready for it, tensing and calling

Rusty's name into the quiet still of the night. He held her tightly as shuddering tremors of passion shook his body.

Spent, they lay together for long moments, their breathing slowly returning to normal. "I love you, Blake," Rusty murmured into her soft wet hair.

"I love you, too, Rusty," she said softly. "But we both knew that, didn't we?"

Rusty rolled off her and gathered her to him. "Will you marry me?" he asked simply.

Blake nodded. "Of course I will," she whispered, turning her head and seeking Rusty's lips with her own. He bent his head and kissed her firmly, sealing the agreement that they had just made. But for Blake reality intruded as she remembered that they were to return to San Antonio and Randolph tomorrow, and she looked at Rusty with eyes suddenly clouded with apprehension. "But what about when we get back to San Antonio and have to face—well—everything there? Do you think it will work out?"

"You mean have to face my flying? I certainly don't see why it can't work out," Rusty replied with confidence. "Listen, any two people who share all that we share—and I don't mean just physically," he added when Blake started to giggle, "those two people can certainly work out a problem like that, now, can't they?"

Blake nodded as Rusty rolled over and covered her body with his own. He was right. Any two people who shared what they did would surely be able to work things out between them. Yielding her body to Rusty's caresses, Blake thought she must be the happiest woman in the world.

CHAPTER TWELVE

"Blake, are you ready to go?" Rusty demanded as he stuck his head into her office. "I'm supposed to pick you up in thirty minutes to go get your ring."

"I'm just leaving," Blake replied as she grabbed her purse and slammed the drawer shut. "What's your hurry, anyway?" she asked, noticing the excitement in Rusty's face. *Isn't that sweet,* she thought as she pecked his cheek. *He's excited about buying me a ring!*

"What's this I hear about a ring?" Colonel Alda asked as he winked broadly at the two of them.

"This woman's got me hog-tied and happy about it," Rusty teased as Blake's mouth fell open.

"Good work, Blake," Colonel Alda said, kissing her cheek and shaking Rusty's hand. "So why haven't I heard about this earlier?"

Rusty looked at his watch. "She only agreed to marry me forty hours ago."

"Well, congratulations to you both," Colonel Alda said as he ducked around the corner.

"Come on, Blake," Rusty said impatiently as he hustled her out of the hangar.

"I'm coming, I'm coming," Blake replied, scurrying to the parking lot, a broad grin on her face. Rusty was more excited about the ring than she was. His color flushed, he hopped into the pickup truck and roared out of the driveway. At a little more sedate pace she followed him out and drove home.

She had barely had time to shower when she heard Rusty let himself in the front door. "Blake, honey, are you ready yet?"

"My God, you must have broken every speed record in Texas," she laughed as she rushed into her clothes and slapped on a little makeup, although with her tan from their week at the lake she didn't need much. Within a few minutes they were at one of San Antonio's most widely known diamond importers, a store where you could get everything from the most reasonable of stones to the very finest.

"What kind of ring do you want?" Rusty asked as they walked through the front door.

Blake shrugged, then her face split into a wide grin. "Can I have one like Suzanne's?" she teased.

Rusty eyes grew wide, then he realized she was teasing, and grinned. "That's more like what I'd spend on a house," he admitted.

At that point they were taken under the wing of a very eager young salesman who agreed that Blake and Rusty were very lucky people to have found each other, then he went into the usual sales pitch about size versus quality. Blake listened attentively and wondered why Rusty was fidgeting beside her when he had been in such a hurry to get here in the first place. The spiel finally over, the young man brought out several trays of matched sets, none of which appealed in the slightest to Blake, who had always preferred simple jewelry.

Rusty picked up Blake's hand and looked at it critically. "You know, I want to buy you a diamond, but I also like

213

the thought of matching rings of some sort. Can something like that be worked out?"

The salesman brightened and suggested several options. Blake and Rusty both liked the idea of a conventional solitaire for now, and then closer to the wedding they would come back and buy matching bands and have Blake's diamond mounted on her band. The salesman went to the back to bring out several loose diamonds that could be mounted in a simple setting for now. Blake grew more and more confused as Rusty kept glancing at his watch and tapping his foot impatiently. He had hurried her over here, and now he acted like he was in a hurry to get out.

The salesman returned with several tissue-wrapped diamonds. He unwrapped one at a time and let Blake inspect them. Although they were pretty, she didn't fall in love with any of the round stones and asked if a fancy cut would be any more expensive for the carat weight. Assured that the shape would not influence the price, she asked if she could see a few of the different shapes. As the salesman scurried away, Rusty scowled at her impatiently. "What was wrong with those?" he asked.

"I—I just didn't like them," Blake stammered. "I am going to wear it every day for the rest of my life, you know."

"Sorry, I didn't mean to fuss," he replied. "It's just that I've got to get home and pack."

"Pack?" Blake asked. "You just got back from your vacation."

"Yeah, but something great's come up and I need to talk to you about it, but I wanted to get you your ring first."

Blake opened her mouth to ask Rusty what had come up, but the salesman brought out another tray of tissue-wrapped stones and Blake's attention was immediately diverted to the stones in the tray. She was enchanted with the marquise, and after a few minutes they had settled on a stone that was beautiful yet within Rusty's budget. Rusty got out his checkbook and the salesman offered to have the stone mounted while they waited, if they had a few minutes to spare. Rusty winced but nodded, and he and Blake browsed the cases while the stone was being set. In just a few moments the salesman returned with a small box which he handed to Rusty, who in turn only gulped a little when he wrote out the check.

As soon as he handed the salesman the check, Rusty popped open the box and drew out the ring. Picking up Blake's hand, he slipped the ring on her finger, then gathered her into his arms and kissed her. Uncaring that she was in full view of some eight or ten people, Blake kissed Rusty right back, blushing only when everyone in the store burst into applause. "I think he loves me," she called out over her shoulder as they walked out of the store, their arms tightly around each other's waists.

"So where is your cross-country tomorrow?" Blake asked as she held her ring up and turned it this way and that.

"That's what I meant to tell you," Rusty said eagerly. "It isn't a cross-country." He opened the door of the pickup and let Blake get in, then got in on his own side and slammed the door. "I'm going to Tactical Air Command for six weeks."

"Tactical Air Command?" Blake asked, astonished. "What on earth are you going to be doing there?"

"Fighter pilot school! They want to let me try it out and see if I'm any good at it. Isn't that the greatest?" Rusty asked with the enthusiasm of a small child at the circus.

"Fighter pilot school?" Blake echoed, bewildered. "I didn't know you'd even applied."

"I'd practically forgotten about it," Rusty admitted. "I applied almost a year ago. I'm amazed that they ever got to me."

"Well, that—that's great," Blake stammered, biting her lip. "When are you leaving?"

"At five in the morning," he replied. "Oh, Blake, this is the most exciting thing that's ever happened to me!"

I thought I was that, Blake said to herself. So he wasn't excited about the ring, after all. Rusty chattered about it all the way to his house. She offered to fix them supper while Rusty packed his clothes for a six-week stay at Holloman Air Force Base. Lucky Rusty! All that great flying. Six weeks of nothing but flying. *Watch it, Blake,* she cautioned herself as she cut up and fried a plump chicken that she found in the refrigerator. *If you're not careful, you're going to find yourself jealous of him again, and that will never do! Besides, you couldn't go on something like this even if you were flying. Combat is still off-limits to women.*

Willing her disturbing thoughts away, she fixed them supper and called Rusty in from his bedroom, where he was blissfully packing his flight bags with enough gear to last him for six weeks. She handed him a glass of iced tea and sat down across from him. "Do you think we should start making any wedding plans?" she asked as she served herself a piece of chicken.

Rusty shook his head. "Not tonight. After all, how much can we accomplish in just one evening? Better let it wait until I'm back from Alamogordo."

"All right," Blake said quietly, her face falling as she served herself a spoonful of green beans.

"Hey, now, don't feel bad," Rusty said quickly as he noticed Blake's face fall.

"I don't," Blake said too quickly. "I—well—I'm going to miss you. Six weeks is a long time."

"That's true," Rusty agreed gently as he sampled a piece of fried chicken. "But we do have to face the fact that if we're both going to stay in the Air Force, periodic separations are the name of the game. Next time it might be you that gets to go off somewhere."

"Maintenance officers don't get to go off anywhere," Blake muttered dryly. "Oh, you're right, and I'm glad you're getting to go. It's just that I had hoped that we could marry soon."

"So had I," Rusty admitted. "But I would like to be in on some of the planning at least." He poked around on the platter and picked out the other drumstick. "So why don't you get together a guest list and do some of the legwork, and we'll be able to pull it together when I get back?"

Blake nodded as she nibbled unenthusiastically on a piece of chicken and forced back tears. She was happy for him, she really was. Most pilots, even Air Force pilots, dreamed of the chance that Rusty had been given. The pilots would go to Holloman and train for a few weeks, and then if they did well and were serious, they would go back for more training before they were selected for piloting a fighter jet. She was going to miss him, that was what was bothering her. She just knew that she was going to be lonely without him, that was all. She couldn't be jealous. This was the man she was going to marry!

"Blake, are you all right?" Rusty asked as she pushed her plate of uneaten food away.

"Sure, I'm fine," she said as she stood up and started to pick up her plate.

"Liar," Rusty said as he reached out and gripped her

wrist, pulling her into his lap and nuzzling her neck with tender lips. "What's bothering you?"

"I'm selfish," Blake owned up freely. "I wish you didn't have to go just now. I wanted to get our wedding ready."

"Oh, hon, so did I," Rusty drawled as he circled the inside of her ear with his tongue. "But this will be for only six weeks."

"You'll be flying a lot, won't you?" Blake asked.

Rusty immediately stiffened under her. "Is it that again?" he asked.

Blake shook her head slowly. Rusty reached around and caught her chin in his hand, tipping her head down so that he could see her face clearly. "If it is, I'll get over it," she promised him quietly.

"Oh, please, Blake, don't feel that way!" Rusty pleaded as he held her tightly in his arms. "We have so much going for us; don't let something like this come between us."

Blake stood up and wandered to the window, staring out at Rusty's backyard and twisting her fingers together. "Rusty, I'm trying," she said in a voice hoarse with tears. "I don't want to be jealous of you, honest to God, I don't. And I don't think that I am. I'm going to miss you, and I'm disappointed that we have to put off planning for the wedding. But I won't be jealous of you."

Rusty stood up and joined her at the window, holding her face between his hands. "I'm sorry if I sounded like a little kid at Christmas earlier," he said as he stared into Blake's eyes. "But I am excited about this and I wanted to share it with you. I'm going to want to share all of my triumphs with you, and many of them are going to involve flying. I want you cheering for me, Blake, not feeling like you're being left out. And you're the only one who can control how you feel about that."

"I said I wouldn't be jealous, Rusty, and I meant it,"

she said as a slight tremor went through her. Although Rusty's words had been gently spoken, there was a message in them that she could not ignore. He was not going to have her jealous of him every time he was called on to fly. What if she couldn't live up to that?

"Good girl," Rusty said, his somber mood instantly vanishing. "How about cleaning up in here while I finish packing, and then we'll get in a little practice for our wedding night."

"Good idea," Blake said, her depression lifting at the thought of making love to Rusty. "Besides, I'd like to see if the diamond helps."

"Come here, woman," Rusty commanded her with arms outstretched. "You haven't thanked me properly for the ring."

"Then I'll have to do just that," she replied, melting into his arms for his kiss.

It's easier said than done, Blake thought to herself as she twirled around in her swivel chair and fiddled with her engagement ring, holding it up to the light and admiring it for the hundredth time. It had been a week and a half since Rusty had left. She had missed him horribly in the last ten days, and in spite of her excitement over being engaged, she was depressed. And jealous, she admitted to herself as she lowered her left hand and sipped a cup of coffee, too preoccupied to even grimace at the bitter brew. In spite of her promise not to be, every time she thought of Rusty up in one of those pretty AT-38s she went peagreen with envy. Damn, why couldn't she have been up there in one of them? She told herself over and over not to be ridiculous, that the Air Force wouldn't let women fly combat, and that she would never have gotten to fly one anyway, but in spite of her continual reminders to herself, she envied Rusty for the chance to do that kind of flying.

"Captain Warner?" Sally asked as she pushed open the door.

"Come on in, Sally," Blake invited her, motioning the girl in with her left hand. Sally stepped in and shut the door behind her, holding a magazine out to Blake. "Ma'am, I thought you might enjoy looking through this," she said as she extended a copy of *Bride's Magazine* to Blake. "I'm through with it now and thought you might enjoy it."

"Why, thank you, Sally," Blake said sincerely as she took the recent but nevertheless dog-eared issue from the young airman. "You said you were finished with it? Have you need of it too?"

"Yes, ma'am," the girl said shyly. "I'm getting married over Christmas." She extended her left hand and proudly showed off her small ring. "Joe just got it out of layaway this afternoon."

"Why, Sally, it's beautiful," Blake exclaimed as she admired the girl's ring.

"So's yours," Sally said. "I bet you'll beat me to the altar, won't you, ma'am?"

"Probably," Blake admitted. "But that's all right. You and Joe are younger than we are, and you can practice your—uh—cooking," she stammered, remembering what she and Rusty had been practicing.

"That and other things too!" Sally piped, then both women blushed to the roots of their hair. Apparently she and Rusty weren't the only couple in the world who had been practicing. "Besides, Joe likes my cooking. Says I make the best coffee in the world. I need to get these to the Taj Mahal for the colonel. See you, Captain Warner. 'Bye!"

220

That young man must really love her, Blake thought as Sally wandered out the door.

Blake took the magazine home and was flipping through it that evening when the telephone rang. She grabbed the receiver, hoping against hope that it was Rusty. "Colonel Prescott here," her C.A.P. commander said crisply. "There's a plane down somewhere between here and Columbus," he said. "We're starting an S.A.R. in the morning. You're piloting. Seven o'clock."

"Yes, sir," Blake replied. She hung up the telephone and quickly called Colonel Alda, who graciously agreed to give her the time off to fly the mission as long as she would put in the missed hours over the next weekend. Great! Blake thought as she cheerfully undressed and showered, climbing naked into bed and trying not to think about how much she missed Rusty's warm body next to her. We'll find the plane, and maybe there will even be survivors! Oh, it will be good to accomplish something in a plane again, she thought as she drifted off to sleep.

Blake reported to Stinson early the next morning and was assigned three teenage observers and an exact spot on the grid where she was to search. Unreasonably excited, she flew to her grid, which was over a pasture about halfway to Columbus, and descended to about a hundred and fifty feet to begin the slow, meticulous process of searching for a downed plane. Back and forth, over and over, she flew until her fuel supply was low. She returned to San Antonio and refueled and began the process all over. By the end of the first day she had only covered a third of her grid and she was exhausted. Her observers, all of whom had been so excited this morning, trudged tiredly to their waiting cars, none of them looking forward to another day of searching. Blake's eyes burned and her back ached, but mostly she was disappointed. None of the search planes had turned up a thing. *Thank goodness tomorrow's Saturday,* Blake thought tiredly as she drove home in the late evening dusk. *I won't miss but one day of work.*

But by the end of the second day everyone was discouraged. Rain had kept them from flying until almost noon, and then no one could find anything even after the weather had cleared. Tired of the small, slow Cessna she was flying, Blake would have given her eyeteeth to take one of the speedly little T-38's out for a joy ride. Falling into bed late on Saturday night, Blake longed for someone, anyone, to find that plane.

Someone did. About two the next afternoon, while Blake was making what felt like her millionth turn, the radio crackled on and informed them all that a rancher had found the plane under the trees lining a creek bed. There were no survivors. Discouraged, Blake flew back to San Antonio and drove home in the hot afternoon sun, changing into her swimsuit and diving into the crowded complex swimming pool. *A lot of good that two and a half days of flying did,* she thought disgustedly. *All we did was waste gas.*

She swam off her frustration and was walking back into her apartment when her telephone rang. "Blake?" Rusty's voice crackled over the wire. "Have you been out of town? I've tried to call you all weekend."

"Sorry," Blake said tiredly. "I've been flying search-and-rescue for the last three days."

"That's great, Blake," Rusty replied.

"Not really," she said. "A farmer found it."

"Oh, well, that happens," Rusty reminded her lightly.

"Blake, you wouldn't believe all they have us doing here! This is the best flying I've ever done!"

For the next fifteen minutes Rusty regaled Blake with the tales of his exploits in the AT-38s and said that in a week or two he might get to take out an F-16. Blake listened attentively and cooed and asked questions in all the right places, only the red tinge of her face, which Rusty could not see, giving away her true state of mind. By the time Rusty finally rang off, she was ready to scream. Damn! He was having a ball in those speedy jets and she had just spent the weekend in a stupid little prop plane on a wild goose chase. Forgetting her promise to both herself and Rusty not to be jealous, she threw a pillow across the room and dissolved into a flood of bitter tears.

Blake's mood did not improve over the next two weeks. She missed Rusty yet at the same time she was jealous of him. He would call her and tell her all about the fantastic, exciting flying he was doing and it was all she could do to keep from slamming the telephone down in his ear. Yet at other times she felt guilty for feeling so jealous of the man she loved so dearly. She wouldn't have been jealous of his flying if she could do some flying that meant something, she thought over and over. When Colonel Prescott called one Wednesday at noon with another search-and-rescue to perform, Blake was almost glad the little plane had gone down, she was so desperate to fly again and to feel some sense of accomplishment from it.

Blake and the others reported to Stinson Field and immediately were assigned their grids. They flew steadily for four exhausting days, battling heat and thunderstorms, and missing work, until the C.A.P. received word that the plane had not crashed at all, but apparently had filed a false flight plan in order to fly across the border and return with illegal drugs. Thoroughly disgusted, Blake considered writing out her resignation to the C.A.P., but decided that she would wait until Rusty returned and talk it over with him.

Blake became short-tempered with everyone around her, snapping at the pilots and earning herself a dressing-down from Colonel Alda, who mistakenly thought that she was simply missing Rusty. The job as maintenance officer, which she had liked in the beginning, became dull and onerous, and she would stare out the window at the jets soaring into the sky and she would have to stop herself from going out and climbing into one and taking off.

Damn, Blake thought one afternoon as she watched Pat taxi a T-37 to the end of the runway and fly off, *I want to fly. I want to fly and I want to do it every day, not just on Saturday and Sunday. I want to do it for a living. I want to accomplish something with it. I'm tired of watching these turkeys do it every day while I shuffle paper around on a desk.* Getting up suddenly, she walked over to the Taj Mahal and found an administrative clerk, who promptly congratulated Blake on her engagement.

"Thank you," Blake replied. "May I have a set of D.O.S. papers, please?"

The airman looked at Blake as though he hadn't heard her correctly. "D.O.S. papers, ma'am?"

"Yes, Airman," she replied firmly.

The airman handed her a set of Date of Separation papers and she bid him good afternoon. Since it was almost five anyway, Blake returned to her office and got her purse out of the drawer. She was about to walk out the door when Colonel Alda walked into her office. He handed her a sheaf of papers and got her signature on them, then noticed the D.O.S. papers on her desk. "Whose are these?" he asked grumpily. "Which one of my hotshots thinks he wants to fly for American?"

"Probably none of them, sir," Blake replied, her lips twitching.

"Oh, you know what I mean, Blake," he returned shortly, not appreciating the joke. "Which one of them thinks he wants to get out?"

"I do, sir," she said in a small voice.

"You?" Colonel Alda bellowed.

"Just me," she replied. "You won't be losing any of your hotshot pilots," she added bitterly.

"No, just the best damned maintenance officer I've ever had. Blake, why do you want to throw your career down the drain?"

"My career went down the drain three years ago," Blake replied. "Colonel Alda, I want to fly. I want to fly every day. I don't want to have to save it just for weekends."

"And you think you can do this by getting out of the Air Force?" Colonel Alda asked. "Do you honestly think you can get a job on the outside?"

"I don't know and I don't care whether I'm working for a charter company or some rinky-dink cargo operation," Blake admitted. "Besides, I haven't filled out the papers yet. I'm still thinking about it."

"Blake, aren't you forgetting something? You and Rusty are engaged now, and he has a right to be in on this kind of decision. You need to call him before you do anything you can't undo."

Blake bit her lip. Colonel Alda was right. She couldn't and shouldn't make that kind of decision without talking to Rusty. He was due to call her in a few days, but she would try to get a call through to him before then.

She drove home and threw the papers on the dining

225

room table, then picked up the receiver and dialed the number Rusty had given her in case of an emergency. The airman who took the message told her that Rusty was out on a survival training session but that he would be back in two days and asked if this was a family emergency. Blake assured him that it was not and gave him a message that Rusty was to call San Antonio the first chance he got.

Blake's phone rang two days later just as she was leaving to meet Pat and Denise at the Officer's Club. "Blake? Hi, honey, I've missed you. What's up?"

"Oh, Rusty, we need to talk, but I'm supposed to meet Pat and Denise at the Officer's Club and I'm late."

"So talk for five minutes. Pat's always late anyway."

"Rusty, I miss flying. I want to fly every day, not just on the weekends."

Blake could hear Rusty exhale an impatient breath on the other end of the line. "Blake, we've been through all this before. There isn't any way you can fly on a daily basis, not in the Air Force."

"But if I got out of the Air Force . . ." she began tentatively.

"Look, Blake, I'm tired and you're in a hurry. If we get into this over the phone, it will take hours. Can't this please wait until I get back?" Rusty begged.

"Oh, all right," Blake sighed. "How much longer until you're through?"

"I might get through by the middle of next week, but it probably won't be until next weekend. I miss you, Blake."

"I miss you, too, Rusty," she said softly as she hung up the telephone.

If Rusty doesn't get back to town before too long, I'm going to run out the door screaming, Blake thought a week

later as she stared at the five o'clock news and sipped a glass of iced tea. The early September sun poured in through her windows, heating up the small apartment in spite of the air-conditioning. Hasn't San Antonio ever heard of fall? she wondered as she stood up and pulled the drapes, shutting out the glare that fell across her dining room table. Glancing down, she spotted the D.O.S. papers that had been sitting on her desk for the last week. She stared at them for a moment as though they were a snake, then picked them up and flipped through them. She had started to fill them out and turn them in a dozen times, but she had promised Colonel Alda that she would talk with Rusty before she did anything.

And Rusty isn't going to like it, she told herself as she wandered into her bedroom and shed her fatigues. A shower revived her physically but not mentally. Rusty wasn't going to want her to get out of the service. But if she didn't get out, how was she going to fly every day? She pulled on a denim skirt and a T-shirt and on impulse picked up the telephone and called Suzanne. If she could spend the evening with Suzanne, maybe she wouldn't spend it brooding about her future.

"Suzy? This is Blake. Are you busy?"

"No, I'm not busy," Suzanne replied absently. "John won't be in for a while."

"Great! Could you use some company?" Blake asked eagerly.

"No—wait, I guess that would be nice. Come on over and I'll get out a frozen pizza."

"Thanks, Suzy," Blake replied as she hung up the phone. Wonderful! An evening of laughing and talking with Suzanne was just what she needed.

Blake grabbed up her purse and headed out the door. In just a few minutes she was ringing the doorbell of her

friend's elegant house. A tired-looking Suzanne answered the door. "How you doing, Blake?" she asked quietly.

"I miss Rusty," Blake replied honestly. "I hope it has been worth his time to go."

Suzanne shrugged. "I'm sure it will be," she said, motioning Blake in the house.

"Look! You were on vacation when Rusty gave it to me," Blake said proudly, nearly scratching Suzanne's nose with her new ring.

"It's nice, Blake," Suzanne replied, admiring the ring. "Cheese or pepperoni?"

"Pepperoni," Blake said as she followed Suzanne out to the kitchen. *Nice? In the old days you would have drooled on it for five minutes, even if it didn't hold a candle to yours. Has all the money made you jaded, Suzanne?*

Suzanne put the frozen pizza into the stove. Together they made a salad and set their feast on the kitchen table. Blake told Suzanne all about their week at the lake and Suzanne briefly outlined their week in the Bahamas, but try as she would Blake could not get her friend to tease and joke like they usually did. *I came over here to get myself cheered up, and it looks like I'm doing all the cheering.* Blake ate her meal with gusto but noticed that Suzanne barely touched hers. What's the matter with her? Is she having problems with John?

Their meal finally over, Blake scraped her dish into the trash and put her plate into the dishwasher, and then took Suzanne's half-eaten plate and did the same. She then asked Suzanne if she was flying the next day, and when Suzanne assured her that she wasn't, Blake poured them each a glass of wine from a bottle in the refrigerator. Handing one to Suzanne, she sat down across from her quiet friend. "Do you want to talk about it, Suzy?"

228

"Do I want to talk about what?" Suzanne asked almost belligerently.

"Uh—about whatever's bothering you," Blake said. "You're just not yourself. Are you having problems with John?"

Suzanne shook her head. "We're fine," she assured Blake.

"Then what is it?" Blake pressed her gently.

"It's all over the base that you picked up D.O.S. papers," Suzanne said sadly. "You've lost your career now, along with your flying."

"What?" Blake asked, astounded.

"Well, you're getting out, aren't you?"

"I don't know. Maybe," Blake replied tersely.

"Don't you see, Blake? It's all my fault. First you couldn't fly anymore and now you won't even stay in the service." Her lips trembled and her eyes filled with tears. "Don't you see? I've ruined your life. You're never going to be able to forgive me for what I've done to you."

Blake stared at her friend as her shock turned to anger. How could Suzanne have so little faith in her? She had long ago forgiven Suzanne what little there was to forgive. Didn't Suzanne know that after their last talk? Is this what she had been tearing herself apart over? Blake clenched her hand into a fist and slammed it down on the table, sending the wine rocking back and forth in the glasses and making Suzanne jump. "Damn it, Suzanne," she said through clenched teeth, her voice seething. "Is that all the faith you have in me?"

CHAPTER THIRTEEN

"Faith in you?" Suzanne asked tearfully. "What do you mean?"

"I mean just that," Blake replied angrily. "We lived together for the better part of a year and you know me as well as anybody does. So how can you keep harping on the bit about me not forgiving you?"

"Well, you haven't," Suzanne replied.

"And whatever gives you that idea?" Blake demanded as she got up and paced the kitchen floor.

"You wouldn't come see me at Williams," Suzanne said, slowly getting up out of her chair and wandering over to the window.

"No, I wouldn't, and I've told you already that I'm sorry," Blake said as she leaned against the counter. "That was about as wrong of me as it could be."

"No, it wasn't, if that's the way you really felt," Suzanne argued earnestly. "I didn't blame you for blaming me then and I don't blame you for blaming me now."

"Damn it, I don't blame you," Blake said slowly and clearly. "I don't think I ever did, really. I just needed someone to take it out on and you were convenient." She stopped her pacing by the kitchen table and took a gulp of her wine. "Suzanne, I told you before that wreck was an accident! How can I blame you for that?"

"But you must!" Suzanne cried, bursting into tears. Blake put her arm around Suzanne and steered her into the family room, pushing her down on the expensive couch and sitting down beside her. "Now, why must I be blaming you?" she asked gently.

"Because you're miserable," Suzanne said softly.

"I'm what?" Blake asked.

"You're miserable," Suzanne stated baldly as she sniffed. "You've changed since Williams, and it breaks my heart. You used to be so happy, so outgoing. Everybody on base loved you. Now you've turned so bitter and resentful that I hardly know you. Frustration and misery are the only two things that would do that to you."

Blake gulped quietly. So Suzanne had seen beyond her words and could feel the attitude beneath it. "Yes, Suzanne, I'm bitter and resentful that I can't fly anymore. I'm frustrated and I'm so jealous of other pilots sometimes that it eats my insides out. But I don't blame you for it."

"But you *have* to!" Suzanne cried. "What else can I believe?"

"The truth, for God's sake!" Blake snapped, getting up off the couch and pacing the floor. "I don't blame you. I don't resent you. It wasn't your fault."

"But how can you separate your feelings about flying from the way you feel about me?" Suzanne asked.

"The way I feel about flying has nothing to do with the way I feel about you!" Blake replied deliberately.

"But you miss it, don't you?" Suzanne said as fresh tears filled her eyes.

"God, yes, I miss it! I miss it every day of my life! Is that what you wanted to hear?" she cried as Suzanne sobbed even harder.

"I seriously doubt that that was what she wanted to hear," John's biting voice said from the doorway. "But, then, it's more fun to put a guilt trip on your best friend, isn't it, Blake?"

Blake stared in horror as John advanced into the room, staring at her with pure hatred in his eyes. Suzanne stood up and tried to shake her head at John, but he advanced on Blake until he was just inches away from her, his dark eyes burning like two coals. "You blamed her then and left her with a guilt trip that it took her months to shake. She had gotten over it and was about to forget it when who shows up here but you, the sainted Blake Warner who was such a wonderful pilot but whose life is ruined all because of Suzanne. I've tried to tell her that you're not worth it, that you're just a selfish bitch who never had a thought for anyone but herself, but Suzy won't listen. You've done your best for the last six months to rub it in how miserable you are because you can't fly. Well, Captain Warner, I've had enough. You're hurting my wife and I'm not going to stand for it anymore. So you can get out of my house and out of my wife's life."

"Gladly, if that's the way that you and Suzanne feel," Blake said coldly as she advanced on John, her eyes burning with wounded anger. Startled by her angry advance, John stumbled backward until he flopped onto the couch, staring up at his wife's friend with astonishment. "But first you're going to listen to me, both of you, and you're going to listen good.

"You decided before you ever laid eyes on me that I was no good, didn't you, John? You judged me on the basis of behavior that I exhibited under very hurting, trying times, and you've decided that I'm to be the villain of the piece. Nasty old Blake Warner, the spiteful bitch who's making Suzy miserable.

"Well, I'm not the one who's making Suzanne miserable. I don't blame her, John. I don't think I ever did, way

232

down deep, and I certainly don't blame her now. That wreck was an accident, and I've spent the last six months trying to convince her of that." Blake stopped and wiped tears from her eyes. "But I don't suppose you'll ever believe that. It was too much fun to tell Suzanne how awful I am, without so much as coming and talking to me, wasn't it?"

John's face turned a dull shade of red and he watched Blake with astonishment.

Blake turned to Suzanne, a heartbroken expression on her face. "I'm leaving now, Suzy. John's told me to go, and if I'm making your life as miserable as he says I am, I'll get out of it. But, Suzy, once and for all, I don't blame you. Yes, I'm bitter and resentful, and I do miss flying, but if I blame anyone, I blame myself for distracting you from your driving. If it's anyone's fault, it's mine. And I guess that's the hardest part to live with. I screwed up my own life. But you didn't, Suzy." Blake picked up her purse and walked out of the front door, shutting it quietly behind her.

She was almost to her car when the flood of tears broke. She fumbled with her keys and unlocked the door, sitting down in the sweltering car and crying harsh sobs into her clenched fists. John was right. If she was making Suzanne miserable, it would be better to get out of her life. But, oh, she was going to miss her!

Blake jumped as the car door opened and John knelt by the car and put his hand on her arm. She jerked her arm away angrily. "Haven't you done enough?" she demanded. "I'm going to miss Suzanne."

"Blake, get out of the car and come back in the house," John commanded her gently. "I believe I owe you the biggest apology in Texas." She looked at him suspiciously, and he had the grace to blush.

233

"All right," Blake said as she sniffed and got out of the car. John handed her a handkerchief and she wiped her eyes and blew her nose. They walked together back into the house and into the family room, where Suzanne was hunched on the couch, a Kleenex in her hand.

"Suzy, she came back," John said quietly as he sat down beside his wife and motioned to Blake to sit down on the other side of him. Blake shook her head and sat down in one of the chairs.

"I wouldn't have blamed you if you never came back into my house again after the way I talked to you," John said as he slid his arm around his wife. "Blake, I'm sorry, I'm just as sorry as I can be. For two years Suzy had told me all about you and how you had turned from her after the accident, and all I could think about was her feelings. I never even gave yours a thought."

"I told you she wasn't a monster," Suzanne said.

"And I should have listened," John admitted. "Then you turned up here, obviously resenting your coworkers. Yes, Rusty told me as much," he added as Blake's eyes widened. "And I assumed that you blamed your unhappiness on Suzanne and were saying and doing subtle things to make her feel bad. I never had any idea that you blamed yourself."

"Why should you?" Blake shrugged.

"No reason," John said. "Anyway, Blake, I'm truly sorry for the things I've thought and the way I've treated you."

"It's nothing," she said as she started to get up.

"Blake, wait," Suzanne said. Blake sank back down in the chair. "Did you really mean it about not blaming me, about blaming yourself instead?"

"Yes, I meant it," Blake replied. "For three long years

I've thought *What if I hadn't been acting such a fool that day?*"

"And what if that car hadn't been trying to pass you on the right? What if that other car hadn't been in the left lane? What if you had been in a larger car, or a smaller car, or you had stayed on base?" John asked quietly. "Blake, Suzy, you both can what-if yourselves to death and make your lives miserable, if that's what you want to do. Suzy, Blake has forgiven you long ago for what you think you did to her. Now, do you think you can put her mind at rest and forgive yourself?"

Suzanne shrugged. "I don't know if I can," she said.

"Suzanne, you have to," Blake said. "If not for your sake, then for mine and John's."

"And how about you, Blake?" John asked. "Are you ready to forgive yourself?"

"That's going to be the hard part," Blake admitted. "It was much easier to forgive Suzy."

"I know that," John said. "But maybe if you forgave yourself, then Suzy would be able to forgive herself also."

Blake swallowed a lump in her throat. "I'll try," she said. "Suzy, I'll come over and we'll talk again," she said as she got up and kissed Suzanne on the cheek.

Suzanne did not get up, but John walked Blake to the car. "How about your feelings about flying, Blake?" he asked as she unlocked the car.

Blake stiffened, fearing another tirade. "What about them?" she asked.

"I'm not going to yell at you again," John said. "I'm sorry I yelled at you earlier. But I am worried about how you feel about Rusty's flying if you're going to marry the guy."

"I love him," Blake said. "I love that man a lot."

"I know that," John replied. "But do you resent his flying?"

Blake turned anguished eyes on John. "I'm trying not to, John. I'm trying very hard."

John looked at her sadly. "But is trying going to be enough?"

"It's going to have to be, isn't it? Look, I'll come by and talk to Suzanne again tomorrow after I leave work. I'll try again to talk some sense into her."

"Thanks," John said as Blake climbed into her car. "I'd appreciate that."

Blake drove home in the quiet, hot night. Tonight had been upsetting, but maybe getting their feelings out in the open had been good for Suzanne, and it had certainly cleared the air with John. Hopefully, now that he knew that she did not blame Suzanne or resent her, he would be her friend also. But his question about Rusty and his flying had disturbed her even more than her argument with Suzanne, because she did not have the answer to it.

Blake pulled into the apartment house lot and parked her car. Climbing the steps, she did not remember leaving the kitchen light on, but she had left in a hurry and there was no reason why she couldn't have left it on. She turned her key in the lock and walked in, then stared in astonishment at the man sitting on her couch, his red head bent over a paper in his hand. "Rusty! When did you get back?" she asked as she rushed into the living room.

Rusty looked up at her, the expression on his face freezing her in her tracks. "Are these your D.O.S. papers?" he asked.

"Y-yes, they're mine," Blake confirmed as she moved more slowly into the living room and sat down in the wing chair opposite Rusty. "I tried to talk to you about it last week."

236

Rusty's expression clearly mirrored his fury. "And why are you ready to throw away a promising career in the Air Force?" he demanded.

Blake looked at his angry face and felt her insides turning to jelly. "I can't fly for them anymore," she explained.

"You haven't been able to fly for them for the last three years," Rusty ground out. "So what's the difference now? Why are you suddenly ready to go out into a recession economy and try to find work?"

Blake swallowed and took a breath. "I want to fly," she said. "I want to fly on a daily basis. I'm sorry, Rusty, but it's tearing me apart."

"You want to fly," Rusty mimicked her angrily. "All right, Blake, let me see if I understand you correctly. You are ready to get out of the Air Force, throw away a promising future with them, just because you can't fly a damned airplane anymore. Good grief, Blake, you're colonel material! If you stayed in, we could be stationed together and travel together and get promoted together and have a damned good life together. And we could retire together and have a great second career doing something exciting. But no, that isn't good enough for you. You want to fly, and you're ready to throw everything else away. That's stupid, Blake, when you can fly all you want on the weekends."

"Weekends aren't enough!" snapped Blake. "Whoopee! Flying dinky little single-engine planes for a do-nothing civilian organization. Yes, Rusty, while you were off having a ball in those fantastic little F-16s I was doing some flying too. But it just isn't enough, Rusty. I want to fly. I want to fly every damned day, and I want it to mean something."

"Well, Blake, even if you get out of the Air Force, do you really think anyone's going to hire a has-been Air

Force pilot with glass scars on her cornea? You're not going to get a job flying, and I think we both know it."

Blake got out of the chair and stared out the window, two tears running down her face. "You're the soul of kindness, aren't you, Rusty? Okay, I may not get a job with the airlines, but I still can fly charter flights or cargo. At least I'd be flying more than I am now."

"And that's all you're going to be able to do if you get out of the service, Blake," Rusty reminded her firmly. "But do you call that a career, compared to what you have now? In time you'll become bored and frustrated with that kind of flying, too, because your real problem is that you haven't been able to accept the fact that you'll never be an Air Force pilot. Why don't you, once and for all, just face it, Blake. The only flying career that has ever mattered to you is over and nothing else will ever take its place. Once you do that, maybe then you'll appreciate what you do have and can still do."

"You're a cruel, hard bastard, William O'Gorman," Blake said through clenched teeth. "Yes, you are," she said as Rusty opened his mouth to speak. "How would you like it if you were the damned maintenance officer and I were the pilot? If you had to watch me fly off every day? If you had to put up with me being gone six weeks while I flew my heart out? You just don't understand the way I feel, Rusty. How could you? You have your career in flying."

"And you have your scapegoat all picked out, don't you, Blake?" he asked quietly. "If I've told you once, I've told you a hundred times, I'm sorry you can't fly for the Air Force anymore. I'm sorry you don't believe that. But you've had three years to get over it and to learn to live with the frustration. And you can fly on weekends doing something useful."

Blake uttered a rude word. "I was coping with it better before I started flying on weekends," she taunted. "That just makes me realize how much I lost."

"Yes, I guess that was a mistake on my part," Rusty said quietly. "I thought you were mature enough to enjoy it for what it is and not to expect it to replace Air Force flying in your life. I guess I was wrong."

"I guess you were," Blake agreed.

"But Blake," Rusty said, standing up and laying the D.O.S. papers on her table. "I'm not going to have you taking your frustration out on me for the rest of my life because I'm a pilot and you're not. I refuse to be your whipping boy every time I have to fly, or every time I get to fly a new plane, or every time you feel bad because you can't fly anymore. I love you, but I just can't take that."

"But what about the way I feel?" Blake asked, close to tears. "What am I supposed to do?"

"I suggest you stop crying for the moon and get on with your life the best way you know how," Rusty replied.

"Thanks a million," Blake replied bitterly. "I should have known better than to expect any support from you."

"If you think I'm going to support something as idiotic as your getting out of the service to fly charter or cargo flights on a hit-or-miss basis, then yes, you should have," Rusty said. "Look, maybe I was hard on you, I don't know. I don't think tonight's the time to talk about it. I'm dog tired, and I promised Bob Merrill that I'd fly with him to Del Rio and go dove hunting with him over the weekend. We'll talk again when I return." He stared into Blake's tear-filled eyes and drew her into his arms, holding her tightly as his own eyes watered. She held on to him for dear life, tears flowing from her eyes as she sobbed quietly on his shoulder.

Rusty gently pushed her away from him and wiped her

eyes. "Please, think about it, Blake. I don't want to lose you." Without waiting for a reply, he left her apartment and shut the door behind him.

Blake stared at the closed door, fresh tears pouring down her face. She should have known that Rusty wouldn't understand. *I'm afraid it's over with him,* she thought as she sat down on the sofa and let the tears fall freely down her cheeks. *He's right—he doesn't need a wife that resents the hell out of him, and I can't seem to help doing just that.*

Rusty, you jerk, why couldn't you have left well enough alone? he asked himself as he slammed the truck into gear and drove toward his home. *She said she didn't want to fly again and you forced her back into it and now she's more miserable than ever.* Why couldn't he have taken her at her word?

I guess I expected too much, Rusty told himself as he wandered into the house and flipped on the light. Sitting down on the sofa, he kicked off his shoes and propped his feet on the coffee table, his relaxed stance belying his inner turmoil. Blake was miserable and to a great extent it was his fault. If he hadn't pushed her back into flying, she wouldn't be at home crying her eyes out. But he had honestly thought that any flying would be better than none—for him it would have been. But maybe Blake was different. Maybe she had to have the daily joy of flying to be happy. Maybe she had expected it to take the place of Air Force flying. Maybe they both had expected too much.

Rusty wiggled his toes and sighed out loud. *Do we even have a future together?* he asked himself as he reached down and pulled off his socks, a film of tears over his eyes making the job more difficult. He had meant what he said to her. Although he loved her more than life itself, he didn't have the temperament to put up with her constant resentment of his career. He would grow bitter, and so would she. *Oh, Blake,* he thought as he went into the extra bedroom to look for his shotgun and a box of shells, *do we even have a chance?*

Blake ran a comb through her hair and dabbed on a little makeup to cover the deep circles around her eyes. She had not slept well the night before, her argument with Rusty bouncing around in her head every time she closed her eyes. How on earth would she ever be able to overcome the jealousy and resentment she felt over his flying? He was right. They could not live together for the rest of their lives if she was going to take out her bitterness on him. *And the solution to this has to come from me,* Blake thought as she left her apartment and climbed into her car. *There's not one thing Rusty can do to alter the situation.*

Blake got on the expressway and drove across town to Suzanne's house, hoping that the dark thunderclouds in the distance signaled rain for the hot city. She parked her car in Suzanne's driveway and rang the doorbell. After her own rocky night she would really have rather let this go, but when John called and told her that he would be on a cross-country and that Suzanne would be alone, she had promised that she would check on her friend and see how she was doing. Blake was about to ring the bell a second time when Suzanne pulled open the door, her hair wet and dressed in a skimpy bikini. In spite of her deshabille, she smiled genuinely and stood aside for Blake to come in. "John told me you might be coming by," she said as Blake walked in the door.

"I didn't realize you had a pool, Suzy," Blake said as she followed Suzanne into the family room.

"Oh, we don't, at least not yet. I was sunning and

thought I'd cool off with the hose. Can I get you anything before I go and get dry?"

"Coke?" Blake asked. "Look, I'll get it myself while you go dry off."

Suzanne disappeared into the back part of the house while Blake helped herself to a Coke in the refrigerator.

Suzanne reappeared momentarily in an old pair of shorts that Blake remembered from Williams. "All that money and you still won't get rid of those old things," Blake teased as Suzanne got herself a Coke from the refrigerator.

"These fit my bottom, I'll have you know," Suzanne replied. Then her face sobered. "I had no idea you felt guilty about that accident," she blurted out. "Why on earth do you feel badly about it?"

"Because I was distracting you from your driving," Blake explained earnestly. "If I had been letting you drive, you would have seen that car coming up behind you and the accident would have never happened."

"So you really don't blame me?" Suzanne asked quietly.

A small smile touched Blake's mouth. "Of course I don't blame you, Suzy. Once I got over the shock of all that happened, I never really did."

"Then you've forgiven me?" Suzanne asked. "You've really forgiven me?"

"For what little there was to forgive, of course I've forgiven you," Blake replied. "Although there was nothing to forgive really. That accident was not your fault."

"But I've felt so guilty!" Suzanne said with anguish.

"Oh, Suzy, there's no point in that! You know, this reminds me of the time when we were at Williams and Jeannie Pewett made that nasty crack about me, remember? I felt bad for a day or two and then forgot about it. Jeannie came up to me six months later and apologized!

242

She had felt bad about it all that time! And you're doing the same thing. I've forgiven and forgotten your part in that accident long ago. It's you who can't forgive Suzanne. And you're going to have to if you're ever going to really be my friend again."

"But what about you?" Suzanne asked. "Are you ever going to be able to forgive yourself?"

Blake sipped her Coke and raised her eyebrows. "That's a good question," she said. "I keep thinking that I screwed up my own life, and I feel like I wasted a year and a lot of the Air Force's money on skills that are now totally useless. I think that's what bothers me. I have all this talent as a pilot and no one wants me to use it for them. And that's a waste."

"I thought you were flying for the Civil Air Patrol," Suzanne said slowly.

"I am, but they certainly don't accomplish much," Blake said wryly. "The last two missions we flew were zeros. I just feel useless."

"Is that why you picked up the D.O.S. papers?" Suzanne asked.

"I guess so," Blake shrugged.

"Do you think you can get a job on the outside?" Suzanne asked as she took a sip of her Coke.

"Maybe," Blake admitted. "Rusty certainly doesn't think so."

"Uh-oh," Suzanne muttered. "You mean I'm not the only one to blame for those gorgeous bags under your eyes."

"Hardly," Blake said as she drank the last of her Coke and crushed the can absently in her fist. "Last night was my night for fights. I left here and Rusty was at home waiting for me looking at the D.O.S. papers. He says I'm throwing a good career away and that he's not going to be my whipping boy for the rest of his life. I'm frustrated and I'm unhappy and I'm about to run off the best man that ever came my way. Is it any wonder I feel guilty?"

"That's ridiculous," Suzanne replied spiritedly. "You certainly don't need to feel guilty on top of everything else."

"And neither do you," Blake said quietly. "All right, I'll make a deal with you. You quit feeling guilty about your part in that accident and I'll quit feeling guilty about mine. We'll call it what it was, an accident, and go on from there. Okay, Suzy?"

"I can do anything as long as I know that you really don't blame me," Suzanne said softly. "But what about your other feelings? What about the resentment? What about Rusty?"

"I honestly don't know," Blake said quietly, her eyes filling with tears. "I'm going to try to work things out, but I may not be able to." She reached up and wiped a tear from her eye. "I do know this much, though, Suzanne. If I can't work them out, I'm going to need you more than ever."

"I'll be here," Suzanne said softly, reaching out and stroking Blake's hair lightly. "What do you say I go out and get us a bag of burgers and fries—some food for the soul?"

Blake sniffed and nodded. "Remember how I like mine?"

Suzanne nodded. "Be back in a minute."

Blake had recovered her poise by the time Suzanne returned with a sack of hamburgers and fries. They ate their meal with gusto and sat on the floor in the family room for a couple of hours, just visiting and talking, their relationship finally back to the closeness they had shared at Williams.

Thank goodness Suzy is going to be all right, Blake thought as she scurried to her car in the brisk wind that had come up while she was at Suzanne's. The thunderheads that had been in the distance earlier were right above her head and as she switched on her engine a few fat drops of rain hit her windshield. *I've managed to make her feel better about things, now what am I going to do about my own life?*

The rain was pelting down fiercely by the time Blake reached her apartment. As she ran to her door, she wondered if it was raining in Del Rio. That hunting trip wouldn't be much fun if it were! She unlocked her door quickly, but by the time she got inside she was drenched. Shedding her wet clothes, she heaped them into the laundry basket and turned on a warm shower. She dried herself with a thick terry towel and found a long cotton nightgown and slipped it on, then curled up on the couch.

What on earth can I do about Rusty? she agonized as she reached out and picked up the television guide. There was an interesting-looking movie on the cable channel, so Blake switched it on, but she turned it off thirty minutes later when she discovered that it was one of those old romantic comedies with a man and a wife and another woman. *At least that's not my problem!* she thought as she brushed her hair and stared at the blank TV screen. As far as she knew, Rusty had not looked at another woman since she had entered his life so many months ago. He just wasn't made like that. *Oh, Rusty, you're so special and I love you so much! Why can't I be satisfied with all that you have to offer? Why do I think I have to fly?*

Blake got up and padded to the kitchen, pouring herself a glass of milk and returning to the couch. She sipped her milk slowly and thought about what she had said to Suzanne. She had talent as a pilot that was going to waste.

She wanted to use that talent, if not for the Air Force then somewhere where it counted. She didn't just want to fly; she wanted to achieve some sense of personal satisfaction from it. At first she had thought that she would be able to do that in the C.A.P., but after the last two missions she seriously doubted that she would find that kind of flying there.

So what could she do? Rusty was violently opposed to her getting out and trying to fly civilian, and he was probably right. Besides, he would be transferred every three years and she would have to go with him if she intended to be his wife, so even if she got a job flying in San Antonio, there was no guarantee that she would have a job at his next tour. Yet if she didn't do something, and they stayed on the path they were traveling at the moment, her jealousy and resentment were going to rip them apart somewhere along the line.

Blake got up and stood at her window, staring out into the raging storm for a very long time. She thought until her head was spinning but simply could find no solution to the dilemma. And Rusty had admitted that he knew of no answers either. But we just have to come up with something, Blake thought as she leaned her head against the doorframe and stared down at the winking diamond on her finger. *We just can't let it go. We have to work it out.* Finally, exhausted from her sleepless night the night before and the torment of her thoughts, she turned out all her lights and crawled into her bed, drifting off to sleep as the storm raged outside.

Blake mumbled in her sleep and swore softly as she reached for the telephone. Squinting at the clock, she promised herself that she was going to give some thoughtless soul a piece of her mind. Five thirty in the morning!

She put the receiver to her ear and muttered a very ungracious "Hello."

"Captain Warner? Commander Prescott here." Blake was instantly awake and a little disgusted. Surely not another search-and-rescue farce for her to fly.

"Yes, sir," she said tiredly.

"There's a plane down somewhere between here and Del Rio and we're going to fly out of here in an hour. Can you be here?"

"Of course, sir," she said, wondering why Commander Prescott sounded so strained.

"Come prepared to stay as long as it takes. This is one of our own."

Icy dread gripped Blake as she clutched at her stomach. "Bob Merrill's plane, sir?"

"Yes, and we doubt that there are any survivors."

CHAPTER FOURTEEN

Blake stared at the receiver gone dead in her hand. No survivors. Rusty was on that plane. She swallowed, staring straight ahead as she slowly laid down the receiver. Mechanically she got out of bed and quickly dressed in a pair of jeans and a shirt. Her hands trembling, she braided her hair and pushed on a pair of shoes and got her sleeping bag and her packed duffel out from under the bed. She packed a little food and threw everything in her car, then she went back into the apartment and dialed Suzanne's number. A groggy John answered. "What?" he asked sleepily.

"John, this is Blake. The plane Rusty was on went down last night somewhere between here and Del Rio. I'm going now to try to find it. Call his mother." She started to hang up the telephone.

"Blake, wait!" John said urgently. "Are you sure Rusty was on that plane?"

"Yes, I'm sure," Blake said.

"Was there any chance—"

"Colonel Prescott said no survivors," Blake replied mechanically. "We're just going to be looking for the plane."

"Blake, are you sure you should be flying the mission?" John asked urgently. "Come over here and stay with us today."

"No," Blake replied doggedly. "We're going to find the wreckage. I want his mother to know for sure." She hung up the telephone and quickly left her apartment.

John stared at the dead receiver in his hand. "What is it?" Suzanne asked groggily.

"Rusty's plane went down last night," he said, dazed.

"Was that Blake?" Suzanne demanded. John nodded. "Do I need to go to her?"

"She's already left to fly the search," John said. "She says she wants his mother to know for sure."

"Oh, God," Suzanne said fervently. "How was she?"

"I think she was in a total state of shock," John replied as he opened the drawer and got out his telephone book with shaking hands. He looked through it for a moment and found the number he was looking for, then dialed 0 and waited a moment for an operator. "Operator, I need to make a person-to-person call to Bitter's Cove, Alabama," he said with a voice that trembled.

248

Completely numb, Blake started her engine and mechanically the Datsun seemed to find its way out to Stinson. NO SURVIVORS. The words crashed around her brain. No, it's not possible, she thought as she took the Mission Road exit. But how could it be otherwise? In that kind of storm it would be almost impossible for a pilot to coast to safety. Too much in shock even to respond emotionally yet, she took Mission Road and turned into Stinson Field.

Blake climbed out of the car and found Colonel Prescott in the small office assigning grids to the various pilots. Blake fought to keep from fainting or screaming out loud and waited, still as a stone, while Commander Prescott spoke to the other pilots. The pilots were silent and grim, knowing that Bob and any of his passengers were probably dead, but none of them were as ashen as Blake. As Colonel Prescott showed Blake her grid on the map, he looked at her pinched features with real concern. "Captain Warner, are you sure you're up to flying this mission?"

"Of course, sir," Blake replied. "Why shouldn't I be?"

"Well, you're reacting rather strongly to the tragedy. We've all known Bob a long time and are upset, but your hands are trembling and you look like you're about to faint. Now, I know you were fond of Bob, but don't you think you're overreacting?"

Blake took a deep breath and stared at the group in bewilderment. "Didn't you know that Rusty was on that plane? My fiancé was one of the passengers," she explained slowly and patiently.

"Oh, my God," Commander Prescott said as he pushed Blake into a chair. "Oh, Blake, we didn't know. San Antonio International didn't release the names of the passengers. Blake, I'm sorry."

"I'm sorry too," Blake replied mechanically. "Now, if

you'll just show me my grid and assign me some observers . . ."

"Blake! You can't fly this mission!" Commander Prescott said. "It would tear you apart."

"I want to fly it," Blake said, raising her head and looking at him pleadingly.

"Blake, no. What if you do find the wreckage? I told you that in that storm last night it's unlikely that a pilot could have come to any kind of survivable landing. There will be no survivors."

"I know that," Blake replied doggedly. "I know that Rusty's dead." She turned stunned eyes on him. "I want the satisfaction of trying to find the wreckage. I want to spare his mother and father the horror of not knowing for sure. Please, Commander, I have to fly this one."

"This is against my better judgment, but if you feel that you can fly it with adequate skill, I won't stop you," Colonel Prescott said.

"Oh, I'll fly it right," Blake replied with grim determination in her eyes. "This one's for Rusty."

Commander Prescott assigned her a grid in brushy pasture near Del Rio and she and her observers gave their gear to the ground crew and were soon in the air. Behind them the sun was rising in all its splendor, but as far as Blake was concerned she didn't care whether the sun ever rose again or not. Rusty was dead. Gone. She would never feel his lips against hers, never have him reach across the bed and pull her close for a good-morning kiss. She felt her fingers start to tremble and her throat tightening and she clamped an iron will down on her emotions. *You can think about all that after you've found him,* she told herself, willing herself to calm down. *You have three observers up here with you and you have a job to do.*

Blake landed in Del Rio and refueled the plane at the

small airport, then she and the three observers flew the short distance to her grid and began the painstaking process of combing the countryside for the downed plane. The plane was a red Piper and should be easy to spot if only it weren't under trees or brush. Methodically Blake flew back and forth across the grid, the three observers straining their eyes for some sign of the wreckage. *Would we have made it, Rusty?* she wondered as she turned the plane in a graceful arc and started back down the grid. *Would I have been able to overcome my resentment? Would we have been happy? Would we have had a little redheaded baby someday?*

Knowing that she would never know the answers to those questions now, Blake controlled her thoughts the best that she could and concentrated on flying their grid. She flew as low as she legally could, sure she was eliciting curses from the avid dove hunters on this first weekend of dove-hunting season. The cabin grew unbearably hot, and she and the observers used thick terry towels to wipe the sweat from their faces. Back and forth, turn, fly it again just a little ways over. *I'm going to find you, Rusty. Either I will or one of the other pilots will. We won't let your mother and father suffer from not knowing. We'll find you, my love.*

Blake flew until her fuel supply was nearly exhausted and reported to the Del Rio airport for refueling. The observers ate heartily of sandwiches and drank soft drinks and with the coaxing of the mother of one of her observers, who was in the ground crew, Blake gagged down a half of a pimiento cheese sandwich and an entire Coke. The woman, who knew that Blake and Rusty were engaged, was sweetly compassionate and it was all Blake could do not to break down into a storm of weeping on her shoulder.

She took a deep breath and she and her observers headed back out to their grid.

As the afternoon sun baked them, the shock of the crash begin to wear off and raw pain started to lick at Blake. He was really gone. No more dancing blue eyes, no more silly teasing, no more gentle bullying, no more tender lovemaking. *Mother, how did you stand it when Dad died?* Blake thought as she wiped her forehead yet again. She would have to call her mother after they found the wreckage and tell her what had happened. Blake, who often had wondered why her mother had never remarried after her father's death, now understood why her mother was still alone. *I'll never be able to marry another man,* she thought as she turned the plane in yet another graceful arc. *I'll always love Rusty.*

Blake bit her lip and fought back tears. Good God, why had she and Rusty parted on bad terms the other day? Why couldn't she have been more mature about his flying? Why had she resented him like a petty child? *Rusty, I wish I could do it over,* she thought as she stared into the sun that was dipping low in the sky. *I swear I'd figure out some way to get over the way I feel about your flying. Oh, Rusty, I wish I had another chance. I would do it differently, I swear I would.*

Blake and the observers flew their second leg of the search for most of the afternoon. The sun was beginning to dip low on the horizon when one of the observers grabbed up the mike and switched it on. "Captain Warner, I've spotted something." The teenager motioned back toward the last strip that Blake had flown. "Down there."

Blake turned the plane around and flew back down the same strip of land. The observer motioned her over a little to the right. "There, do you see it?" he asked excitedly.

Blake's hands started to tremble as she looked out the

252

window and spotted the red Piper, surprisingly still somewhat intact. It had cut a ragged path through about thirty yards of brush and was laying on its side, one wing sheared off and lying several yards away but the rest of the plane still together. *Well, we did it,* she thought as she switched on the radio. "Del Rio? This is flight 783 on S.A.R. for the C.A.P. We've located the wreckage." Blake radioed the exact location and circled the plane once more, preparing to fly back to Del Rio and refuel for the flight back to San Antonio. She had accomplished her goal. She had found Rusty's tomb.

The young observer grabbed up the mike and yelled in it excitedly. "Look, under the wing! Look! There's something moving down there!"

Something moving! With trembling fingers Blake banked the plane and continued to circle the wreckage. "Where?" she demanded. "Where did you see movement?"

"Down under that wing," the young man replied. "The wing that's still attached to the plane."

Grimly Blake continued to circle the plane, straining her eyes to see down to the wreckage. "There it goes again!" one of the observers in the back shouted over the noise of the engine. "It's moving again."

"My God, you're right," Blake said, her voice quivering. She grabbed the radio and shouted into it. "Del Rio, tell that ground crew to get a move on. We can see something moving under the wing! We might have survivors!"

Del Rio assured her that they would come just as quickly as they could. Her mind in a spin, Blake tipped her wings as she flew past one last time, hoping that if there was a survivor under the wing, that he would see her and know that they spotted him. *Do I dare hope that it's Rusty?* she asked herself as she landed the small plane at Del Rio.

No, that would be hoping too much. Besides, it might not have even been a survivor. It might have just been a wild animal under the wing. *Don't get your hopes up, Blake.*

Nevertheless, her hands trembled as she refueled the plane. Most of the other planes had already refueled and left and the ground crew had left for the accident site. Commander Prescott came out to the plane and greeted her and the observers tiredly. "Good work, folks," he said.

"Should I wait here for—well—until we know something?" Blake asked.

"No, I don't think so, Blake," Commander Prescott assured her. "If there is a survivor, the news will be relayed both here and to Stinson at the same time. Besides, it will probably be hours until we know something for sure. It's going to take them a while to get across that brush. You would do better to wait it out with your C.A.P. friends at Stinson."

"Will do, Commander," Blake assured him.

Commander Prescott reached out and touched Blake's arm lightly. "Please, don't get your hopes up, Blake," he warned her. "The chances are—well, not very high that it's him."

"I know that," Blake replied, her eyes dimming. "But I can't stop hoping some, now, can I?"

Blake and her observers flew back to San Antonio, Blake hoping against hope in spite of Commander Prescott's warning. She landed the plane and they tied it down quickly, then she and the observers crowded into the packed meeting room, quiet except for the low hum of whispered conversation. Blake poured herself a cup of coffee and sat down on one of the folding chairs, staring down at her engagement ring as though it were a good-luck charm.

Blake and the others sat patiently for nearly two hours,

waiting for some word from the ground crew. Some smoked, some got up and wandered around, and some, like Blake, merely stared into space. Since most of them knew that she and Rusty were engaged, they would make a point of sitting down for a moment beside Blake and encouraging her, assuring her that the ground crew matched the air crew in skill and efficiency. Still, as Blake stared out the window into the dark night sky, she wondered if the ground crew had found the wreckage before night fell. If they had not, the search would have to be abandoned until morning. Oh, what if Rusty were alive and had to spend tonight out there! Forcing that thought out of her mind, she reminded herself that those folks trying to reach him were the best.

Finally, at nearly ten, the radio crackled on and Commander Prescott's voice crackled on the radio. "Stinson, do you read me?"

"This is Stinson. We read you."

"Great. Now listen closely. The ground crew has just radioed me with the identities of the survivors."

Survivors? Are there more than one? Blake thought excitedly.

"One of the survivors is Bob Merrill."

A loud cheer went up as Bob's name was announced, then the group quieted down quickly. Blake bit her lip and stared at the radio.

"And the other survivor is Rusty O'Gorman."

Rusty. He was alive. *He was alive.* "Oh, my God!" Blake said out loud. "Did you hear that? He's alive, oh, thank God, he's alive!" The pent-up emotion that she had been bottling up all day poured forth. Blake collapsed into her chair, uncontrollable sobs racking her body.

Colonel Prescott continued to speak on the radio but Blake was oblivious to it all. Rusty was alive! She hadn't lost him after all! Some kind soul, Blake was not sure who, let her cry on his shoulder for long minutes, relief and joy robbing her completely of her usual iron control. When she was finally able to compose herself, her good Samaritan lent her a clean handkerchief and she wiped her eyes and blew her nose and went over to the radio operator. "Excuse me, did Commander Prescott say where they were taking Rusty and Bob?"

"Bob, being civilian, will go to Medical Center. Rusty, of course, will go to Wilford Hall."

"Was he hurt badly?" Blake demanded, her joy in Rusty's survival turning into concern for his condition.

"Commander Prescott didn't say too much, just that they both needed medical care."

"How do I get to Wilford Hall from here?" she asked, a tired smile on her face.

"Four ten to Military," the radio operator replied. "I guess you're one happy woman tonight, aren't you?"

"You bet I am," Blake replied.

She quickly telephoned Suzanne and John with the good news, then she climbed into the Datsun and headed out to Wilford Hall, her heart singing. Even if he was hurt, Rusty was still alive! Praying that he would be all right, she followed the simple directions across town and in about a half an hour she was driving onto Lackland AFB and pulling up in front of the huge military hospital that served all the Air Force bases. She parked her car and fairly ran inside, where she pleaded with the clerk to tell her where Rusty was. The clerk, looking at the wild-eyed, disheveled officer a little strangely, checked her records and informed Blake that Rusty had just been brought into the emergency room. Blake got directions from the clerk and trotted through the huge hospital corridors as quickly

256

as she could, almost knocking down a pregnant aide with a basket of blood samples.

She burst into the emergency room and ran up to the desk. "Is Captain O'Gorman here?" she begged. "Where is he?"

The clerk picked up the telephone and punched a button. "Have you taken Captain O'Gorman up to surgery yet?" he asked. "Friend here wants to know." The young man turned to Blake. "You Captain Warner?" he asked.

"I'm Captain Warner," Blake replied crisply, the command in her voice a direct contrast to her rumpled appearance.

The clerk looked at her a bit disdainfully, then returned to the telephone. "Captain Warner is here," he replied. He turned to Blake. "The doctor will be with you in a few moments."

Blake sat down in one of the plastic chairs that lined the room and watched anxiously for a doctor to appear from the maze of cubicles down the way. Finally a young major appeared. "Are you Captain Warner?" he asked as Blake stood at attention.

"Yes, sir, I am," she said. "How is Rusty?"

"Well, he didn't come out of a plane crash with just a few scratches, as I'm sure you know, but we aren't going to lose him or anything like that. I did his preliminary workup, but an orthopedic surgeon will have to take care of his right arm and leg, plus he did have a punctured lung and some internal bleeding there."

"He's hurt pretty badly then," Blake replied, her face falling.

"Yes, but he's young and he's going to recover," the doctor reassured her. "He sent a message for me to give you. He said to tell you that was some flying today."

"He did?" Blake asked in astonishment.

"Yes, he did," the doctor replied. "Although I have to admit that it doesn't make any sense to me."

"I was flying the search-and-rescue plane that spotted him," Blake admitted quietly.

"Well, Captain Warner, I guess you know that you saved him," the doctor replied.

"I did?" Blake asked.

"Of course you did," the doctor said. "He had lost a lot of blood and he probably wouldn't have made it another night out there. You folks did your job and then some today."

I saved him, Blake said to herself. *We all saved him. My flying actually saved Rusty's life.* "When can I see him?" she asked.

"I'm afraid he's going to be in surgery for a long time," the major admitted. "Why don't you go home and get—uh—fixed up?"

"No, I'll wait," Blake replied. "Where can I wait to see him?"

The doctor gave her instructions for finding the surgical waiting room and Blake wandered through the hospital corridors, a bemused expression on her face. She had saved Rusty's life. The doctor had said so. She and the combined efforts of the Civil Air Patrol had saved the life of the man she loved so dearly. Her head spinning, she found the waiting room and sat down on the functional couch, staring straight ahead as her mind raced. Her flying had actually saved a life. No, make that two lives. Bob had been in that plane too.

It meant something, Blake thought in wonder. It really meant something. Her flying today had been important. In fact, it couldn't have been any more important! For what could mean any more to her or anyone else than saving human lives? Blake stared at her reflection in the window pane with a sense of awe on her face. Even if she never flew again, never got into a cockpit and roared down a runway and up into the sky, her training and her expertise had not been for nothing.

Maybe that was the reason behind it all, she thought as she tucked one sneakered foot under her. Maybe out there somewhere it was written she would be needed today to fly that mission. And she had used every bit of her talent and skill to sweep the ground for that downed plane. A lesser pilot might have flown too high and missed it.

Blake sighed as a deep sense of satisfaction enveloped her, the first real satisfaction she had known in three years. Yes, she could still accomplish a lot with her flying, even though she could no longer fly for the military. Even though her flying with the Civil Air Patrol was voluntary, she could perform an important service within its ranks. Today was not an isolated incident. The Civil Air Patrol would save lives again, and she would be a part of that! No wonder Rusty wanted to be a part of it. No wonder he wanted her in it.

Blake's brow creased in a frown as she thought of Rusty. How badly were his arm and leg injured. What about his lung? Was he going to be all right? Her own euphoria fading, Blake winced when she thought of the agony Rusty must have suffered until the ground crew got to him. *Oh, I wish we had found you sooner, Rusty. I wish we could have spared you some of the pain.*

Blake jumped as the swinging doors of the waiting room flew open and John and Suzanne rushed in. "How's Rusty?" they demanded.

"He's going to be all right," Blake said as she rose from the couch. Suddenly light-headed, she swayed as her legs buckled under her, and if John had not caught her, she would have fallen. Noting her pallor, John sat her down and Suzanne pushed her head down between her knees.

"Are you all right?" John demanded a few minutes later when Blake tentatively raised her head.

"I—I think so," Blake replied. "It's been a long day. What time is it?"

"Almost one," John replied. "When's the last time you ate?"

"A half a sandwich and a Coke at noon," Blake said.

"No wonder you're reeling," John said. "I'm going to go out and bring you a hamburger and you're going to eat it," he said in his best commanding voice. He stood up and turned to go.

"John," Blake called across the room. He turned around, prepared for an argument. "Will you bring me two?" Blake asked sheepishly. "I hope you won't think I'm awful, but I'm starved!"

"I can't believe the commander let you fly that mission," John said as Blake polished off the last of her second hamburger. "I'm sure he knew you were in shock."

"I begged him to let me go," Blake admitted as she drank a huge swallow of her Coke. "I didn't want Mr. and Mrs. O'Gorman to suffer the way Mom and I did when we had to wait to hear any word on Dad." She looked down at her engagement ring. "I never honestly thought I'd find him alive."

"You found him?" Suzanne asked. "Your plane spotted the wreckage?"

Blake nodded as John's eyes widened. "Yes, we had already radioed the position when one of the kids spotted something moving under the wing and I radioed another message to get a move on, we thought we saw a survivor."

"So how do you feel about your flying now, Blake?"

260

John asked with a twinkle in his eye. "Being as how you saved my best friend's life with it today?"

"Real good, John," Blake said as her eyes started to fill again. "Oh, John, I really saved him! He's really alive! I haven't lost him!" she sobbed as the tumultuous emotional upheaval she had been through that day caught up with her again and tears provided the release she needed.

John took the sobbing woman into his arms and let her cry, a smile on his face. "Just like a woman," he informed Suzanne over her shoulder. "I'll bet she flew the mission as cool as a cucumber and now that he's all right she's crying her eyes out. Oh, not you too," he said as Suzanne's eyes began to fill with tears and his own became suspiciously moist. "Come on, Suzy. Don't you cry on me too!"

Blake cried until she was spent, then composed herself and blew her nose. She gratefully accepted John and Suzanne's offer to wait with her until Rusty was out of surgery and she could see him. John went to the lobby for magazines to pass the time, but as the hours crept by Blake became more and more anxious.

"Do you think the doctor told me everything?" she asked finally as she put her magazine to one side.

John put his paperback aside and looked her in the eye. "Are you thinking what I'm thinking?" he asked.

Blake nodded. "His flying?" Suzanne asked.

"Yes," Blake said. "He could lose that even if he recovers." She fiddled with her braid. "Wouldn't that be the ultimate irony? Two grounded pilots in the same family!"

"He would adjust," John said gently. "You had to, and you did it."

"Yes, but I still wouldn't wish it on him," Blake replied. "He loves to fly, John! Even more than I do."

At that moment a tired surgeon in rumpled greens came through from the surgical suite. Three pairs of anxious eyes turned to him. "I'm Colonel Magarsky. Are you Captain O'Gorman's friends?" he asked.

"I'm Captain Warner, his fiancée," Blake said. "How is he?"

"Groggy and in pain right now," Colonel Magarsky said frankly as the three of them winced. "His right arm and leg were pretty badly mangled and it required surgery to fit all the pieces of bone back together. That leg's going to have to be in traction for at least three weeks, and he'll need several months of therapy after that to regain bone and muscle strength in both his arm and his leg. We did the lung too—no problem up there."

"I guess his flying's over, then," Blake said as her face fell.

"Oh, no," the tired doctor assured her. "There's no nerve damage. He'll recover full use of his arm and leg with no problem. Granted, it will be a number of months before he's back up there, but Captain O'Gorman will fly again."

"Oh, thank God," Blake breathed in relief. "When can I see him?"

"Well, I guess you can see him now just for a minute or two," the doctor said doubtfully. "But then you better get home and rest a little yourself." He looked at the tatty officer in front of him with distinct amusement in his eyes. "You look worse than he does."

Blake followed the doctor back into the surgical suite and a kindly nurse showed her into the recovery room. Blake bent over Rusty's bed. His eyes were just barely open and dazed from all the medication. A tube was still in his nose and a large bandage covered part of his bare chest. Numerous small cuts and scratches covered his left arm, and his right arm and leg were swathed in huge casts, a pin extending from the one in his leg. Blake blinked back tears and reminded herself that the doctors had assured her that he would be all right. She leaned over him and touched his forehead lightly.

Rusty's eyes snapped open and he tried to speak. "No, Rusty," Blake said as she held her fingers to her lips. "You'll hurt yourself by talking. They won't let me stay long. I just wanted to tell you that I love you. I love you so much!" Her throat closed with tears and she reached out and took his left hand and squeezed it tightly. He squeezed back, ever so faintly, then drifted back into that twilight world where he needed to take refuge. Blake reluctantly let go of his hand, then left the hospital and drove home in the early dawn.

CHAPTER FIFTEEN

Blake woke slowly and blinked her eyes, wondering why the room was so light and why her back ached so badly. She glanced over at the clock and stared at it in wonder. Noon? Why had she slept until noon? As she fell back on the pillow, a spasm of pain caught her in her lower back and she remembered that she had spent most of yesterday flying, looking for Rusty's wreckage. Rusty! How was he this morning? She crawled out of bed and hurriedly thumbed through the telephone book for Wilford Hall's number, but the information clerk could give her only a general condition of satisfactory and Rusty's room number. Swearing softly, she grabbed up a bra and panties and ran for the bathroom.

She showered and dressed in record time, slipping on a simple elegant shirtwaist that was a direct contrast to her disheveled appearance of the night before. She neatly wound her damp hair into a chignon at her nape and carefully applied cosmetics, liberally using a cover stick to reduce the circles under her eyes. Picking up her purse from the dining room table, she spotted her D.O.S. papers sitting just where Rusty had thrown them three nights ago. Blake stared at them for a moment, then picked them up and deliberately tore them in half, throwing the pieces neatly in the kitchen trash. "I guess I won't be needing those, and it's a shame to clutter up the apartment," Blake told Calico as she left the kitchen.

Blake got instructions from the desk and found her way to the orthopedics wing of the huge hospital. She knocked quietly on Rusty's door and was rewarded with a hoarse "Come in." Blake stepped inside and closed the door behind her, suddenly feeling very shy.

"Come here, beautiful," Rusty called weakly across the room. "I want to look at you."

Blake obediently crossed the room, standing on the left side of the bed beside Rusty's good arm and leg. She reached out and took his hand, squeezing it tightly. "You look better," she said honestly. "Are you in much pain?"

"No, those little white pills do wonders," Rusty admitted in a low voice. Blake pulled up a chair and sat by the edge of the bed, her head close to his so he would not have to strain his raw throat. "Damn, this contraption's confining," he complained, referring to the elaborate traction device from which his right leg was suspended. "This is going to be a very long three weeks."

"But it's necessary to get your leg back in shape," Blake

264

admonished him. "The sooner your leg's healed, the sooner you'll be back in a cockpit."

"You're right," Rusty agreed. "And I do look forward to that." He pulled her closer with the hand that was holding hers. "I need to thank you, lady, for saving me yesterday."

"Any time, Rusty," Blake replied, her eyes filling with tears. "But how did you know it was me?"

"Who else could it have been?" Rusty asked. "The minute I saw that plane arcing and coming my way, I knew it had to be you. Believe me, Blake, nobody can make a turn like you can up there! I knew way down deep, as soon as our plane was down and I was still alive, that you'd be the one to come for me."

"I thought you were dead," Blake admitted as tears flowed from her eyes. She picked up the edge of the sheet and wiped them gingerly, trying not to smear her mascara. "They called me and told me there were no survivors. I had to beg them to let me fly the mission."

"If you thought I was dead, why did you want to fly it so badly?" Rusty asked softly.

"I didn't want your mother and father not to know for sure," she explained. "Oh, Rusty, I'm so sorry!"

"Whatever for?" Rusty asked. "For thinking I was dead? You could hardly be blamed for that."

"No," Blake said. "For being so jealous of your flying all this time. Believe me, if I could have made a bargain with the devil yesterday, he could have had my soul and my flying forever if I could have had you back." She fished around in her purse for a tissue and blew her nose. "I've made you miserable and I'm sorry."

Rusty reached out with his good arm and pulled Blake's head onto his shoulder. "You couldn't help it," he said. "I know that now." He lovingly stroked her hair with his

265

hand. "All day yesterday, under that damned hot wing, hurting and wondering how long it would take you to find me, all I could think about was whether I would be able to fly again. I'd look down at my arm and my leg and I'd wonder if they would be able to put them back together well enough to pass a physical. And then, finally, I understood how you must have felt when the Air Force told you that you would never fly for them again." Rusty kissed the top of Blake's head. "I was terrified that my flying days were over."

Blake raised her head and kissed Rusty's lips. "Did they tell you that you would be all right?"

"Yes, and I broke down and cried like a baby. But how did you know?"

"That's the first thing I asked the surgeon," she said. "I was scared to death that you wouldn't fly again. I wouldn't want you to lose that. Oh, thank God you're going to be all right!" she said, tears filling her eyes as she looked up at Rusty. "I'm sorry, I just can't stop crying!"

"I think you've earned the right to a few tears, don't you?" Rusty asked as he pulled her close and let her cry, her tears of joy and relief wetting his shoulder and the edge of the sheet.

Blake spent the rest of the afternoon and evening with Rusty, leaving only long enough to grab a bite to eat in the cafeteria. She helped him eat the meal he was brought, teasing him about the bland, tasteless food, and helping him wield his fork in his left hand. When visiting hours were finally over, she left him reluctantly, kissing him lingeringly on the lips, not wanting to leave him, although exhaustion was about to claim her again.

Back at her apartment, she called Rusty's parents to give them word on his progress. A sweet-voiced woman answered the phone and when Blake identified herself the woman broke down in tears, thanking Blake for saving her son. Blake could tell that Rusty's parents were not really reassured that Rusty was all right, so Blake impulsively invited them to fly out and see for themselves, saying that they could stay with her. The O'Gormans didn't need much persuasion and agreed to come. Blake had just hung up when the telephone rang again and a tearful Margie Merrill thanked Blake for finding Bob before it was too late. Margie explained that Bob's insides had been creatively rearranged somewhat, but said that he, too, would recover completely.

Blake spent a busy week while Rusty lay in traction at Wilford Hall. She insisted on making the long drive over every evening to see Rusty, who admittedly only made a token protest to her doing so. As he progressed to a regular menu, she would cut his meat and do anything else for him that he couldn't do with just one functioning hand. She kept him supplied with books and magazines, slipping in a few girlie magazines as Rusty began to get better and his complaining increased accordingly. She brought him fresh pajamas and laundered his dirty ones, teasing him about looking good for the sexy night nurse who always made it a point to linger at his bedside for a few extra minutes.

Blake took over the care of Rusty's lawn, watering it often. Since Rusty felt that his parents might be more comfortable in his home, Blake stocked his refrigerator. She picked the O'Gormans up at the airport on one rainy afternoon at the beginning of the second week of Rusty's hospitalization. She was immediately taken with the quiet couple, who both kissed her cheek and thanked her again for her part in Rusty's rescue. Since they found her car more comfortable to drive than Rusty's truck, she lent the

Datsun to them and drove the pickup herself during their week-long stay.

Blake spent a lot of time talking with Rusty during the three weeks that he was hospitalized, but he did not bring up the issue of their future together and neither did she. At first all Blake's attention was focused on making Rusty comfortable and all of his was focused on getting better, but as the days went by and Rusty said nothing about making wedding plans, Blake began to become anxious. Had he changed his mind? Had he decided that he no longer wanted to spend his life with her? Although they shared many kisses and caresses and Rusty frequently told her that he loved her, not once did he say a word about what the future held for them.

Oh, Rusty, I hope you haven't given up on me, Blake thought as she scrubbed out Rusty's bathtub and swirled a mop around the bathroom floor. He was being released tomorrow and would be recuperating at home for a few months, until his bones had knit completely and he was able to go back on active duty. The doctor had suggested that he stay a couple of weeks longer, but when Blake unblushingly volunteered to move into Rusty's house, the doctor had agreed to let Rusty go. So Blake had filled the refrigerator with plenty of food and was cleaning the house thoroughly after his parents' brief stay.

Her body occupied but her mind available to run free, Blake's anxiety grew until she was positively on edge. What if Rusty thought she was still jealous of his career? She had meant what she told him the day after the crash. She would have cheerfully given up flying if she could have had him back, but what if he didn't believe that? Yes, she was cured of her jealousy, and she was also finally at peace about her aborted career. But she hadn't had a chance to explain any of this to Rusty. Would he give her a chance to do so?

On the day Rusty was to be released, she borrowed Suzanne's big Buick with the spacious backseat and parked it in front of Wilford Hall. She made her way to Rusty's room and found him sitting on the edge of the bed, his arm and leg in smaller, more maneuverable casts. He was wearing the short-sleeve shirt and cutoffs he had instructed her to bring yesterday, and although he was pale, he had never been more appealing to Blake. She leaned over and kissed him fully on the lips, gasping when Rusty brought his good arm around her and pressed her to him, flicking open her lips and capturing the sweetness of her mouth. His heart thumped against her palm and Blake was suddenly aware of how very long it had been since they had made love. Color swept her face as desire swamped her body. "We better quit this," she murmured.

"Yeah," Rusty replied, thrusting her away and grinning at her impudently. "I think they have a regulation against doing that in here."

"They probably do," Blake agreed as Colonel Magarsky walked through the door and signed Rusty's walking papers. He admonished Rusty not to do too much too soon and made him promise to let Blake wait on him some, then an orderly wheeled Rusty to the door while Blake ran ahead for the car. She and the orderly helped Rusty into the backseat where he could stretch out his leg with the cast, and the orderly handed Blake a set of crutches to put into the trunk.

"Where'd you get this limo?" Rusty asked as Blake pulled off the base.

"Don't you recognize it? Suzy lent it to me to get you home in," Blake said. "They've been super through this whole thing."

"They waited with you all night while I had surgery, didn't they?" Rusty said.

Blake nodded. "And Suzy offered to drive the Datsun as long as we needed this to transport you in."

"That was good of her. John tells me she's getting over all that guilt about the wreck, thanks to you."

Blake shrugged. "I only did what any friend would have done."

"No, you did what Blake would do," Rusty corrected her.

Rusty chattered to Blake all the way home and into the house, insisting that she install him on the couch in the den rather than in bed, but he fell asleep almost immediately, tired lines of strain showing on his face. *See there, you're a lot weaker than you thought you were,* Blake chided him silently as she tucked a pillow under his head and kissed him gently. She unloaded the suitcase and the flowers from the Buick, then she crawled up in the recliner in the den intending to rest for only a few minutes, but within a moment she, too, was asleep.

When Blake's eyes finally opened the sun streaming in the windows was coming from low in the sky. She blinked sleepily and looked around, her eyes widening as they met a pair of dancing blue ones from across the room. "Afternoon, sleepyhead," Rusty drawled from across the room.

"Good grief, how long have I been asleep?" Blake demanded as she popped the recliner down and sat up.

Rusty shrugged. "Since I just woke up myself, it doesn't really matter."

"What can I do for you?" Blake asked as she stood up.

"The crutches," Rusty suggested as he struggled to a sitting position. Blake rushed to the couch and helped him up. "These damned casts are heavy," he complained as Blake retrieved the crutches from the entry. As she handed him the crutches he pulled her down on the couch beside him. "You look tired," he said as he ran a gentle finger around the circle under her eye. "You've been just great, Blake. I would have gone crazy in that place without you."

"I was glad to do every bit of it, you know that," she said as he pulled her close and kissed her cheek gently. "But I must admit I'm glad you're out."

"So am I," Rusty admitted as he struggled to his feet, balancing precariously on the crutches. "Now I'm going to check out how well you can clean a bathroom." Blake stuck out her tongue at his retreating back.

"What do you want for supper?" Blake asked when Rusty returned.

"Oh, something that you don't have to kill yourself making," he said as he awkwardly lowered himself to the couch. Blake's heart went out to him as he struggled with the casts, but as she made a motion to go to him, Rusty waved her away with his good arm. "No, I've got to learn to manipulate these damned things myself."

"If you say so," she replied. "Could you manage home-made ravioli?"

"Blake, I said something that wouldn't put you out to cook it," Rusty warned her.

"Well, then, how about Stouffer's homemade?" she teased.

"I have a feeling that's what you had in mind all along," Rusty said suspiciously as Blake winked at him.

Refreshed from her nap, Blake went into the kitchen and found the two packages of ravioli she had bought yesterday and popped them into the microwave. As she tore up lettuce and sliced tomatoes for a salad, she wondered if she should bring up the subject of their future herself. It was killing her not to know if Rusty had

271

changed his mind. But what if he said no, that he no longer wanted her to be a permanent part of his life? How could she stay here while he recovered, knowing that? No, she wouldn't say anything. Maybe it would be better not to know.

Blake set their plates on TV trays in front of the couch so that Rusty would not have to maneuver his way under the kitchen table. She flipped on the evening news and they watched together, with very little conversation between them, although the silence was companionable rather than strained. *I hope it can be like this for us always,* she thought as she carried their plates to the kitchen and loaded them into the dishwasher.

By the time she had returned to the den the news was over and Rusty had gotten up and turned off the set. "You shouldn't have done that," she admonished him gently. "I would have turned it off for you." She sat down beside Rusty and he reached out and took her hand.

"I wanted to talk to you, and I didn't want to have to compete with some good-looking anchorman," Rusty teased, then his face sobered. "We do have to discuss the future, you know."

Blake swallowed and nodded. "Yes, I know," she said. *Here it comes,* she thought.

"I had a lot of time to think while I was laid up in there," Rusty began slowly. "Nearly dying did affect me more than I thought possible at first. It made me realize how precious life itself is. And it made me realize just how much I do love you."

"I already knew that," Blake said, her heart thumping.

"But I didn't," Rusty replied. "Anyway, I do love you and I want your life to be as happy as it can be." He stopped and hesitated.

"And?" Blake prompted.

272

"And I'm willing to get out of the service with you if that's what you want," Rusty said in a rush of breath.

"You're *what*?" Blake asked as she sat up and stared at him with astonishment.

"I'm willing to get out of the service with you if that's what you want," Rusty replied. "Look, I love flying, but I love you more, and I want to spend my life with you, whatever it takes. You do still want to spend your life with me, don't you?" he asked with anxiety in his voice. "You haven't said anything about it since the crash."

"Of course I want to spend my life with you, if that's what you want," Blake said as she squeezed his hand, relief surging through her. "I was beginning to think that maybe you didn't, since you never brought the subject up," she added.

"I thought you might not want me anymore," Rusty admitted in a low voice. "I wasn't really very nice that night when I got back from Alamogordo."

"I was scared you didn't want me," Blake said. "After the hell I put you through with my jealousy." She reached over and looped her arm around his neck and hugged him tightly. "I thought I'd lost you with my pettiness."

"I think we both could have been a lot more understanding," Rusty said as he rubbed her thigh thoughtfully. "But that's water under the bridge. Anyway, I do most certainly want to spend my life with you, and I want to do it in such a way that we'll both be happy. So I'm willing to get out of the service if that's what you want."

Blake shook her head slowly. "No, that's most definitely not what I want," she said. "I tore up the D.O.S. papers the day after I found you."

She got up from the couch and paced the room slowly, stopping in front of Rusty's airplane models and touching one of them gently with her forefinger. "I don't think either of us really should get out of the service—you because that's the best place in the world for a pilot, and me because I'd like to make colonel before I retire." She turned around and grinned sheepishly. "I think I'm colonel material too."

"What about the flying?" Rusty asked urgently.

Blake stared for a moment at the model planes, then turned back to Rusty, a hesitant expression on her face. "Rusty, I'm always going to envy you a little bit, and I'll always be a little sorry that I didn't get to fly." As Rusty's face fell she hurried on. "But I know I can handle it from here on out," she said confidently as Rusty's eyes flew up to meet hers. "I may live for Saturdays and Sundays, but I don't think you'll mind that too much, will you?"

"Of course not," Rusty said. "But what made your feelings change so radically? Before the crash it was eating you alive."

"The crash, what else?" Blake said. "And it isn't because I had thought I'd lost you," she tacked on honestly. "Even up there in that plane, thinking for sure that you were dead, I was still wondering if I would have ever gotten over the jealousy, even though I was berating myself for it at the same time. Even then, I was wondering if we would have made it."

Blake walked up and down the den, voicing her thoughts carefully. "Then I spotted your plane and we thought we saw you alive, and sure enough, you were and so was Bob. I had the rare privilege of saving two lives, one of a dear friend and one of the man who means everything to me." Blake's eyes swam with tears and she wiped them away impatiently. "And I have my flying to thank for that. That weekend flying I used to think was so silly actually meant more to my happiness on a single hot afternoon than a twenty-year career in the Air Force would have, because it gave you back to me. I'm feeling very fulfilled these days about my flying, Rusty. I'm not frustrated anymore, because flying with the C.A.P. can be just as rewarding, if not more so, than military or commercial flying." Blake smiled through her tears. "Saving lives is a real joy."

"Come here, Bebe," Rusty said as he held out his hand, happy tears in his eyes.

"Bebe? You haven't called me that in ages," Blake said as she took his hand and snuggled down beside him. She had almost forgotten that he remembered her nickname.

"That's because you weren't Bebe for a long time," Rusty explained. "I've thought of you as that though. To me, Bebe was that warm, loving person I met that first night at the Officer's Club. Then when you found out who I was and what I did for a living, you froze up on me and never quite let down your guard, even after we fell in love and I had asked you to marry me. I really despaired of ever getting back to Bebe." He reached up and wiped a tear out of his eye. "But now she's back."

"And she's back to stay," Blake promised him solemnly as she placed her hand in his. He pulled her to him and kissed her gently, binding her to her promise with his lips and his heart.

"Rusty, I love you," Blake said when he finally released her lips. "And I want very much to spend my life with you." He pulled her to him and started unbuttoning the top button of the blouse she had on. "Rusty, what are you doing?" she demanded.

"You said you wanted to spend your life with me," he said as he undid the second button. "I just thought we might start spending it together tonight."

Blake pulled out of his arms and looked at him worriedly. "But you're sick," she objected.

"No, I'm not," Rusty replied as he flicked open the third button and thrust his hand inside, finding the nipple of her breast with unerring speed and accuracy.

Blake gasped at the intimacy of his touch. "That feels so good," she whispered. "But you're tired and you've been hurt," she protested. "You need to rest."

"Nonsense," Rusty murmured as he pushed her blouse back off her shoulders, baring her to the waist except for the thin wisp of bra that she wore. "I'm not tired, I slept all afternoon. And I didn't get hurt *there*."

Blake started laughing, then shrugged her shoulders helplessly. "What am I supposed to say to Colonel Magarsky if we hurt you or something?"

"I'll tell him it was worth it," Rusty replied wickedly. "Oh, please, Bebe, can't we even try?" he pleaded. "I can hardly live in the same house with you and not want to make love to you. I've wanted you so badly for so many weeks now. First in Alamogordo and then in the hospital."

"How can I say no to that?" Blake said, more to herself than to Rusty. "I've missed you, too, Rusty. I've wanted you so badly sometimes I've ached."

"Then what are we waiting for?" Rusty asked as he levered himself up off the couch with only a little help from Blake. "Of course, we'll have to be careful, and I'm afraid you'll have to do most of the work," he added as she handed him his crutches, "but I think we can work something out."

"Sounds great," Blake muttered under her breath.

Rusty swayed on the unaccustomed crutches and Blake placed her hands in the middle of his back to keep him from toppling over on her, then slid her arm around Rusty's waist as he dropped the crutch from his bad arm. With Blake on one side and the crutch on the other, they

276

made their way to the bedroom awkwardly, Rusty banging his crutch into the hall twice and cursing loudly both times, Blake giggling at his ineptness.

She reached out and switched on the light and helped him to the bed, where she whipped back the cover with one hand as she helped him down with the other, picking up his heavy cast and laying it gently on the bed. "Oops, we forgot to take off your pants," she said.

"That's going to be fun," Rusty admitted as he moved to sit back up.

"No, don't," Blake said as she motioned him back down. "Your sweet lover-girl can manage." She turned on the table lamp and switched off the overhead light. "Now, let's see, how can I get these off?" she teased as she slowly unzipped the cutoffs, pausing every so often to caress Rusty's soft stomach.

"Bebe, watch those fingers," Rusty warned her as her fingers made light patterns on his vulnerable hips. She slowly drew down his cutoffs and his briefs, easing them down over the cast and off his body.

"Kind of got my order reversed, didn't I?" Blake teased as she tickled the skin of his hip, then moved upward to unbutton his shirt, lightly flicking open one button after the other until all the buttons were open and easing the shirt over the cast on Rusty's arm. Totally naked except for the casts, Rusty stared at her with unconcealed longing in his eyes.

Blake reached out and with tender lips kissed the new red scar on his chest, the short, bristly hair where they had had to shave part of his chest contrasting with the luxurious pelt where it was unshaven. Rusty stiffened as her lips touched the scar and Blake reared back in alarm. "Did I hurt you?" she asked.

"No, but it's ugly," Rusty said. "And the ones on my

277

arm and leg are likely to be worse. Will you mind looking at them?"

"Oh, Rusty, of course not!" Blake assured him, his vulnerability touching her deeply. "I love you—all of you. Those scars are a part of you now. Besides, they'll fade."

"You really think that?" Rusty asked.

"Of course," Blake told him as her lips traveled back down to the scar. "Besides, someday you're going to have to look at a big tummy and stretch marks, and I'm afraid I'll have to look at a bald head, and we both may get to look at a few sags and wrinkles. So what's a couple of scars between lovers?" She nibbled at all of his chest lovingly, not avoiding the blemished area.

"You're really something, Bebe," Rusty said as he grasped her head in his good hand and brought her face up to meet his, crushing her lips to his and plundering her mouth with his own. "Oh, I've missed kissing you," he whispered after long moments. He reached out and caressed Blake's breast through the lacy bra. "And I've missed touching you."

Blake looked down at her partially clothed body. "I'll make it a little easier," she volunteered as she slid away from Rusty and quickly stripped, her pale skin glowing in the lamplight.

"Your tan's gone, but you still look beautiful," Rusty whispered as Blake stretched out beside him and pressed her body intimately against his, the blood singing through her veins at the touch of Rusty's warm body next to hers. They hadn't made love in such a long time, and Blake was starved for his touch. "Slide up some," Rusty instructed her. "I can't reach your breasts from here."

Obediently Blake slid up and was rewarded with the touch of Rusty's lips on her breasts. She cradled his head in her hands, running her fingers through the thick red hair as he nibbled her lightly at first and then with increasing erotic intimacy. Blake whimpered softly as his hand crept downward and found its way to her waist and her stomach, drawing small circles of pleasure there before creeping lower, finding the center of her desire and tormenting it with his knowing touch until Blake writhed away. "No, not yet," she whispered.

"Yes, yet," Rusty whispered as he cupped her bottom and drew her back to him. His loving fingers tormented her until she arched beside him, stars shooting behind her eyes as her body pulsated with pleasure.

"Why did you do that?" she whispered, her breathing labored.

"I wanted to give you that," he replied, guiding her hand to touch him.

"Now it's your turn," Blake promised as she willingly played her fingers intimately upon Rusty's body, tormenting him much the way he had done her. Her lips crushed against his. Her fingers were free to roam his body, finding all the intimate spots that needed her attention, and caressing them until he moaned deep in his throat. She raised herself and bent to touch him in all the ways that pleased him so, drawing from him the same uncontrolled ecstasy that he had drawn from her. When she sensed that he was near the brink, she moved over him and swiftly made them one, rocking with him until he cried out and arched into her, shuddering with release. She too found delight again, whimpering with pleasure.

"That was over too quickly," Rusty complained as Blake moved away from him. "I meant to make it last, but I couldn't."

"Give me a minute and we'll have another go at it and see if you can get it right," Blake teased as she snuggled down beside him. "So how soon do you want to set the wedding?"

"Oh, three or four months from now," Rusty suggested.

"Three or four months!" Blake demanded. "That's too far away!"

"Not if I'm going to marry you without crutches or a cane," Rusty reminded her. "It will be at least two more months before these come off, and then I'll be in therapy for a month or two after that and won't be able to get away for a honeymoon."

"Boo on you, you sensible creature," Blake complained as she thumped his arm lightly. "I wanted to start spending my life with you now, not in three or four months."

"Looks like you're doing a pretty good job of that already," Rusty teased. "Let's see how the therapy goes and plan it for whenever that's over."

"All right," Blake agreed as she gently caressed Rusty's chest. "We're going to make it, you know," she whispered as she kissed him lovingly. "We're going to be so happy together!"

"I know that," Rusty said tenderly as she moved over him and made love to him yet again, bringing him to the heights of pleasure one more time. "Yes, Bebe, I know that," he whispered as he gathered her spent body close and together they drifted off into sleep.

Blake turned over and snuggled deeper under the covers, smiling in her sleep as she dreamed of soaring over sparkling water, Rusty in the small cockpit beside her. She slapped at the tickling on her nose, unwilling to relinquish her lovely dream just yet, but as a pair of warm lips captured hers her eyes flew open, blinking for a moment as she stared up into Rusty's sleepy face, a feather dangling from his fingers. "Good morning, Captain O'Gorman," he whispered as he touched her lips lightly with his own.

Blake pulled her arm out from under the covers and saluted sleepily. "I like all those interesting things you kept calling me last night better," she smiled as she gently caressed Rusty's cheek.

"You mean like wanton hussy and unbelievable sexpot?" Rusty teased.

Blake nodded. "I liked the wife one too. And love of my life. Those really turn me on."

"Okay, wife," Rusty whispered. "You really are an unbelievable sexpot though. Bebe, what are you doing?"

"Living up to your image of me," she chuckled as she felt for him under the covers. "Want that wanton hussy back?" she asked as she found his waist and slid her hands around it.

"You bet," Rusty said as he ran his hands slowly down Blake's body, down her sides and her hips and her thighs. "It's good to have two arms to hold you with again," he said as he caressed her breast with one hand and rubbed her stomach with the other.

"It's good to have you well again," Blake murmured as her tongue found the sensitive spot behind Rusty's ear. She ran her hands down his arms, both strong once again, only a five-inch-long scar on his right one serving as a legacy of the crash. "And it's great not to have to run all over the house for you."

Rusty reared back and looked at her teasingly. "What makes you think that's going to stop?" he demanded as he bent his head and captured the tip of her breast between his warm moist lips.

"Because, oh, I'll think of why later," Blake breathed, moving closer to Rusty's marauding lips. "Good grief, are we going to do this again?"

281

"You started it," Rusty said as he teased her breast and then captured her other breast in his mouth, rolling it between his lips and his tongue as Blake ran her fingers down the sides of his body, cupping his hard bottom in her hand. "I just can't seem to get enough of you. This last week has been miserable."

"Well, I couldn't very well stay the night with you with your parents at your house and my mother at the apartment," Blake protested as Rusty's lips traveled lower.

"We should have let them all have the house and you and I holed up in the apartment," Rusty teased as his tongue ran a circle around her navel. "Anyway, I think Mom sort of caught on when she found a pair of your panties in my drawer."

"What did she say?" Blake asked, turning crimson.

"Well, I blushed and tried to explain and she laughed out loud at me," Rusty admitted. His fingers found her soft warmth and stroked it enticingly. Blake squirmed under his touch, her own fingers busy stroking and touching Rusty with feverish need. Although she loved for Rusty to touch her, she also loved to touch him, to see his face as her knowing fingers drove him to distraction.

"Are you ready for me yet, Bebe?" Rusty asked after long moments of kissing her and caressing her lovingly.

"You know I am," Blake murmured as Rusty parted her legs with his and claimed his bride. Blake moved beneath him, pacing herself so that she complimented Rusty's actions. As always, the ecstasy began to build for both of them, rising higher and higher until they exploded together in a mutual celebration of delight. It was always this way for them now, Blake thought as she snuggled down beside Rusty and caressed him gently. "You know, it's nice to have a little variety back in our lives," she said musingly.

Rusty leaned over and kissed her cheek. "I'm glad, too, but some of my sweetest memories are of the way you made love to me when I had those casts on and couldn't move much. Some of the things you thought up to do!" He sat up and threw back the covers. "Let's get a move on, if we're going to make that flight!"

"Our flight! I'd forgotten!" Blake said as she leaped out of bed and ran for the shower.

She and Rusty shared a shower and in record time they were dressed in their traveling clothes and ready to go. Blake carefully laid her wedding dress across the bed, knowing that Suzanne would pick it up later today and see that it was cleaned and stored away. "Now are you going to tell me where we're going for our honeymoon?" Blake demanded as they left the house and locked it behind them.

"Nope, not until we get there," Rusty said as they put their suitcases into the truck. A cold February wind whipped around them, but as far as Blake was concerned it was the first day of spring.

I wonder why Rusty sold his boat? Blake asked herself for the hundredth time as they drove toward the airport. He had made some excuse about not having time anymore to use it, and despite Blake's objections that she didn't mind his fishing, he had sold it two weeks ago to a fellow pilot. She just hoped he didn't miss it too much.

Rusty drove into the entrance to San Antonio International, but instead of parking in the lot he took a side road and circled the airport as Blake looked around in confusion. "Where on earth are you taking us?" she asked.

"Oh, a buddy of mine said we could park back here and he'd keep an eye on the truck for us," Rusty explained nonchalantly as he wound his way through the maze of small buildings and drove around a small hangar. Sitting in front of the hangar was a small plane. A Beechcraft Bonanza, used but in mighty good shape, Blake thought as Rusty parked the car beside the hangar. "Want to take a look at the plane?" he asked.

"Sure, if we have time," Blake said as she hopped out of the car. They walked together to the small plane, Rusty's arm around her shoulders.

As Blake expressed her admiration of the small plane, Rusty reached in his pocket and pulled out a set of keys. "I thought this might suit you," he said as he put the keys into her hand. "Happy honeymoon, Bebe."

Blake stared at the keys in her hand and at the plane, then over at her husband, her jaw hanging open in astonishment. "You bought this for me? You bought me an airplane?"

Rusty grinned sheepishly. "Well, both our names are on the title and the note, but yes, I bought it for you."

"Oh, Rusty!" Blake squealed, throwing her arms around him and hugging him tightly, her eyes moist. "This is the best wedding present I could have! Oh, thank you!" She stepped back and stared at him. "The boat?" she asked.

Rusty nodded. "I have a suspicion I'll enjoy the plane more. Now, I filed a flight plan yesterday for a flight to Taos for skiing, and we're due to fly out of here in ten minutes. We better get moving."

"Who gets to fly today?" Blake asked.

"You want to?" Rusty asked.

"You bet!" Blake said as they ran to the truck for their luggage. In just a few minutes they had gone through the preflight routine and Blake was radioing the tower for permission to take off. As permission was granted, Blake leaned over and kissed Rusty, then she let out her throttle and sped down the runway, flying away with her husband on the wings of their love.

LOOK FOR NEXT MONTH'S
CANDLELIGHT ECSTASY SUPREMES